THE RISING OF ④ THE SHIELD HERO

Aneko Yusagi

Fitoria

The High Priest

The Queen

Myne

Motoyasu Kitamura

Filo

Melty

Naofumi Iwatani

THE RISING OF 4 THE SHIELD HERO

Raphtalia

Characters

Her eyes were red, and her gaze carried an air of authority about it.
Her face was small and well-composed. Quite beautiful, really.
She was dressed in a red and white gothic-style dress.
"Allow me to introduce myself. I am Fitoria, the Queen of the Filolials."

Table of Contents

Prologue: On the Run

"Jeez! That brain-dead harem sure is persistent!"

I was so annoyed that I was spitting insults involuntarily.

But it was only natural. We'd been accused of abducting and brain washing Melty, and we'd been on the run for a while.

We'd turned onto some overgrown mountain roads in an attempt to lose the soldiers chasing us.

But they were still close behind.

"Dammit! Nothing good has happened since I came to this world!"

My complaint brought everything that happened over the last few months freshly back to my mind

My name is Naofumi Iwatani.

Back in the modern world I'd been, I admit it, an *Otaku*. I was a 20-year-old university student.

But that was before everything changed. I was killing some time in the local library when I found an old book called *The Records of the Four Holy Weapons*. I had been flipping through the pages when, all of a sudden, I passed out and woke up in a completely new world.

Not only that, I'd been summoned there as one of the four heroes that the book had been about. I was the Shield Hero—the only hero that couldn't attack.

In the beginning I was thrilled. The world was like a dream—and I was a hero! I couldn't wait to get out and start adventuring. But some wicked, cowardly people set a trap for me and framed me for a crime I didn't commit. My reputation was completely ruined, and I was heavily persecuted. They accused me of rape and sent me out into the world on my own, even though I couldn't attack, and I didn't know anyone. I had to find some way to make it on my own.

However, there was a strange phenomenon called "The Waves" that were threatening to destroy the world.

When the wave occurred, I was automatically (forcibly) transported to the scene of destruction. I had to fight monsters to protect a world that had treated me so poorly.

Even worse, the Legendary Shield that was attached to my arm was impossible to remove. It felt like a curse of some kind.

So not only did I have to put my own life on the line to save the people that had hurt me, but I couldn't even run away if I wanted to.

Because of the shield, I couldn't use other weapons at all, and even if I punched enemies with my fists, I wasn't able to deal any substantial damage.

On the other hand, the shield had the ability to absorb defeated enemies and materials, and doing so would unlock new abilities and new shields. The Legendary Shield was capable of transforming into different shields with different attributes.

This new world I found myself in functioned, in many ways, like a video game. There was a type of magic called "status magic," and it basically let me level up by defeating enemies. When I leveled up, I got stronger.

The abstract concept of levels might not make sense immediately, but basically the harder you worked, the more powerful you got—typically in proportion to the difficulty of the task you completed. I was pretty used to the way that the system worked from reading manga, anime, and games, so I was able to pick it up pretty quickly.

I was at level 39. I'd leveled up that much after all that I'd been through.

"Did we shake them?"

"No, they're still coming."

"Damn!"

I was being chased by a person named Motoyasu Kitamura. He was 21-years-old.

Like me, he had also been summoned to this world from another place. He was from a modern version of Japan too, but it was different from my own Japan. He was the Spear Hero.

Among the four of us heroes, he was the best looking. We are both guys, but I can admit that.

But he was a womanizer of sorts. He only thought about girls.

Motoyasu and the other two heroes all seemed to know

about this world as they had played games similar to it before. They knew where to go and what to do to level up as fast as possible.

Despite knowing all that stuff, Motoyasu refused to teach me anything, and he played a big part in having me framed.

If he had enough free time to bother me, shouldn't he be fighting to save the world or something?

There were two other heroes. The Sword Hero was Ren Amaki, and the Bow Hero was Itsuki Kawasumi. Both of them had also been summoned from other modern versions of Japan.

Ren was 16 years old. He had black hair and looked very "cool." He was the silent swordsman type.

Itsuki was 17, I think. At first he looked kind of quiet and boring, but he seemed to be very good with his hands.

It didn't look like Ren or Itsuki were chasing me. They must be harboring some suspicions about all that had happened.

"Should I hide us with magic?"

"Sure."

The girl suggesting the magic was named Raphtalia.

She had the ears and tail of a *tanuki* because she was a raccoon-type demi-human girl.

She looked to be around 18 years old. Standing a little shorter than I did, she looked healthy, and attractive, and serious. You didn't have to be friends with her to notice how attractive she was.

Her hair was long and brown, with languid curls and a notable sheen. Her arms and legs were long and slender. She really did look like a model.

After I was summoned to this world and framed and left to my own devices without friends or equipment or money, I met Raphtalia. Actually, I bought her as a slave with the spare money I was able to make on my own.

She was under a slave curse that gave me complete control over her, including whether she lived or died. I could set rules for the curse, and it would cause her pain when she broke them. After I was betrayed and framed, I completely lost the ability to trust people, and that was why I bought a slave, because they had no choice but to do as I said. With the slave curse on her, Raphtalia wouldn't be able to lie.

I wasn't able to inflict any damage on enemies, so she held a sword and fought on my behalf.

When I bought her, she was just a young girl—around 10 years old.

But demi-humans grow up differently than normal people. When they are young, their bodies mature with their level.

She leveled up quickly enough, and that's why she looks older these days.

That maturation process is probably why demi-humans and humans are treated so differently here.

Before the first wave came, Raphtalia and I were able to

level up and get good enough equipment to survive the disaster. But later on Motoyasu heard that I was using a slave, and he challenged me to a duel—even though I wasn't capable of attacking at all.

The king of the country that summoned us, Melromarc, demanded that the duel take place, and he even saw to it that I lost through some cowardly intervention. So Raphtalia was freed from the slave curse, but she decided that she still wanted to stay with me. She's still here by my side as my slave.

However, she never does anything that would activate the slave curse, and I took off all the curse settings that could have impacted our relationship. So she was really just a slave in name only.

Raphtalia wanted to fight with a hero to save the world... She wanted to fight against the waves.

In the past, before the waves came, Raphtalia lived in a village with her family. She lost everything when the waves came, including both of her parents and the village itself.

That was why she wanted to do something about them.

The heroes were charged with fighting against the waves, and she had lost everything to the waves—our goals were perfectly in line.

Originally I thought of Raphtalia as an easily usable slave, but now she is my dependable partner, my right hand, and I have parental feelings toward her. I really wanted to protect her, and keep her out of harm's way, but Raphtalia was driven to battle, and I couldn't stop her.

She was at level 40.

"Leave it to me."

"Thanks—sorry."

"What are you talking about? We're on the same side here. You don't have to feel bad."

"You're right. It's just… this guy is so damn persistent!"

"I know."

There I was again, complaining without thinking.

"What should Mel and I do?" asked Filo.

"Good question. Filo, you stay in human form. If there's trouble, turn into a Filolial. Melty, you just stay quiet."

"Okaaay!"

"The way you phrase that, it's like you think I'm making a racket back here!"

"Yeah, yeah… Okay, Melty, you keep watch to the rear."

The two people yelling at me were both young girls.

The first one was Filo.

She was a 10-year-old girl with little wings, blonde hair, and blue eyes.

She had wild, innocent blue eyes, soft cheeks, and a naïve demeanor.

She wore a one-piece dress with a large ribbon on the chest. It was a simple dress, but it brought out the cuteness factor of her little face and wings.

But she was really the Queen of the Filolials—giant carriage-pulling bird monsters. Something like that anyway.

In her real form she was a giant owl… or penguin… some kind of bird bigger than a person. She could run very fast.

Her feathers were mostly white, with little flecks of pink mixed in.

Personality-wise she was very childish and innocent. She ate like a pig, though, and was downright crazy compared to what her composed appearance would suggest.

She was such a glutton that she'd eat anything. Once she even tried to eat the rotting flesh of a dead dragon.

We met when Raphtalia and I went to have Raphtalia's slave curse reapplied. The slave-trader had a booth set up at the back of his tent where you could pick a monster egg from a large box of eggs. I picked an egg, and out hatched Filo.

She was born only two months before.

For some reason that I don't really understand, she gained the ability to transform into a human girl with little wings on her back. Now she spends most of her time in human form when she isn't pulling the carriage.

More than anything, she loved pulling heavy carriages. She'd always look over at me when she did it, as if she wanted me to give her approval.

But she had recently made a friend and discovered that there are more important things in life than eating, sleeping, and playing.

Still, it was because of Filo that we were able to travel around selling things, and that was how we'd made all our money.

Filo thought of me as her owner, and of Raphtalia as her big sister. Honestly though, I had started to think of Filo as a daughter of sorts.

She was at level 40—the same as Raphtalia.

"Mr. Naofumi. Your hand, please…"

"Sure."

Raphtalia's tail fluffed up as she prepared to use a magic spell.

I took her hand and squeezed it.

"Hey! Big Sister and Master are cuddling! I want to cuddle too!"

"We are not CUDDLING! Think about the situation we are in, please."

"But… But, Sister! You're keeping Master all to yourself!"

"That's fine, but if you don't stay quiet we won't get away from the bad men. Melty—help keep her quiet."

"Very well. Filo, you have to calm down for a second."

"Booo! Big Sister! You know that Master likes me best!"

"What are you talking about?"

"If you don't hurry up, they'll catch us!"

That was Melty.

Her real name was Melty Melromarc.

She was the same size and age as Filo, but her hair was a bright blue—very noticeable.

She kept her hair in pigtails. Her face always portrayed a look of heavy purpose. She normally dressed in frilly gothic dresses, but at that moment she was dressed in cheap, tattered, farmer's clothing.

She was as attractive as Filo or Raphtalia. You could tell that she'd be a real beauty when she grew up. As for her personality, I didn't really understand her that well. She was picky with her words and ended up sounding sarcastic at times.

A few moments ago I told everyone to be quiet, and she told me to stop freaking out.

When we first met she spoke very politely and considered her language—but the more time we spent together the less patient, and more stern, she became.

That was only natural when you thought about it.

This Melty girl was the younger princess of the country that was currently chasing us. Her life was in danger, and so she didn't have any other choice but to run away with us. But by sticking with us, she put us in danger too. It's why we were being chased.

Melromarc did not think well of the Shield Hero. When I started traveling around and helping people, the populace started to question if I was really as bad as they said. Those were doubts the Crown wanted to suppress. To do so, they framed me for yet another crime, and now I was a wanted man.

The story went like this: Melty, the younger princess, also happened to be first in line for the throne. So she was the heiress to the kingdom, and they accused me of kidnapping her.

You might think that we should just turn her over to the authorities, but unfortunately it wasn't that simple. There was another person in line for the throne after Melty, and there were reasons to think that that person was plotting Melty's assassination. If we were to just hand the princess over to someone like that, they were sure to have her killed.

So in the end we were forced to cooperate with one another.

If we wanted to prove our innocence, we were going to have to bring Melty to her mother, the Queen of Melromarc. Just to make matters worse, the queen was not currently in Melromarc but was on a diplomatic mission in a foreign country. We weren't going to just run into her on the street.

Furthermore, Melty and Filo had become best friends.

Melty was borderline obsessed with Filolials, and she and Filo were clearly on the same wavelength. They were fast friends.

Her mother, the queen, had apparently sent Melty back to Melromarc to improve relations between the king (her father) and me.

But lots of things had happened since then, and we weren't exactly on the best of terms.

I'd been calling her "Princess" for a while, but then she screamed at me and demanded I call her by her name. So now we are on a first-name basis.

Like Filo, Melty seemed to think of Raphtalia as a dependable older-sister type.

She was at level 19. Since she started traveling with us, she'd leveled up once.

"So, Ms. Raphtalia, what spell are you using?"

There she was, being polite to Raphtalia. Why wasn't she polite with me anymore?

I was mulling that over when Raphtalia finished casting her spell.

"I am the source of all power. Hear my words and heed them. Hide us!"

"All First Hiding!"

A tree appeared, formed from magic, and dropped its leaves over us. We were completely hidden from view.

I ducked down inside the leaves and held my breath.

A moment later Motoyasu and his retinue came running around the corner.

"Where'd he go?"

That was Motoyasu, the Spear Hero.

"Mr. Motoyasu, don't you think they have moved on?"

Motoyasu had three party members with him. They were all women.

The one that ran over and spoke to him was someone I didn't know.

"Let's move on."

"Sure, but don't forget that Naofumi has Raphtalia with him. They could be hiding around here somewhere."

How obnoxiously intuitive, he was right.

Still—if he was going to find us, he'd have to use magic of his own, or at least a skill from his legendary weapon.

If he did, we might be in a tough spot. But without a defined target he'd never be able to hit us with a spell.

"Huh? Footprints! I found footprints over here!"

Motoyasu shouted for the three women.

The footprints he'd found were not ours, and they led him in the opposite direction of our hiding place.

We'd sent Filo around to make fake tracks leading in the wrong direction. It was a good enough plan, and it looked like Motoyasu was going to fall for it.

"Let's go after them. Ah... my precious Melty. I can't believe you've been kidnapped and brain washed by the Shield Demon! I swear I will save you!"

The person who just spoke, who called Melty by name and called me a demon, was the very same person that had originally framed me and had me kicked out of the kingdom: Bitch, the princess herself. She went by the "adventuring name" of Myne Sufia, but her real name was Malty S. Melromarc.

She was Melty's sister.

She was a real monster—a bitch if I've ever met one. She loved to watch others suffer while, at the same time, she lived a life of luxury.

I had plenty of good reasons to suspect that she was behind everything that was going on with Melty and us—that she was the one pulling the strings behind the scenes.

Because of her wretched behavior and personality, her parents had decided to make Melty the heiress to the throne, despite the fact that Bitch was older.

Actually, the last time we fought she basically made her intentions as clear as could be when she started hurling attacks directly at Melty.

I hated her, and I'd taken to calling her "Bitch."

Someday I'd make sure that she got what was coming to her.

"We should get going, Mr. Motoyasu. I want to catch them as soon as possible."

Bitch sent Motoyasu off first, and after he'd gone she started snooping around the area.

"Why do we have to go through all this trouble? We could just burn the whole area."

She said, slipping a bottle from her pocket. She uncorked the bottle and proceeded to sprinkle the contents around.

I had a really bad feeling about that bottle.

If I jumped out of our hiding place to stop her, then Motoyasu would catch us for sure—so I had no choice but to sit and watch.

"Naofumi…"

"Shh!"

Melty was shaking my shoulder. She looked worried. I had a pretty good idea of what Bitch was up to, though.

"First Fire."

She waved her hand, and flames leapt from her palm to the spilled contents of the bottle.

The area affected by the spilled contents burst into flame.

I knew it. Bitch! She would burn a whole mountainside to smoke us out? What was wrong with her?

Is that how a princess should behave? Everything she did was criminal.

She was immoral!

She left the flames behind and ran off after Motoyasu.

The flames spread further, and soon they were licking at the trees. Flames were everywhere. I turned to see where Motoyasu had come from, and there was a column of smoke rising in that direction too.

"Mr. Naofumi!"

"Melty, can you use magic to take care of the fire?"

"I can put this one out, but I can't do anything about the fire she's already started. It would spread too much by the time I got close enough."

Damn… Bitch was hanging behind Motoyasu and setting fires as she went.

How miserable did she have to make us before she could be satisfied?

She was sure to pin the fires on me afterwards.

What should we do? Did we have enough time to hang back and play firefighter?

"Master! It's so smoky!"

"I know. Filo, turn into your Filolial form. We need to get out of here fast."

"Okay!"

"What are you going to do about the fire?"

"I don't know if it would help much, but can you use your magic to make it rain?"

Melty was good with water magic. That's why I wanted to know if she could do something to try to prevent further damage.

"I can try, but I won't promise anything."

Melty concentrated on casting a spell.

"I am the source of all power. Hear my words and heed them. Drop rains of mercy!"

"First Squall!"

When she finished casting the spell, rainclouds covered the sky, and heavy drops began to fall.

But the rain didn't cover a very large area.

I guess it was better than nothing.

"This whole place will be on fire soon! Raphtalia, Melty, do you have anything against running?"

"My sister is crazy! What was she thinking?"

"She's going to try to frame us for this!"

The area was beginning to fill with smoke. If the rain would come a little harder...

Filo turned back into her Filolial form with a puff of smoke, and we climbed onto her back. I kicked my heels, and we took off running in the opposite direction that Motoyasu had gone.

In the ensuing chaos of the wildfire, we had a chance to shake Motoyasu off of our trail.

Chapter One: Demi-Human Adventurer Town

We got rid of Motoyasu and escaped from the fire, but we didn't know where to go from there.

"I know he said the southwest—but where, exactly, are we supposed to go?"

In order to clear our names, we were heading to meet the queen in a country to the southwest, but no one had told us where she actually was.

It wasn't anything more than just grasping at straws, but I was hoping that if we just headed southwest and crossed the border, things would be clearer.

What I couldn't figure out was how Motoyasu had been able to find out where we were going in the first place.

My best guess was that he was asking around for eyewitness reports or something.

Could there have been a shadow on the enemy's side too?

"Shadow" was the name of the queen's secret service soldiers. They had shown up to help us a couple of times.

But from what I hear, the shadows were far from a singular organization. The enemy might have been employing them too.

According to the Shadow, the queen's group (who was trying to save us) and the Church of the Three Heroes (who accused me of kidnapping Melty but is actually trying to have her killed) were in the middle of a dispute. If the Church was as good at snooping around as I suspected, they might have been feeding Motoyasu information about our whereabouts.

The shadows that were helping us were dressed like ninjas. Apparently the group was divided into spies, and soldiers, and other specialties.

"We don't have the time to let our guard down. If we don't wait for Motoyasu to get far away from here, then we'll have to keep running for days on end."

Thanks to Motoyasu and Bitch, Melromarc's road to the southwest had been heavily damaged.

By the time we had the chance to stop and think, we'd gotten far off of our intended path.

"Filo."

"Whaaat?"

"Can you figure out where Shadow went?

"Um… I can try, but Big Sister Raphtalia is better at finding hidden things!"

"Is she?"

"Is that true, Ms. Raphtalia?"

Melty chimed in on the conversation.

"Please don't put so much pressure on me. Sometimes I feel… I feel like something strange is going on… but I wouldn't be able to tell unless I was really close."

"Yeah, good point. Sometimes I feel like we are being watched from far away. I don't know how we can hide completely."

It would be very difficult to completely escape the gaze of the shadows. Still, there was a shadow on our side too, and he was drawing attention away from us. There was a high probability that we could shake off Motoyasu.

Even better... Motoyasu stopped tailing us once night fell. Bitch probably didn't like to fight in the dark. She probably complained that a good night's sleep was the cornerstone of proper skin care, the fire-starting monster.

Whatever. As long as they weren't still chasing us, I didn't care.

"Ah."

Melty looked as though she'd had a realization. She was staring at me.

"What?"

"I know a wealthy family in this area. They might let us hide out until Motoyasu has moved on. Then we could escape without being seen."

"You want to head into town? You? And me? Even Filo is pretty recognizable these days."

My face was very well known. The crystal ball they had used was like a 3-D photograph back in my world. There wasn't a soul alive in Melromarc that didn't know my face.

If someone saw Filo, they'd report that too. She'd been turning into a more average-looking Filolial these days, but she still stood out just by being pink.

We'd seen the village from a distance, and there were clearly a number of guards posted there.

"And you say they are wealthy?"

I had a good reason for asking.

The powerful families of Melromarc tended to really hate the Shield Hero. According to what Melty said, and as far as the teachings of the Church of the Three Heroes were concerned, the Shield Hero was Melromarc's enemy. It didn't matter how many people's trust I managed to earn on my mercantile wanderings. The nobility and the powerful families would still hate me.

"I think it will be fine."

"Why?"

"This particular family always worked very closely with my mother. I think they share her way of thinking."

"What do you mean?"

"They were very involved in demi-human to human relations in Melromarc. They tried to help everyone get along."

"Then why don't they speak out against your father, Trash, and the Church?"

If they were so enlightened and active, why did everyone still disbelieve me? Why did they all hate me?

If they had really worked so closely with the queen, then they certainly couldn't claim ignorance about Melromarc's internal affairs.

"They were a noble family in charge of managing a territory called Seyaette. But they died in the wave."

"Oh…"

Why did the good people have to die so quickly?

"They were vacationing in their lands when the wave happened. They fought to protect the people who lived there… until the end."

"That's terrible…"

"Yes. We lost them in the first wave. It was a great sacrifice."

Huh? The first wave?

I looked over at Raphtalia. She had met a hard fate during the first wave too.

Raphtalia nodded.

"My village was under the protection of the governor. But the governor died, and we tried to rebuild… the village was…"

So it was all true.

"When we lost that family, we lost the last voice that spoke for the compassionate treatment of demi-humans. Any remaining powers that held the same views were given reassignments by my father. That's not the worst of it either. I've heard that the inhabitants of Seyaette met a hard fate in the ensuing violence."

"Violence by the Crown's soldiers."

Raphtalia was unable to hide her irritation.

Melty silently nodded. She appeared to understand what had happened.

"I believe my mother, once she returns, will see that they are punished. She sent a letter, but it seems to have been ignored. Once all this is over, Raphtalia, please tell me about the soldiers that did these things."

"I will."

"Your father is up to no good."

"Father…"

Melty looked disappointed.

She should be disappointed. One of her parents and her sister were after her life.

Melty says that he's just being used, but could Trash, the king, really be innocent?

Still, the real mystery was the queen and this noble family. Were they really working for demi-human liberation? Here in human-supremacist Melromarc? I didn't have enough information to fathom a guess at their true intentions.

But I digress. Back to the topic at hand.

"Ok, and you say there is a noble family in these parts with ties to the past governor of Seyaette?"

"I think so. They were not close with my father, and I believe they were forcibly removed from their lands."

"That's a real gamble."

It sounded like this family was having a rough time. But it wasn't like I knew nothing about the area.

I guess it happened gradually over a few weeks, but with Filo pulling the carriage, I'd managed to travel most of the country. There were even times when I knew people and places that Melty mentioned.

I didn't travel as the Shield Hero though. I pretended to be a holy saint of a bird-god, and I traveled around selling cheap accessories for handsome prices.

I remembered a rather intellectual-looking, young family. I'd met a young guy that seemed very kind. My private nickname for him was "Nice Guy."

I'd secretly snickered to myself at the time, but could it be that he'd done business with me—and he'd known that I was the Shield Hero?

He might have. He had seemed affable. Thinking back on it further, I remembered seeing some demi-human adventurers around town too. Raphtalia might be able to walk around without arousing suspicion.

"It's a risk to enter the town, especially for Melty and Filo."

"Why?"

Melty cocked her head inquisitively. Filo did it too—I wished she wouldn't copy Melty like that.

"Your blue hair stands out too much."

Melty's hair was noteworthy. It was a deep blue… almost navy.

It was rare to come across people with deep blue hair, so she stood out even when she wore a disguise.

As for Filo: her Filolial form, and of course her Filolial Queen form, drew the attention of anyone walking by. Don't even get me started on her human form. She was impossible to hide. If we all walked in wearing heavy robes to hide our identities, that would look suspicious too.

"You stand out too, you know."

"You're right."

"Hey, Master! How about we wait until dark. Then everyone can sit on my back, and I'll jump over the city gate!"

"That's not a bad idea, but we'd be caught if there was a single guard on duty."

"Raphtalia could use her magic to help us…. but I guess that if we used advanced magic, that would draw attention too…"

"What should we do then? It seems like we can count on support. And yet…"

Running away probably wasn't a bad idea. But constantly running away from Motoyasu had me exhausted.

My body was telling me that it needed rest. Motoyasu was not our only enemy. We might have to fight with adventurers, soldiers, or bounty hunters. We needed to rest up.

"Um…"

Raphtalia raised her hand.

"What is it?"

"What if they've been following the news, and they are expecting us to stop by?"

Hm… that very well might be the case.

After all that happened, it seemed like the country was divided into two factions over how to deal with me.

"Good point. And you know, Naofumi, a demi-human adventurer might be more willing to listen to us."

"Why do you think so?"

"Did you forget? If the Shield Hero is the enemy of human-supremacist Melromarc, then what would the demi-humans think of him?"

She had a point. Among the countries that were on bad terms with Melromarc, one of them was a nation of demi-humans.

It seemed like the Church of the Three Heroes was the national religion of Melromarc—which meant that any nation that stood in opposition to Melromarc might be more willing to cooperate with us.

And that meant that demi-humans might be more inclined to listen to us.

Thinking back on it, I recalled then some of my first customers had been demi-human adventurers. It might be worth a shot.

"All right. When we get to the town, let's try talking to a demi-human adventurer."

"Okay."

"I hope it goes well."

"Here we go!"

We made for the nearby village, careful to stay hidden on the way.

"Ex… Excuse me!"

"Hey!"

As we drew closer to the town where we expected to meet the nobility, we found a demi-human adventurer on the road. We hid in the shadows and called out to him, but…

"Oh man… that's the tenth time! Naofumi, what did you do?"

"I don't know!"

When the demi-human caught sight of my face he made an exaggerated apology and ran away.

But why? Had my demonic reputation spread even to them?

Things were not going as smoothly as I'd hoped.

"It doesn't look like he reported us."

"You're right. He ran, and then we ran—but no soldiers have shown up."

I had been worried that the town guards would find us and

chase us away. But so far no one seemed to be around.

Honestly, as we were walking down the road, it looked like even the demi-humans would run off to a different path when they caught sight of us.

"Maybe I should approach them?"

"Will you do it for us, Raphtalia?"

"Sure."

"If anything happens, call for help immediately."

"All right."

"You can do it, Big Sister!"

So Raphtalia stepped in to approach some demi-humans we encountered.

It had me a little worried. The demi-humans in Melromarc always seemed to be on their toes—always ready to dash off.

It must have been very uncomfortable for them to be in Melromarc. They were always aware of their status.

I wondered what they were doing here, but the sheer number of people seemed like a good enough explanation.

Raphtalia came back from talking with the demi-human adventurers.

"I'm back."

"What happened?"

"Well, I found out why they won't talk to you. It seems that they have been ordered not to speak with you directly."

"What's that supposed to mean?"

"I thought it was weird too, so I asked in a way that seemed natural. They said that the Shield Hero told them not to speak with you."

The last Shield Hero had told the demi-humans not to talk to me? That could be a problem.

So the only reason Raphtalia talked to me was because, at first, she didn't know that I was the Shield Hero? And because she was in trouble? It's like this whole world was set up to make me miserable!

"Naofumi, didn't you once tell demi-humans to stay away from you?"

"I don't remember that."

"That's strange. My mother once said that the Shield Hero had ordered everyone to stay away from him. Demi-humans worship the Shield Hero, so they were only obeying his wishes."

What?

"You mean because Master said to stay away?"

"Could that be it?"

"I don't remember saying that. Was it a previous Shield Hero?"

"No. So you mean that it's not true? Could it all be a misunderstanding?"

It had to be the Church of the Three Heroes!

"I heard that this happened a few days after you were summoned here, Naofumi."

I was pretty messed up then, and I don't remember much about the first couple weeks.

It was when I had just been framed and arrested. I didn't trust anyone, and I told off anyone that tried to talk to me.

Could it be that someone who sincerely wanted to team up with me had approached me? Could I have told them to stay away from me?

"Naofumi? You don't think…"

"Anyway, can we get into the town?"

I changed the subject. I couldn't tolerate the way that Melty was staring at me.

"Well, they seemed friendly for as long as we spoke. They know how foolish Melromarc is being. They said the Church was crazy."

"Did they mention any reports about us?"

"They said that everyone has been told the Shield Hero is close. But they also said that all the demi-humans were in agreement that they wouldn't say anything if they saw him."

"Huh… Well, it sounds risky, but should we try it?"

If things turned sour, we could always escape on Filo. We could throw capes over our faces…

"Hello?"

"What?"

We were hiding in the bushes, but did someone just call out for us?

I looked out to the road, and Nice Guy was there. He wore glasses, and was sitting in a high-class carriage. He stopped it and called out to us.

Yeah, I remembered. Nice Guy had been nobility in that town.

"Could that be Princess Melty and the Shield Hero in there?"

"Um… yes?"

"Yeah."

"It's dangerous to speak here. Would you accompany me back to my residence?"

Judging by the direction he'd come from, he must have come out here to meet us. So he HAD been thinking about us.

"If you try to hand us off to the other heroes, we'll cause a big ruckus."

"Naofumi, you shouldn't…"

"And by 'We,' I mean my subordinates and this barbaric princess."

"What was that?!"

Melty shot me an ice-cold glare.

"YOU'RE the barbarian!"

"What are you saying? I'm the most sophisticated hero by a long shot."

"You once sold me an item, for which I am very grateful. The materials are quite simple, so you see pieces like it everywhere, but your design, Hero, makes it much more valuable to me. It cost five times more than similar items, but I still feel like it was worth it."

Melty was really glaring at me now.

"I'm very sorry."

Raphtalia held her head in her hands.

"Anyway, Naofumi, we should go with this man for now. We can hear all about how you've behaved later."

"Why do I have to talk with YOU about MY behavior?"

"Because these issues are going to keep popping up. Could it be YOUR fault that people call you the Shield Demon?"

"Any stories you hear will be stories of my valorous deeds."

"Don't act like you are proud of your crimes!"

Whatever. I can deceive my enemies all day long and not feel a bit of guilt for it.

It's all about perspective. Modesty can look like cowardice to an enemy.

"That's enough for now. If you cause a fuss here, the Spear Hero will find us."

Hm… Raphtalia was right. We silently crawled into Nice Guy's carriage.

I looked out the carriage window to get a sense of what was going on outside. We had only been on the run for a few days, but I was already finding myself nostalgic for hustle and bustle. The town outside the carriage window had a backwater character.

It really did seem like there were more demi-humans around this town: lots of adventurers out and about.

Before long we arrived at Nice Guy's residence. We left the carriage and snuck inside.

"Excuse us."

Melty was sure to pardon herself before stepping inside.

Whenever she had to act as the official princess she became very polite. She spoke that way to the other heroes too.

Actually, come to think of it, she was only rude when she spoke to me.

Granted, I hadn't exactly gone out of my way to earn her respect—so I suppose I couldn't blame her.

"You must be exhausted. Please take this time to rest up."

He led us to a dining room and stepped out before reappearing with food for us.

Filo didn't have the best table manners, but Nice Guy smiled and looked genuinely pleased.

"So you have been on the run this whole time? You ended up in my territory and decided to stop by?"

"That's right. We were looking for a way to shake Motoyasu… I mean, the Spear Hero, off of our trail. We thought this might be a good place to hide out."

"I have something I'd like to ask you. I've heard that you set fires in the mountains around here to try and cover your tracks and escape from the Spear Hero. What really happened?"

Bitch. She did it all herself, but of course she blamed it on me.

"Your sister doesn't hesitate for a second, does she? She did exactly what I thought she would."

"Sister... How could you...?"

"So it's not true? I thought so!"

"Yeah, it wasn't me. It was the princess that's traveling with the Spear Hero. We were hiding from them in a bush, and I saw her set the fires myself."

Nice Guy sighed deeply.

How much worse could Bitch get?

"Very well. I hope that I can be of some use to you... Do you have any other ideas?"

"We are trying to meet with the queen, but we don't know where to go. We've had to spend all our time trying to avoid Motoyasu, and so we aren't making much progress."

The noble stood there thinking for a moment before nodding.

"Very well. I think I've understood the situation. We'll do whatever we can to help you. However, my own position is not exactly secure, so I'm not sure how much I can actually do."

"I'm not expecting much. Whatever you can do is a help."

Besides, I didn't really know how much we could trust him. I wasn't planning on staying very long anyway.

"We'd just like to rest for a little bit. Oh, and do you know anything about what the other heroes are up to?"

Motoyasu wasn't the only person we had to worry about. I had no idea what Ren or Itsuki were up to—since they didn't seem to be chasing us. It was best to try and figure out what they were doing.

I was well aware of the possibility that the Church was watching Nice Guy closely, so once I had the information I wanted I planned on escaping as soon as I could.

We had to cross a border too… I wanted to figure out the safest course we could take.

"Very well. I think I can find out how the other Heroes are occupying themselves. Please wait a little."

"We're putting you at risk. We'll leave in the morning."

"We're leaving that quickly? Shouldn't we rest up a little more?"

Melty had to make sure we all knew how she felt about it.

"There's a good chance they will come looking for us here. If we stay, we'll put these people in danger."

"Yes… Well…"

"Very well, I will look into the actions of the other Heroes, so please take this time to rest up."

"Thank you."

"I kind of wanted to rest for a few days…"

"Ms. Melty, you seem to have changed during your travels with the Shield Hero."

"What do you mean by that?"

"Before, you always put duty first when you spoke. Your true emotions never made it past your official proclamations. I think the people will prefer the new you."

Nice Guy smiled at Melty. He looked genuinely happy.

"That's… That's not true…"

"What's up, Melty?"

"Don't listen to them, Filo. This man has just decided to evaluate me."

"Oh…"

Nice guy turned to Raphtalia.

"How did Melty used to behave?"

"She always spoke very politely, and she always forced herself to be perfectly composed. She always behaved as though her position as princess was at the forefront of her mind. But as she's been traveling with us, and with the Shield Hero, she's begun to mature in a different direction. It has made me very happy to watch it happen."

"Sh… Shut up!"

"Very polite… Yeah… that is how she was. I wonder what made her change."

"Don't you think it's your fault, Mr. Naofumi?"

"MY fault? I don't think so."

It wasn't that traveling with me had changed her. It was that her true nature finally came to the surface. The outer skin had just been peeled back.

Still, that's not to say she was so bad. Compared to her father, Trash, and her pyromaniac sister, she was in a different category altogether.

"It's your fault, Naofumi!"

"Oh, don't go pinning that on me. You're the one with arsonists in the family. Hysterical traits are inheritable, you know?"

"What was that?! Are you seriously comparing me to my sister? I can't STAND that!"

Melty was glaring at me with fire in her eyes.

She must have really hated her sister. Granted, she was impossible to like.

Looking at it from that perspective, Motoyasu was very impressive, not that I'm trying to stick up for him or anything.

Still, Melty was her sister, so she was definitely working with some of the same material.

I guess it just meant that she never developed a taste for the misery of others. That's what I thought, anyway—but of course I wasn't going to tell her that.

"Apologize."

"Oh fine. Fine! Melty, you're nothing like that fire demon sister of yours. There, happy?"

"You didn't really mean it!"

"You're right."

"What?!"

She was starting to get on my nerves.

"Now, now… Relax. You know Mr. Naofumi doesn't mean the things he says in times like these."

Raphtalia, acting like an enlightened angel, tried to calm Melty down.

Filo was nodding along with her. What was up with these three?

"You've finished eating, so please go to your rooms and rest up. I should have all the information I'm going to get in the morning."

He led us to our rooms, and we all started to relax.

But everything had gone so smoothly that I couldn't shake the remains of my doubt. I looked out the window at the town.

Apparently there hadn't been any poison in our food, but I wasn't sure how far we could trust this guy.

"Naofumi. Why don't you relax a little?"

"I made up my mind a while ago not to let my guard down in times like this. That's what this world has taught me."

"But if you don't rest, you'll just get more and more tired out."

"I've had all my things stolen while I slept. If you don't

watch your back, people will betray you."

"Oh come on... Why can't you just trust someone for once?"

"Because of your sister and father!"

"I understand that! I'm just saying you could try to trust a little more!"

"Whatever. I will rest up as I see fit."

"You're not the only one upset with Father and Sister! So just relax!"

"Who else is?"

"My mother. Before we parted ways, she would take paintings and statues of Father and Sister and burn them whenever they behaved this way."

"Well, you reap what you sow. If she doesn't know how to choose a man, she doesn't know how to raise a daughter."

"Are you speaking ill of my mother?!"

It's been like this since Melty started traveling with us. She was always freaking out about something.

She even behaved this way knowing full well that people were after our very lives. If I let my guard down, she was going to get us all killed.

"Ok, Mr. Naofumi. We will all keep watch while you get some rest."

"Huh? Oh... okay then."

"Why do you listen to everything that Raphtalia says?!"

"Because I trust Raphtalia."

"Oh, and you don't trust me?!"

"Not particularly…"

It's just that we were in a situation where she couldn't turn on us.

People were after our lives, and she helped us in battle. It wasn't that I didn't trust her—not exactly.

She behaved as she should, as the second princess and first heiress of the kingdom.

So in that regard, I suppose I could trust her.

But that is not what this was about.

Sure, I'd been traveling with Raphtalia for much longer, but even setting that aside, Raphtalia was far more experienced than Melty.

Trust had a lot to do with that.

"Hey Mel! I want to check out the rest of this house!"

Filo jumped into the conversation with something completely unrelated.

"Good idea. It might be good to go for a walk to improve my mood. Okay then, Raphtalia. Filo and I are going for a walk around the house.

"An adventure!"

Filo wanted her to say "adventure," but Melty just smiled, waved, and left the room.

Finally—some quiet.

When she left the room I realized how tired I really was.

I lay down on the bed, trusted Raphtalia to keep watch, and drifted off to sleep.

Urm… I could feel someone approaching. How long had I been sleeping?

Ever since Bitch betrayed me, I've started to come out of my sleep whenever I feel someone approaching.

"If you get any closer, Mr. Naofumi will wake up."

"But! But! I want to sleep with Master!"

Filo must have returned from her adventure around the house.

…Which must mean that Melty was back too.

Everything was so noisy these days… and I'd finally managed to fall asleep.

"You can't. We already talked about this."

"But! Big Sister, you said that you slept with him once."

"You can get close while he's still awake. You have to do it before he falls asleep."

"Okay, then I'll ask him when he's awake!"

"…I don't think he'll like it."

Raphtalia really understood me.

If someone approaches while I'm sleeping I won't be able to get any real rest.

Just like what was happening now. I was asleep, but I woke up when Filo came over.

"…Yawwwwn."

Raphtalia yawned deeply. She must be sleepy too.

"Ms. Raphtalia, you should get some sleep too. I'll keep watch."

"Are you sure it's okay?"

"Leave it to me."

"Okay then. Good night."

Raphtalia lay down on the next bed over, and it was only a minute before she was sleeping soundly.

Shortly afterward, I could hear Filo and Melty whispering back and forth.

Melty kept trying to quiet Filo down.

"Hey, Filo."

"What?"

Melty was whispering now.

"I know they were just talking about it, but it's true. I used to always be very careful to speak politely."

Yeah, Nice Guy had mentioned that.

Sure, she had always used formal language before… was she trying to say that her real self was that polite character?

"But ever since I started talking with Naofumi, my language has gotten more coarse… more vulgar. I used to be able to speak with him properly, but now all I do is complain…"

It kind of sounded like she was crying.

Could it have been that hard for her?

"Earlier, when Naofumi was telling me what to do, I even surprised myself. I sounded so hysterical... It's like I'm not myself anymore! Filo, am I... am I going crazy?"

"Um..."

For the first time ever, Filo didn't seem to know what to say.

Melty had picked the wrong person to confide in. What kind of advice did she think that Filo was capable of offering? Raphtalia might have been able to help, but Filo? I could have gotten out of bed and talked with her, but she didn't know that I was listening, and she would probably freak out if I stood up now.

"You pretended to sleep and eavesdropped on me?!"

...She'd say something like that. That would only make her worry more.

I don't know what caused it, but it sounded like somehow, through spending time with me, Melty had stumbled upon some kind of honesty switch, and now she couldn't stop herself from complaining all the time. Best to let sleeping dogs lie. It wasn't my problem to fix.

"Mel? What do you think of Master?"

"Huh? What do you mean?"

"Well, you only act that way to him, right? You're still polite with other people."

"Maybe..."

"Do you feel like you can say anything to him?"

"Huh? Y… You think?"

"Cause when I watch you talking to him, it looks like you are excited, like you are really into the conversation."

Well, well. Filo had really grown up.

Did it mean that Melty, that the REAL Melty, was a hysterical psycho?

Her place in the nobility had given her education, manners, and virtue—all the things she needed to hide her true self. But when she was with me, she couldn't hide her inner bitch. Is that what Filo wanted to say?

"Th… That's not it at all! Filo, don't say things like that!"

"Mel, I didn't mean to say anything weird. Let's both just let Master spoil us!"

"What are you saying? That's not me."

"It's not?"

It sounded like they were about to get into an argument.

This… this had to be a dream. Melty wouldn't talk that way. She wouldn't sound so weak…

That's what I told myself.

The next time I woke up, Raphtalia was sleeping in the other bed with Filo, and Melty was looking out the window. It was twilight.

I raised myself up in bed, and Melty looked over at me.

She looked composed, meek. I had a flash of the dream again.

"You're up."

"Yeah. Ready to switch shifts?"

"I'm not that tired, so I'm fine."

"Okay."

Still, I couldn't picture the two of us just gazing out of the window in silence. The whole room was still, silent.

"Hey, Naofumi?"

"What?"

"I've been thinking about it since we got here. I've been thinking... maybe I should just ask this family to deliver me to my father."

"Really?"

It was true that we were being chased, but Melty herself wasn't accused of anything. The Crown was still treating all this as a kidnapping.

Even if Trash had reassigned this noble family... if they delivered Melty to Trash then she would be okay... maybe?

Of course, she'd only be okay if they could get her into the castle and give her directly to Trash.

Anyway, it would be more effective than meeting Trash with me.

"Maybe... I don't want to drag you guys down... And I want to do what I should."

She was really thinking—despite being so young. She needed to clear her name, and if she went back to Trash then she could prove my innocence too.

"If we could prove it was safe, then it might be a good idea."

"Of course, I already know that it will be dangerous. Still, it might be less dangerous than traveling with you, considering how my sister is on your tail."

For Melty, anyone connected to her sister was a sure source of danger. So traveling with us was a guaranteed series of dangerous battles.

If that was true, then it really might be best for her to sneak back to Trash while we drew attention away from her.

It wasn't like we needed Melty to be with us when we met with the queen anyway.

"It's only an idea. Just keep it in mind."

"I know. You sure are thinking about things."

"Are you treating me like a child?!"

"That's not what I meant. I was just realizing how much you've thought it through."

"But you said it like…"

And there she was again, picking a fight with me. At the time, I had no way to know that we'd have to put her plan into action very soon. The catalyst was already on its way.

Chapter Two: Noblemen

Dusk fell.

I was looking out the window, and I saw a carriage drive onto the premises.

Melty and Filo were off exploring the mansion—apparently they hadn't seen much of it last time.

Raphtalia was asleep. I woke her and told her to prepare for a fight.

What was happening?

A small, portly man jumped out of the carriage and knocked on the door of the mansion. He was followed by a large group of soldiers.

A few minutes passed. Then came a knock on our bedroom door. It was the noble's maid.

"What is it?"

"You have to run away from here."

"I can see why. If you turn us over to them, I'll kill you."

I hadn't completely rid myself of the nagging doubt that Nice Guy had invited us here as a trap.

Depending on how she answered, I'd kick out the window and run.

"A noble family from a neighboring town began to

suspect that the Shield Hero was hiding here. They've come to investigate."

"What?"

So that fat guy was a noble? It didn't look like she was lying.

"Mr. Naofumi."

Raphtalia was trying to tell me something. I looked out the window.

The fat man had tied up Nice Guy with ropes and was loading him into the carriage.

Yeah. I guess he hadn't been trying to trick me after all.

He really had stood out. It looked like he had been watched, and now they were carting him off.

What should we do? If I kicked out the window and ran, that would only put Nice Guy in further danger.

"Please, think of my master. Is there no way that you can escape from here without being detected?"

The maid was standing in the doorway, pleading.

She was right. For Nice Guy to stand a chance, we'd have to sneak out without getting caught.

"If you don't hurry, the soldiers will find you. You can still make it out the back door. Please…"

"Where are Filo and Melty?"

"Both of them are preparing to run."

"Fine. But if this is a trap of some kind, I'll make sure that you suffer for it."

We quickly collected our things, opened the door, and made for the back door the maid was pointing to.

The kitchen was between the door and us.

"Hide in here!"

The maid felt someone approaching, and she stuffed us into to a secret servant room.

A second later, and we could hear people talking on the other side of the door.

"There you are. Are you hiding something?"

A man was speaking, but I didn't recognize his voice. It was probably one of the soldiers working with the noble from the next town over.

"I have a feeling that the Shield Demon is nearby. Get over here!"

"Ahh!"

The maid screamed.

"Please wait! The kitchen is our…"

"Shut up! Are you going to stand in the way of our orders?!"

The maid screamed, and the soldier laughed. It was disgusting.

"Anyway, we have reason to believe the Shield Demon is in this mansion. You will stand aside and let us investigate."

I could hear their footsteps moving off into the distance.

It didn't seem like they were coming back to the kitchen… but still.

It would not be good if they found us. Where were Filo and Melty? Even if we found them... We couldn't run away and leave them here. I prepared for the worst and turned to Raphtalia.

She placed her hand on the hilt of the sword at her waist. She was ready.

If it were a numbers game, we'd lose. But that didn't mean we couldn't win. I didn't want to get Nice Guy hurt, but...

The door in front of us rattled. Someone grabbed the doorknob and a shaft of light appeared at the doorframe.

"The younger princess is over there!"

I heard someone shout.

"I am the second Princess of Melromarc, Melty Melromarc! What are you doing with all these soldiers?!"

That was Melty. She was speaking with grave authority.

It wasn't that hysterical voice she used when she spoke with me. I could tell what she was thinking.

I couldn't hear Filo at all, which meant that they must have split up.

The door clicked shut again.

What should we do? They'd found Melty. Should we jump out of the room and save her?

"Where is the Shield Demon?!"

The soldier was shouting at Melty.

"Silence! Who do you think you are addressing?!"

"I believe it's the little Princess Melty."

I heard him shuffle his ankles together.

"Ah…"

Raphtalia had to clamp a hand over her mouth to remain silent.

What was going on? Raphtalia's face was very pale, and thick globs of sweat were streaming down her shaking face.

"Are you okay?"

I whispered to her, but she just nodded. She was still shaking.

She certainly didn't look okay.

"Have you been playing hide and seek here? Can you tell me where the Shield Demon is?"

"I'm sorry to tell you that the Shield Hero is not here."

"What does that mean?"

"I begged him. 'Please, please,' I said. 'Please leave me here and escape.' I told him that I would stay in Melromarc and clear his name."

Was she trying to do what she'd talked about earlier? That was too reckless!

"Very well, that makes sense. So, Princess, you are here alone. And the Shield Demon is not here?"

"That's correct. And I have no idea where he went."

"Did you all search the mansion?!"

"Y…Yes! We didn't find them!"

The man who'd been talking to Melty, the noble from the next town, sighed in frustration.

"Then I suppose we have no other choice. Princess Melty, please come with us."

"Very well."

They continued speaking, but they had walked away, and I could no longer hear them.

Were they just going to take Melty? Were we just going to leave her?

"Mr. Naofumi."

"Yeah."

I reached for the door.

"The Shield Hero is not here!"

Melty exclaimed loudly.

"She must have thought that we were hiding nearby. Had she sensed that we were about jump out of hiding?

Damn... If we jumped out now, did that mean we were going against Melty's wishes?

"I would very much like to speak with my father to clear all this up. Please bring me to the castle immediately."

"First I would like you to accompany me to my mansion. Then we will decide how to proceed. Everything is in accordance with God's plan."

Melty gasped. The man had explained himself enough. There was nothing left to hold me back!

I went to open the door, only to find that the Maid was standing there to block it.

"Please, you must not ignore the wishes of the princess. If you don't, my master will only receive a worse punishment."

"But we can prove our innocence—"

The maid went right on talking.

"Please, at the very least, wait until she's shown that my master has nothing to do with the Shield Hero."

Right. If they found out that Nice Guy was harboring us, they'd kill him right on the spot.

We were a small group, so we still had some flexibility. If we pulled Nice Guy and everyone into things, then it would be much harder to act.

So if we wanted to give Nice Guy a good chance of surviving this, we'd have to swing back around later to pick up Melty. That would prove that he hadn't been involved.

I hated betraying someone as much as I hated being betrayed.

It was easy enough to say it, but I owed him. I didn't want him to suffer needlessly on my account.

"My master was able to find out some information for you. The Spear Hero is currently looking for the Shield Hero far away from here. The Sword and Bow Heroes are also nowhere nearby."

Motoyasu wasn't our only enemy. The nobility scattered

around the country was going to be a real problem.

The maid slowly opened the door.

"Where is Filo? Did she go with Melty?"

"The blonde girl who was with the princess? She wasn't with Melty when she was discovered."

We went around Nice Guy's mansion looking for Filo.

I swear—you'd think it was bad enough that Melty was taken away. But now Filo was missing too.

So where did we find her? She was hiding up in the attic.

I called for her but she kept hiding. I didn't see any other option, so I activated the monster control magic and got her to come out.

At least she hadn't run far.

"Ouch! Master! You're the worst!"

"No, YOU are. You should have come when I called."

"He's right, Filo! What were you doing?!"

Raphtalia scolded her, but Filo answered with a smile on her face.

"Huh? Where is Mel?"

"You didn't notice?"

"Huh? After everything got loud and crazy, Mel said we should play hide and seek. So I hid. Mel said that I shouldn't come out for anyone."

Filo didn't understand what had happened…

If we left Melty and made for the border, if we found

asylum in another country, then we might be able to find some way to fix all this.

Melty must have known that she'd be killed if the Church got its hands on her.

If she was going to survive, Shadow would have to intervene. From what the nobleman had said, it seemed reasonable to assume that he was connected with the Church.

He'd either kill her himself, or he'd give her to Motoyasu and Bitch, and then they would kill her.

The guy wasn't a fool. He must have realized that Melty wasn't being totally honest with him.

He probably wanted to lure us out of hiding. He might torture Nice Guy.

If we left Melty and ran away, our chances of meeting the queen seemed pretty good.

That's what Melty had done. She'd given us more time to escape.

Now I just had to decide what to do with that time.

Should I tell myself that I wasn't abandoning her? Should I prioritize our lives over hers?

Melty was Bitch's sister. Still, she'd never betrayed my trust.

She'd actually put herself in danger to buy us more time, to give us a chance to survive.

There was only one thing to do.

Even if it was dangerous, I had to do what I could for someone who'd believed in me. I had to save her.

"Filo, I need you to listen very carefully."

"Okay. What?"

"Melty was taken away. She went with them to protect us."

"What?!"

Filo quickly processed what had happened, turned into her Filolial Queen form, and was ready to run.

"Wait. Where are you going?"

"I'm going to save Mel!"

I turned to Nice Guy's maid.

"I just want to check. Where did they take her?"

"Probably to the mansion in the next town. It's not very far away, but I imagine that they have already arrived."

I was familiar with the area from my peddling days. She was right. The next town was very close. Everyone there had been mean to Raphtalia, and we didn't sell anything, so we had moved on quickly.

At the time, we'd had a lot of eyes on us when we made our way into the town. They'd been very concerned with our entry—but they made it very easy to leave.

I hadn't really understood why at the time, but now it all seemed clear enough.

I remembered that, even though demi-humans were treated poorly all over Melromarc, the discrimination had been especially bad in that town.

I didn't know all that much about Melromarc, but it seemed to be that way.

Another explanation might be the notable difference in power between the nobility in that town versus the nobility in this town.

I remember the neighboring town being much larger.

To be honest, the town we were hiding out in was more of a little village. Looking around at the state of the houses, I nodded to myself. Yeah, this place didn't have the same authority as the other town.

I'd heard something about the nobility in that town too… There was some sort of legend associated with the place…

What was it? It had something to do with a previous hero defeating a monster and sealing it away…

I remembered that they'd made some kind of attraction out of the site.

"Do you have a sketch of the mansion they took Mel to?"

"We know someone that has been there many times. Maybe you could listen to their description of the place and make a map of sorts?"

That was a good idea. Better to trust those who had already been there.

Shortly afterwards, I had a simple map in my hand.

The mansion was three stories tall, and built around a central courtyard. They said that Melty was probably being held in a room near the back of the second floor.

"Got it. I'm sorry about all this. We're leaving now. Filo, Raphtalia, let's go."

"Okay!"

"Yes!"

The owner of this mansion, Nice Guy, had been taken too.

I didn't want to put him in any more danger than he already was. What could I do?

I couldn't let them know that he had helped us... I'd have to say that we had come to take Melty from him.

I'd have to get them to think that Nice Guy had somehow taken Melty from us.

If I couldn't convince them, they might torture him to death.

This town had a reputation in Melromarc for being full of demi-humans. I had to do what I could to protect it.

A few moments later, and we were chasing after the carriage that had taken Melty.

"Damn..."

The demi-humans around Nice Guy's town were out in the streets and agitated. Nice Guy must have meant a lot to them.

If I told them all that I was the Shield Hero, they might have jumped in to help, but at the same time I didn't want to involve more people than necessary. Besides, if it became common knowledge that Nice Guy had been harboring us, he'd only end up in worse trouble than he already was.

If I went with just Raphtalia and Filo, the small size of our group would give us flexibility and speed—both of which were necessary if we wanted to stand a chance of saving Melty.

Soon enough, I was riding on Filo's back, and we had jumped over the wall and snuck into the neighboring town.

Luckily, thanks to Raphtalia's magic, we'd been able to deepen the darkness of night and sneak in undetected.

"Think it's that big mansion over there?"

There was a large hill in the center of town, and a large mansion stood on the top of it. It only seemed natural that the governor would live there.

"Yeah… That's got to be it."

Raphtalia silently nodded.

"What's wrong?"

"It's nothing."

Raphtalia was definitely acting strange.

"I didn't notice the last time we passed through here. But now… now I'm sure."

"What do you mean, Big Sister?"

We were still perched on the wall around town. Raphtalia was glaring at the mansion. She looked very agitated.

"I'll make it darker. Then we should hurry up and make our approach. If we don't hurry, who knows what will happen?"

Raphtalia cast a spell to darken our surroundings, and we made our way to the mansion by jumping from roof to roof. I couldn't be sure that no one had seen us. But then again, who walks around town at night looking up at the roofs?

"It doesn't look like any of the town guards have noticed us yet. You think they would be on closer guard, considering the situation with the princess."

"I think it is because, at nighttime, these nobles do things that they can't tell others about. Even if they heard that you were approaching, I doubt they'd be able to respond very quickly."

"What are you talking about? What do you know?"

"Yes… This town is different from other places. The nobility here don't want the guards to keep too close of a watch."

"Are you talking about what happened when you were a slave?"

"Yes."

Raphtalia silently nodded.

This nobleman… He was the one that had tortured her… the one who had finally broken her spirit.

If a guy like that had his hands on Melty… who knows what he was capable of?

"Did you hear that, Filo? If we don't hurry, Melty will be in trouble."

"Yeah! Let's go save her!"

On Filo's back, we jumped over the mansion's fence.

"Woof! Woof!"

Monsters that had been raised to guard the premises had noticed a strange smell on the wind. They were basically oversized guard dogs.

They were called Guardia. They were black creatures with fangs like wolves.

There was some kind of device on their backs that emitted a noise like a whistle. Their barking and the whistling were enough to alert the dullest of guards to our presence.

"Shut up!"

"Hawooooo!"

A Guardia came running for us, but Filo reared back and kicked it across the face. It flew through the air, silent.

Filo was taking out monsters quicker than they could bark. It was kind of scary.

"What was that?"

Drawn by the noise, a guard came running.

"What the— hey!"

"I'm sorry! Please be quiet!"

Raphtalia quickly jammed the hilt of her sword into his stomach, knocking him out.

Everyone seemed perfectly accustomed to what they were doing. We were like robbers.

"Master, we have to hurry."

"We got a quick sketch of the place, but… Raphtalia? Do you know your way around?"

"All I really know is the basement."

"Do you think they are keeping Melty there?"

Raphtalia said nothing but shook her head.

This nobleman was the kind of person who took joy from the torture of demi-humans.

If he had access to the second princess of Melromarc, would he torture her? The answer seemed clear: yes.

We had to find some way into the building.

I stopped to think. Our immediate goal was rescuing Melty.

There were no other heroes around. Any soldiers of the Crown that happened to be in the area should be easy enough for us to take care of.

Or so I was thinking when the gate of the mansion swung open. A large group of guards came rushing out.

"What's that?"

"Filo, do you see?"

In response to Raphtalia's question, Filo rose up onto her toes and turned to the crowd of guards.

Behind us, at the wall surrounding the town, I could see the flickering light of torches, and smoke was rising from the town gate.

"Huh? Are they, um… fighting?"

"Who? Who's fighting who?"

"Um… The demi-humans and the soldiers?"

So the demi-human adventurers were so upset that Nice

Guy had been taken they teamed up and came after him. The soldiers mistakenly believed that I was leading them. I had to find some way to put this situation to use.

"Perfect timing. All the soldiers have come out and are running to the battle at the gate. Before they can come back, we are going straight through the front door and saving Melty!"

"Yeah!"

"Huh? Mr. Naofumi, are you sure we shouldn't sneak in?"

"We can take these soldiers. They're weak. You know we can take them."

Both Raphtalia and Filo were at level 40, and that was the highest level they could get to without going through a class-up ceremony. But I had seen the soldiers fighting during the wave. They were not nearly strong enough to defeat Raphtalia or Filo.

If they came after us, we'd take them out. If they attacked the mansion, we'd take them out.

"We need to have the first move. Think about it. We are running away from the Crown to meet with the queen. If none of the heroes are nearby, we can get away with causing a little fuss."

"That makes sense."

"Okay! Let's go!"

Boing!

At my signal, Filo bounded forward, kicked out a window, and jumped into the house.

"Don't hold back, Filo! Just keep charging! You can knock down the walls if you have to!"

Still, we needed to go slow enough to make sure we found the room where they were keeping Melty.

The sketch seemed to indicate that she'd been on the second floor—but that could be wrong.

"Filo, you just keep breaking things! Raphtalia and I will keep looking for Melty."

"Okay!"

Filo turned left and charged down a hallway. I turned to the courtyard, ran through it, and made for the second floor.

On my way through the courtyard, I noticed a strange boulder of sorts.

What was it? Some kind of gravestone?

Who would put a gravestone in their garden? This guy had issues.

Granted, he tortured people in his basement for fun. There was no use in trying to understand him.

I could hear Filo crashing through the house.

Now we just had to wait and see how the nobleman would respond.

If he noticed the excitement, what would he imagine the cause to be? Sure, he might deduce that it was the Shield Hero coming after him to take back Melty.

If that's what he thought, he'd probably make a hostage of her.

The other possibility he might think of was that the demi-humans were revolting after he took Nice Guy.

If that's what he thought, he'd probably make a hostage of Nice Guy.

It was like we were participating in the demi-human revolt. Sure, once he saw Filo he would figure it out soon enough.

"Mr. Naofumi! Over here!"

Raphtalia had made it through the courtyard and was pointing to a hallway. There was a door at the end of it.

"This door leads down to the basement."

"Do you think he's keeping Melty down there?"

"No. But he might be keeping a captured slave down there."

"Do you think we have the time to save them? It will only make more trouble."

"But still… I…"

If there was a slave down there, they were definitely demi-human.

Before she met me, Raphtalia experienced true horrors down there.

I heard about the terrible things he'd done. She must have wanted to save her past self, her old friends.

We didn't have the time. But if we could free them, we might be able to save a life.

At least that's what I thought Raphtalia was thinking.

"Fine. But we have to save Melty first. The enemy probably knows that we are here."

"Okay!"

There was a loud crash, and a series of explosive booms.

What was Filo getting up to?

"Melllllllll!!"

Filo's voice was echoing through the mansion. Yeah, no one was going to give Filo any trouble.

Considering that the other heroes weren't around, I figured it was safe to assume that Filo could handle herself.

"Take care of the intruders!"

A few guards were running for us. They looked ready for a fight.

"The... The Shield Demon! Tell the governor!"

"Raphtalia!"

"Yes!"

She drew her sword and ran for the guards.

I followed her. The foolish guards drew their swords and came after me.

I was currently using the Chimera Viper Shield.

As the Shield Hero, I didn't have the ability to attack. But I WAS able to use counter attacks.

The Chimera Viper Shield had a counter effect called Snake Fang (medium).

It meant that whenever successfully blocking an enemy's

attack, the snake on the shield would animate and sink its fangs into the enemy. It also poisoned them.

"Damn! That shield is so hard... Is it... Is it moving?! Argh!"

As I just explained, the snake on my shield lashed out and bit deep into the soldier who'd attacked me.

Once poisoned by Snake Fang (medium), you had to be careful. It you weren't, the poison could kill you.

"You better get the hell out of here and find yourself some antidote. If you don't, that'll kill you."

That's what he got for assuming I couldn't hurt him.

"Ugh..."

"Damn the Shield Demon!"

The other soldiers picked up their poisoned comrade and backed away.

I could have gone after them and taken them down—but our goal was saving Melty, not killing soldiers.

Nice Guy had only been protecting Melty. The Shield Hero had nothing to do with it... but that was getting harder to believe by the minute. Especially now that the demi-humans Nice Guy fought for were revolting.

Still, I had to do what I could.

I turned on the fleeing soldiers and shouted at them like a madman.

"Where is Princess Melty?! And don't even think about

lying to me! I don't care if she's here or there, but mark my words: we're taking her back!"

The soldiers agreed to take us to Melty. When we got there, Filo was locked in a death-stare with the plump nobleman.

The fat guy was holding a knife to Melty's throat. He held her tight against himself so that Filo couldn't get any closer. Nice Guy was collapsed on the floor between them.

He looked like he had been tortured. Melty looked like she had been crying.

This guy was evil.

"Governor!"

"You fools! Who told you to bring the Shield Demon here?! You've betrayed me!"

"Aren't you haughty?"

Filo had apparently made it all this way by herself, so he couldn't have had many guards.

"Mel!"

"Filo! Stay back! I made up my mind! This man… He's going to take me to meet with my father."

"Do you think he will really take you there?"

"…"

Melty was silent in response to my question.

Had this guy been a healthy person, he might have kept his promise. But how could I forget that, when he loaded her into his carriage, he said, "Everything was in accordance to God's plan"? He was probably a fanatic.

The national religion in Melromarc was the Church of the Three Heroes, and they were the ones who'd had me framed.

If I gave Melty's idea credence for a second and assumed that the king really didn't know what had been happening, how would he behave when he found out?

And if this guy was part of the Church, then it was doubtful he was really going to take her straight to the castle.

"Ha, ha, ha! I dare you to take a single step! This knife might slip into the princess's throat!"

"So we're okay as long as we don't take a step?"

"What?"

"Air Strike Shield!"

I sent the skill so that the shield appeared between the nobleman and Melty, forming a wall.

"Wh…?!"

"Now!"

"Yes!"

The shield had forcibly separated Melty from the nobleman. Noticing the small gap, Filo immediately ran over to him and planted a firm kick into his groin.

"Ugh!"

The fat man flew backwards and slammed into the wall.

"Raphtalia!"

"Yes!"

In a flash, Raphtalia was at Melty's side. She checked to make sure that Melty was unharmed.

"Finish the job! Take him out!"

"Mr. Naofumi. I completely understand how you feel, but I believe we should first see to Melty and the other man's wounds. Filo has taken care of the fat man for now."

"Has she?"

"Yeah, I held back a little because Mel was so close. But that fat guy is kind of strong."

He was a nobleman after all. He had probably gone through the class-up ceremony.

I ran to Nice Guy's side. He had wounds. I immediately began chanting healing spells over him.

Then I held him close and pulled him up, whispering into his ear:

"I'm sorry. We've brought you so much trouble. Remember, you had nothing to do with us. If they find out that you helped us, they might torture you further."

"I'm... sorry for everything. Don't worry... That man, he... he had no intention of letting me live. I am just happy that the demi-humans have this chance for freedom."

"Oh..."

"I negotiated all that I could. Please... Stop it."

Good. I wasn't planning on crying myself to sleep anyway.

Still, once word got out that I'd raised a hand against a Melromarc nobleman… that would only put me in a worse situation than I already was.

I still held out hope that Ren and Itsuki would eventually figure out the truth. In the meantime, I really wasn't happy about being vilified even further than I already was.

The guards looked over at the fat man and made various expressions of shock.

I finished my first aid work on Nice Guy and helped him to his feet. He turned to Melty and smiled at her.

"Both Princess Melty and the Shield Hero have treated me so kindly. Of course there was nothing to those rumors about you…"

"If you hang out with us, you'll only get wrapped up in more of these bad situations."

I didn't need any other party members. He was clearly not skilled in battle—and it's not like I was all-powerful. I couldn't guarantee his safety.

"I understand. I will simply rely on my connections to keep me hidden and safe until all of this blows over."

"Good idea."

"Excellent."

It was a relief to hear him say that. I'd been worried that we had ruined his life.

Raphtalia checked to make sure that both Melty and Nice

Guy were okay, and then she turned and glared at the collapsed nobleman. Her tail stood on end, and it was clear to Filo, Melty, and I that she was livid.

"You... How could you do this to me? Torture is not a suitable punishment for your like. I'll see to it that you pay with your very lives!"

"All the demi-humans who have died at your hands could say the very same thing."

Raphtalia said it coolly. She slipped her sword from its scabbard.

"Could they? The disgusting creatures, they aren't even human! They sneak into my town... It's like they are begging for death!"

"Yes. That's how it was. That's the sort of man you were."

"Huh? Do you... do you know me? That's right! I remember you. You're that slave I disposed of."

"Yes. We spent a lot of time together."

"Heh, heh... And look at you now. You've teamed up with the Shield Demon. I can still remember your crying face, your shouts of pain. They brought me so much satisfaction. Now I see... You've come back to me. You wish to taste desperation again!"

"No."

Raphtalia turned back to look at me. Then she returned her gaze to the nobleman.

Her sword appeared to be softly glowing.

She had an illusion sword. She was able to hide herself, appearing behind the enemy to attack. She had an attack like that anyway... but her sword seemed to be pulsing with another power all together.

"I'm not a strong enough person to help you, Mr. Naofumi. That's why I... I never rid myself of this need for revenge."

I had warned her before, but I had never stopped her.

She was always a very kind girl, but I'd known for a while that something wasn't quite right.

That's it. I'd completely forgotten. Raphtalia had wanted to get revenge on someone.

If she wanted revenge, I wanted to help her.

I wanted to help.

Even if it wasn't right, even if it wasn't the ethical thing to do, I wanted to stand on Raphtalia's side.

That day—that time when Bitch and Motoyasu and Trash were all against me, when everyone was blaming me and hating me, she'd stood up for me. She'd protected me. She'd saved me.

And now the man that hurt her was right there in front of me. I couldn't forgive him.

"I... I'm not like you, Mr. Naofumi, I can't protect anyone. I know that nothing I do will bring back my village. But I..."

She pointed her sword at the fat man.

"If I don't stop you, right now, then what happened to

me and Rifana will happen to other children. I cannot let that happen!"

"Heh... So the demi-human turns her fangs on me? Fine. I'll make sure you understand your folly!"

The nobleman took a whip from a guard and readied it.

So he fought with a whip?

Something about the whip felt bad... felt wrong.

"Master! I don't like that whip he's got!"

Filo and Melty came running to my side.

"Heh, heh... This whip has been absorbing the blood of demi-humans for years. I doubt that even the Shield Demon can stand up to it."

Wow... so it was like a cursed object?

It seemed like the kind of weapon that would curse you if a hit connected.

"Take this!"

The nobleman swung the whip.

Raphtalia and I ducked under it before it cracked.

The room was too small for Filo to maneuver, so she turned into her human form and protected Melty.

Nice Guy ducked under the swinging whip too.

Damn. The room was small enough that he could cover most of it with that whip.

"Ugh!"

The whip accidentally connected with one of the guards.

His armor warped dramatically before he threw up blood and collapsed to the floor.

It was just a whip, but it seemed to have an enormous attack power. We'd better avoid it.

"G…Governor?"

"What are you doing? Kill the Shield Demon!"

"Y…Yes sir!"

The guards came running at us.

Raphtalia swung her sword wide, and they fell.

"You're in my way!"

Raphtalia turned and dodged the whip. Then a guard thrust his sword at her. Defending with her own sword, she turned, twisted, and then flicked her wrist.

The guard's sword went flying and stuck itself into the ceiling.

"Ah…"

While the guard was processing his newly emptied hand, Raphtalia delivered a roundhouse kick to his stomach, and he flew into his master.

"You worthless trash! If this were a war zone, you'd be dead!"

The nobleman was clearly agitated now. He kept swinging his whip and trying to hit Raphtalia.

But she dodged it and turned her sword on him.

"Ugh!"

She'd dodged the whip, but it continued to swing in an arc before getting caught on the leg of a table. It swung there, turning, and the tip flew toward Raphtalia's back.

He really knew how to use the thing.

To use it in such a small space, and then to use tricks like that—he obviously had a lot of experience with the whip.

"Nice try! Air Strike Shield!"

I read the trajectory of the whip and deployed an Air Strike Shield to block it before it could hit Raphtalia.

"Move!"

Damn… The whip just wrapped around the shield and kept flying in Raphtalia's direction.

It moved like a snake.

It wrapped around Raphtalia's sword, and almost wrapped around her wrists.

But she dropped her sword before it could and jumped back to get some distance.

"Well, you've got determination. I'll give you that. But do you think you can fight me barehanded?"

Barehanded… Raphtalia was very strong. But was she strong enough to take down this nobleman without a weapon? I didn't think so. I was worried.

The fat man snapped the whip and Raphtalia's sword flew into his hand. He brandished it against us.

Raphtalia avoided his thrust with a deft backbend then

pulled out the other sword at her waist… the magic sword. She held it out at him, but there was no blade there, just an empty hilt. The magic sword had been a present from the old guy at the weapon shop—it was pure magic fashioned into the shape of a sword.

"I'm not barehanded."

The nobleman burst into laughter.

"What are you going to do with a toy sword?!"

But he was forgetting something important. I wasn't just going to sit back and watch them.

"Don't think it'll go so smoothly!"

I reached out and grabbed his whip.

My hand felt strange. It was like the whip was burning me. Pain pulsed into my hand.

I knew the thing was cursed.

"You must be a very foolish Shield Hero to reach for my whip!"

"You think? It's not so bad."

It was burning me, but I could handle the pain.

"And since you're focusing on me…"

"I can attack!"

Raphtalia's magic sword suddenly had a blade, and she quickly directed an overhead swing at him.

"Whoops!"

The nobleman abandoned his whip and jumped back to avoid her thrust.

"You're pretty quick. Not as quick as I am, though!"

He was small and plump, but he really was pretty powerful.

Judging from how he knocked out that guard with one hit, he should be fighting in the waves by himself.

Melty looked to Nice Guy.

"That man… He fought with my father a long time ago in a war against the demi-humans."

I was starting to get it. So he used to be a military man. That would explain his strength and resolve.

And if he had been in a war against the demi-humans, he probably knew more about battle than we did—considering that we had only ever really battled with monsters.

"But don't think that taking care of my whip means you're going to win this."

"That's my line. I might not be able to attack on my own, but Raphtalia here is more than powerful enough."

"Heh. If you would make a demi-human your party member, then you are obviously not taking this seriously enough."

"Raphtalia."

"Yes!"

She nodded deeply then held her hands over the point of her sword. The blade started to glow brighter.

"Filo!"

Raphtalia called for Filo.

"What?"

"To take this guy down, I need both you and Melty to chant magic spells."

"Okay! C'mon, Mel!"

"But… Oh, all right!"

Confused about something, Melty looked from the nobleman to the rest of us.

Then she nodded, apparently having made some decision, and began to focus on her magic.

"What's this? The Shield Demon really must have brain washing powers. To think he would use the princess as a pawn!"

"I have not been brain washed. I believe that your behavior is evil, and so I will punish you as the princess."

"You fool…"

"I am the source of all power. Hear my words and heed them. Shoot him with a ball of water!"

"Zweite Aqua Shot!"

"I am the source of all power. Hear my words and heed them. Cut him with the blade of sky!"

"Zweite Wing Cutter!"

Melty and Filo cast their spells at nearly the same moment.

A ball of water shot from Melty's hands, and a blade of air shot from Filo's. Both flew at the nobleman.

"Ha!"

The nobleman dodged Filo's blade, then produced another

whip from somewhere and knocked the ball of water off course.

"Now!"

While he was avoiding the spells he left a weak spot unattended. Raphtalia readied her sword and ran at him.

"You think that will do me in?"

He cracked the whip at her.

I wouldn't let that happen. I stepped forward and swung the whip I'd taken from him, catching the tip of his new whip in mid-flight.

"What?!"

"Hiyaaaaa!"

Aligning her timing with my own, Raphtalia let out a shout. Using her foot, she flipped a sword that the guard had dropped into the air and caught it. Then she readied her magic sword like a javelin and threw it at the nobleman. It plunged deep into his chest.

The magic sword can nullify its opponent's magic. She'd used it to knock out Bitch before, so it should have had some kind of effect.

"Ugh… not yet!"

"No, it's over! HIYAAAAAAAA!"

There was a dull sound, and suddenly Raphtalia's sword was buried to the hilt in the nobleman's shoulder.

"Noooooo! Damn you! You think it's all right for a demi-

human to hurt me?! I survived the demi-human war!"

"You fought demi-humans in the war? Then save your complaints for the war. You're not in a war anymore."

"I'll never forgive you! I'll kill you!"

"You're a coward! You only attack people weaker than yourself! What were the demi-humans you fought like? The ones I know were all women and children. Disadvantaged people! Don't talk to me about how you fought them!"

Still incensed, she pushed him to the window, broke it, and pushed him out. As he fell, she let her sword stay in him, but kept her grip on the magic sword and the blade pulled from his falling body.

"AAAAAHHHHHH!"

"NOOOOOOOOOO!"

I immediately dropped both of the whips and watched the nobleman plunge through the window.

That was close. If I'd waited, the whips would have pulled me through the window with him.

"The… The governor lost to the Shield Demon!"

The remaining guards all quickly ran away.

"I'll get that flag back… the flag from that day…"

Raphtalia stood in the window, whispering to the sky. She then recovered herself and ran over to me.

"Are you all right?"

"Huh? Yeah. No problem."

We still had a little holy water left over from treating Raphtalia's curse.

The curse itself wasn't so bad. The holy water would be sufficient to heal it.

I went to the window and looked down at the courtyard. The nobleman was lying there, face turned to the sky.

I think he was… dead?

When I thought about the things that Raphtalia had told me… how he'd tortured demi-humans, it seemed like a fitting end.

"Okay. If we hang around here we'll get caught up in the confusion. We'd better be on our way."

"But first…"

"Ah… right."

First we had to save any demi-humans he'd imprisoned.

That was what Raphtalia wanted, so I wanted it too.

I turned to Nice Guy and made a request.

"This man used to buy demi-human slaves and keep them in his basement so that he could torture them."

"Unfortunately that is not such a rare thing in this country. It could be that…"

"Even if we saved them, we are on the run. I don't think we will be able to provide the things they need while we are running from the Crown. I know it's a lot to ask, but…"

I knew that I was asking too much. I was putting him in further danger.

But if I was going to grant Raphtalia's request, there was no other option.

"I understand your situation. I will do anything I can to help you."

Nice Guy smiled.

He hadn't lied to us yet, so I didn't see any choice but to trust him.

"It will be okay. I have many demi-human allies, and I know that they will help me."

"That's good to hear."

Raphtalia led us to the basement room.

The door was locked, but Filo used her powerful legs to kick the door down.

The second we walked in, we were overcome by a powerful stench.

It was the same smell that came from the slave-trader's tent. It was that smell of death and decay that told you to keep your distance.

This… this wasn't good.

"I have a bad feeling about this…"

Filo looked really worried.

Melty was shaking, obviously scared. Then she settled herself and seemed ready to accept whatever we found.

"It's a little further."

"We walked down the stairs in the dark and came to the basement. It was filled with various torture instruments. I saw a skeleton in the corner.

How many people had met their ends here?

I turned to see Raphtalia praying before a small skeleton in the corner.

"This girl was… She was a friend from my village. Her name was Rifana, and…"

Raphtalia was looking down at the skeleton. She seemed about to cry, and turned her face away.

They must have been close.

"Rifana was a bright, happy girl. She liked to talk about legends."

Listening to Raphtalia, Melty looked ready to cry herself.

She was the princess of this country. It must have been hard to see this kind of misery happen within her own borders.

So much tragedy could be blamed on the waves, but this was different.

This was nothing more than an evil man taking advantage of the chaos around him. Really, everyone around here seemed rotten to the core.

"She was more girly than me… She was so nice…"

"I'm sorry."

To think of the end that Raphtalia's friend had met… It made me sad.

Had things been different, we might have met when she was alive. We might have been friends.

"She always said that she wanted to marry someone like the Shield Hero."

"…"

But her dream never came true. She'd died in this cold basement. Just thinking about it filled me with rage.

She probably wanted to live. She probably died wishing for escape.

He'd done this to her simply because she was a demi-human.

I couldn't even imagine what went through his mind.

I don't know what kind of person I was in comparison to the children that died here. But I could say one thing:

We avenged them.

"What should we do with them? Should we take them?"

We could take their bones and give them a proper funeral somewhere.

"Yes… It's too cold and sad here."

"You're right."

We silently picked up the bones and put them into a bag.

"Were there any slaves?"

"Yes."

Nice Guy answered from the back of the room.

After we'd gathered the bones, we made our way to the back of the room.

The slave was covered with bruises and cuts. It looked like he'd been badly tortured.

His eyes were devoid of life.

He looked to be around 10 years old, and he had dog-like ears.

Despite being a boy, he was kind of cute. You know how some guys are like girls when they are only 10 years old?

"Who are you?"

"That voice…"

"Who's that?"

"Do you know him?"

"Yes. Keel, that's you, isn't it?"

"Who are you? How do you know my name?"

"Did you forget me? I've grown a little since we last saw each other. It's me, Raphtalia."

"What?!"

Keel raised his head in surprise.

"It can't be. Raphtalia is shorter than me. She's not some tall beautiful woman. I mean, she was cute and all…"

Keel was muttering to himself like a dead man.

"You'd pretend to be a friend?! Why? How are you trying to trick me?!"

His eyes filled with tears. He was overcome with despair. He was just like Raphtalia when I'd met her.

"I'll prove it to you then. Two months before the wave

came, you went to the beach looking for a pretty shell. You wanted to surprise your dad for his birthday. But you nearly drowned, and Sadeena had to jump in and save you..."

He seemed to smile, like the memory brought him joy.

It did seem like the sort of thing that only the real Raphtalia would know.

"Could it be?! Raphtalia..."

He was looking her over very carefully.

"It's me... Do you remember eating that poisonous mushroom out in the field? You got sick and hid so that no one would know! I found you that day, and you told me to keep it a secret. You were shaking..."

"Ahhh! Yes! I believe you! It's you! Raphtalia!"

Finally, the slave, Keel, recognized Raphtalia.

"Raphtalia... Why are you so big? Why are you so pretty?"

Even if you knew that demi-humans grew as they leveled up, seeing it with your own eyes was another thing.

Raphtalia had been so small when I found her. I was shocked when she grew up before my eyes.

Had I grown up with her myself, it would have been all the more surprising.

"I'm actually Mr. Naofumi... The Shield Hero's slave right now."

"What?!"

Keel, the demi-human slave, looked at me.

But he was so weak that he couldn't lock his sight onto one thing. I must have looked blurry to him.

I reached into my pocket for some ointment and made to treat his wounds.

"Don't touch me!"

"It's okay. Relax. This is medicine."

Next he would need some nutritional medicine. I knew that I really shouldn't use it in situations like this, but I couldn't ignore a crisis right before my eyes. I had to help him.

Not that I was actually a holy saint with a beautiful heart or anything, but this was Raphtalia's friend.

"Ugh…"

He resisted at first, but he realized I wasn't trying to hurt him, and he slowly drank the medicine. My shield had many strange powers. One of them increased the efficacy of medicines. In times like this, I was grateful for how useful it was.

He looked a little better already. A little color returned to his cheeks.

I wasn't very good with recovery magic. I had been able to treat his wounds, but he hadn't recovered any energy. Realizing that he was safe, he suddenly fell forward, exhausted, and began to snore.

"I cannot believe that my country allowed this to happen."

Melty whispered to herself.

"I'd watched my mother work in other countries, so I thought that I understood demi-humans and humans. But this… I… I cannot forgive this."

"You have to be a little more hysterical. Why not scream, 'I CAN NEVER FORGIVE THIS!' That would be more like you."

"That's not who I really am! Just what kind of person do you take me for?!"

Melty suddenly realized what she was doing and clamped her hands over her mouth.

"Sometimes you get hysterically angry, and your face gets all red. That's you, Melty."

"What was that?!"

"Okay. We can't stay here forever. Let's get going."

Nice Guy picked Keel up and held him over his shoulder. We turned and left the basement.

We talked as we climbed the stairs.

"First we need to focus on getting out of town. It's not like we can all fit on Filo's back."

It was hard enough to fit three of us on there, much less five.

"Why don't we have Filo take the nobleman, Keel, and Melty out of here first?"

"Good idea."

They could jump over the wall and get out easily.

The town entrance still seemed to be embroiled in an uproar. What was going on?

I was wondering that when I noticed blood pooling on the stairs. I followed it up and saw that it was coming from the courtyard, and the blood continued out to…

"What?!"

"What is it?"

I was silently pointing to the courtyard. Raphtalia understood and nodded.

"Ah, ha, ha, ha! Now I finally have a way to kill you!"

The nobleman who'd fallen from the second floor, the nobleman we thought was dead, was standing there, laughing.

Dammit! What's next?

The nobleman's shoulder was bleeding profusely. He was facing the gravestone-like boulder, chanting some kind of spell.

This wasn't good. Keel was still that man's slave—which meant he could use the slave seal to kill him.

What should we do? We'd just managed to save Raphtalia's friend. If he died now then it was all for nothing

But the slave curse didn't need a spell to work. He could just order him to die, or choose to do so from his status magic.

So was he… doing something else?

"He's… We have to stop him!"

Nice Guy turned to me and shouted.

"What is it?"

"Shield Hero, do you know the legend of this town?"

"I heard they chased something away and then sealed it up. It's still here."

I was getting a bad feeling about this.

"It couldn't be…"

"It's true. The sealing stone has been watched over by this town's nobility for generations. And now…"

I could tell where the story was going. The fat man was attempting to break the seal.

"Back up."

"Okay."

Nice Guy took Keel and ran while the rest of us approached the fat man as he chanted at the sealing stone.

"You've finally come, Shield Demon!"

He was screaming like an insane person now.

"I don't know what's sealed inside that thing, but you better stop that right now."

Raphtalia and Filo readied themselves for battle.

Now that we were outside, it would be easier to fight than it had been in that small room.

"You're too late. If only you hadn't shown up, this town would still be peaceful!"

"Peaceful, ha! If you hadn't stolen Melty and dragged her

here, none of this would be happening!"

"It's all your fault, Shield Demon!"

"I don't have time to listen to the complaints of a coward who gets his kicks from torturing children."

I didn't know what was sealed away in there, but I had to find some way to stop him.

The longer we waited, the worse things were going to get.

The other heroes would probably look on with relish. They would want to fight a monster to get its rare items and experience. But I say it's better to let sleeping dogs lie.

"I am not a coward! I am purging the world of its lower life forms! I am a righteous man!"

Dammit… there was no reasoning with him.

I knew how it felt to find joy in the misery of people you hated, so I'd thought that maybe we could come to an understanding. But I was wrong. I never truly wished for the death of anyone, ever.

Even if it was about a specific person, maybe that was understandable, but to hate an entire class of people made no sense at all!

Anyway, who knew what this guy was up to?

Looking at the sealing stone made me very nervous. We had to stop him.

I stepped forward and began to prepare a skill that would restrain the nobleman.

But before I could use it, the stone cracked and fell to pieces.

"It is finished. If I can kill the Shield Demon, my place in God's heaven will be secure! Ah, ha, ha!"

The nobleman let out a laugh like a broken toy. The ground began to shake. Cracks appeared in the earth.

"What's happening?"

"Yes! Destroy it all! The sealed monster will destroy the Shield Demon!"

The sky over the mansion was filled with purple light.

I looked up to see cracks appearing in the sky, like a tortoise shell. It was at that very moment that the sealed monster appeared.

"Master!"

All of Filo's feathers stood on end. She was staring at the sky.

"What is it?!"

Large reptilian feet, tipped with large, sharp claws, slowly stepped through the crack. They were followed by a large, muscular body, then an enormous eyeball, and finally a massive jaw appeared, rimmed with teeth so large and sharp they could shred metal. I saw what the monster was.

It was a 20-meter tall, carnivorous... dinosaur.

Chapter Three: Tyrant Dragon Rex

"Oh… Oh…"

A huge dinosaur appeared in the sky. I didn't call it a dragon on purpose. It looked exactly like a dinosaur.

To be more specific, it looked like an overgrown Tyrannosaurus Rex, but meaner and scarier.

It wasn't like a normal monster in the field. It was a dinosaur. A rift opened in the sky above us, and the massive beast came crashing down into the mansion.

"Ha, ha, ha! For the glory of God!"

The mansion collapsed under the weight of the dinosaur. Then, with insanity still in his eyes, the nobleman was instantly crushed under the foot of the advancing beast.

He was crazy all the way until the end. And he did crazy things until the end. How were we supposed to defeat such a huge monster?

"We're all escaping together! Filo, you understand?!"

"Yeah!"

Filo ran back to the courtyard entrance, and picked up Nice Guy and Keel before running away.

Raphtalia, Melty, and I all took off running in unison. We made for the property exit.

"GYAOOOOOOOOOO!"

The dinosaur roared and started to destroy what remained of the mansion.

"I come to a new world and have to deal with DINOSAURS?!"

I didn't think there were monsters like that here.

But, thinking a little more, there WERE dragons here. So I guess dinosaurs weren't such a stretch.

Dragons and dinosaurs were in pretty similar categories, after all.

"Why would he summon something like that just to kill Naofumi?!"

"The fool. He didn't think through this at all."

He would see his whole town destroyed just to kill one person?

So he would rather see me die than survive himself? What was wrong with him? Just how much did he hate me?

"Hurry! If you don't hurry, he'll chase after us!"

Raphtalia was right.

"Filo."

"What?"

"Can you make yourself big enough for all of us to ride you?"

"Naofumi! Don't ask for impossible things!"

"I'm not. I think Filo can do it."

"Really? Can you do that, Filo?"

"Yeah… Filo might be able to do it."

Filo, with Nice Guy and Keel on her back, ran up to us.

"Um… I don't think I can… I can't get much bigger than this.

"Damn."

I guess I should have expected that.

"What if you were bigger?"

"I wonder."

Wasn't she still growing?

"See, it's not impossible."

"Don't you think she could?"

"GYAOOOOOOOO!"

Melty turned to see the beast then turned back to me. She nodded.

I'd heard that dinosaurs like moving targets… We ran, but that only attracted it. Now it was chasing after us.

We didn't have time to sit and chat. We were about to end up as dinosaur food.

With such a large monster chasing us, it felt like we were in the middle of an earthquake. The ground shook with every step.

I was starting to understand why people always fell over in movie chase scenes like this.

Running was hard enough. I felt like I'd lose my footing.

And if we fell, that would be the end.

The debris from the destroyed mansion was cluttering the path, which slowed the dinosaur's progress. But once we cleared the debris entirely, Filo was the only one who stood a chance of outrunning the beast.

"What should we do? Fight?"

"Here!? In the middle of town? Think of all the damage we'd cause!"

"That's true, but…"

I wasn't sure that we could win. But I did know that we didn't stand a chance running.

"All right then, we run, and lure the beast after us. Once we get to somewhere we can fight without endangering others, we do it."

We left the mansion grounds to find the streets filled with panicking pedestrians.

I could see the headlines now: "Shield Demon destroys town, causes uproar."

Damn! This was all the proof I needed to see that Ren and Itsuki weren't nearby.

The dinosaur was sniffing around to see where its prey had vanished too.

This didn't feel right. There, I caught sight of its name: Tyrant Dragon Rex.

Something on the dinosaur's chest began to glow. At the same time, Filo's stomach started glowing too.

"Um… Filo?"

"What?"

"The dinosaur is looking straight at us, and I think it might have something to do with your glowing stomach."

"Hm…. Well, you know what? I think that big gecko wants to eat me!"

"Okay, Filo, you run! Lure the monster out of town!"

"What? Naofumi? Are you going to abandon Filo?"

"No, I want her to lure the monster somewhere away from people and then come back!"

"But he's after Filo, so I don't think he'll just let her go!"

"…You're right."

I'd thought that Filo was fast enough to make it, but I shouldn't use her as bait.

"No! I want to stay with you, Master!"

"Mr. Naofumi, you shouldn't ask that of her."

"I know, but…"

"It must be hard to be the Shield Hero."

Nice Guy chimed in like nothing was going on.

"Still, the monster is drawn to Filo. We need to lure him out of town, then fight and defeat him."

If we fought in the center of town, the damage would be tremendous.

The nearest exit was… Actually it wasn't very far at all. And Filo could jump over walls.

"Okay, so we are going to lure the monster out of town to keep the civilians safe. What are you going to do? We should probably split up."

I was asking Nice Guy and Melty.

Keel was unconscious, so there was no asking what he wanted. I don't think we could take him with us though.

"I'm going to run away with this kid... But first I'd like to help evacuate the town."

"Can you do that?"

"The demi-humans from my town are here, so I think we can do it together."

Nice Guy climbed down from Filo.

"I feel like we are abandoning you here. I wish we didn't have to."

"It's not like that. All this happened because I reached out to you, Shield Hero. Don't worry about it."

"Okay then, I won't. Melty, what will you do?"

"I'm going with you, obviously."

Back at Nice Guy's place, she'd thought that she could sneak off back to her father and fix things, but after having her life put in danger by that crazy nobleman, it really only made sense for her to stay with us. Entrusting herself to an authoritative nobleman put her in just as much danger as she was in with us. So nothing changed.

"Looks like we're all set."

"Ugh…"

Keel moaned, and his eyes blinked open. Maybe he still wasn't totally unconscious. His eyes seemed to have trouble focusing.

He held his hand out to Raphtalia.

"Keel. Really terrible things are happening right now. But we're going to take care of it—so you have to go on living."

"Raphtalia… No… Don't go…"

"Keel, it will be okay. I have to go do what I can. I'll get our flag back, Keel. Wait for me!"

She slipped off the bangle that I'd made for her and put it on Keel's arm.

"Let's go, Mr. Naofumi. We have to stop this before anyone else gets hurt."

"Yeah… But are you sure you want to give him that bangle?"

"I should have asked you first. I'm sorry."

"Don't be. It's yours. Do whatever you want with it."

She must have meant to signify that she was making him a promise. If so, I wasn't going to step in and ruin it.

"Keel! Good-bye!"

"But… but, Raphtalia!"

"GYAOOOOOOOOOOOOO!"

The Tyrant Dragon Rex's roar was so powerful it made my head ring.

"Let's go!"

"Okay!"

"Roger!"

We all immediately set about our duties.

As if to break the silence, the dinosaur came crashing after us.

I couldn't see where Nice Guy had gone.

We climbed onto Filo's back and took off running. We slipped through town and jumped over the wall to escape.

"GYAOOOOOOOO!"

The Tyrant Dragon Rex was right behind us. It crashed through the town wall.

We ran through a field bathed in moonlight. The town behind us was smoking.

This wasn't my fault. I wasn't to blame for it.

"Good thing he keeps chasing Filo."

"Yeah."

"Naofumi! If we don't hurry, he'll catch us!"

"I know! Filo, can't you go any faster!"

We had to get as far from town as we could.

Even if we fought well enough to defeat it, if it ran off through another town then the casualties would only get worse.

So we ran, the dinosaur on our tail.

"Think we've gone far enough?"

The town looked far in the distance now. Had we put enough distance between us?

"We better start fighting soon. Are you all ready?"

"Yes. I'm ready."

"If I stick with you guys my life will be a short one!"

"Filo, are you ready?"

"Yeah! I'll do my best!"

"Right!"

When I shouted, Filo stopped running and spun to face the monster.

The Tyrant Dragon Rex was crashing after us, shaking the earth with each step.

White breath puffed from its mouth, and its teeth dripped with saliva.

If it sunk its teeth into me, there was no way I'd survive.

…Not that I was going to let that happen. We jumped off of Filo's back and readied ourselves for a fight.

"GYAOOOOOOOOOOO!"

The beast didn't slow down at all. It kept running at us but lowered its head to attack.

"I don't think so! Air Strike Shield!"

The Tyrant Dragon Rex was running straight for me when the shield materialized in front of it.

Something about this reminded me of the way we'd fought the Zombie Dragon.

We'd done all right for ourselves back then—so things should be fine this time too… right?

With an echoing crack, the beast bit right through my Air Strike Shield. It crumbled and fell.

…But it left itself open for attack.

"Hiya!"

Filo lead the charge.

She reared back and swung a powerful kick into the dinosaur's jaw.

But she was wearing iron claws now, so her attack was higher than it had been back when we fought the Dragon Zombie.

Still, the kick didn't seem to affect the dinosaur the way it had hurt the Dragon Zombie. He didn't seem to hesitate.

"Ugh! It's so hard!"

"Be careful!"

When Filo fought the dragon, she'd left herself open for a second, and the dragon had swallowed her. Luckily the dragon didn't have teeth, and its organs had been rotting. What would happen this time?

"Yeah!"

After delivering her kick to the beast's jaw, she immediately jumped back, gaining distance before rushing forward in a flash and kicking at the monster's stomach.

She was acting like a skilled fighter now.

"Zweite Aqua Slash!"

Melty sent a magic spell flying at the Tyrant Dragon Rex.

It was a sharp blade of water.

"Take that!"

Raphtalia was with them now, and she thrust the magic sword into the beast.

All of their attacks produced satisfying sounds of connection, but the monster was too big... None of them were able to take the beast down.

"Master! Platform!"

"Got it! Air Strike Shield! Second Shield!"

Two different magic shields appeared before the dinosaur.

My Air Strike Shields would remain deployed for fifteen seconds. Honestly, it wasn't very long. But Filo was fast...

"Hiya! Hoo! Pop!"

She was flipping and jumping from shield to shield, delivering powerful kicks each time.

"GYAOOOOOOOOOO!"

Finally unnerved, the Tyrant Dragon Rex let out an enraged howl and began to violently thrash its head and tail. Filo jumped out of the way before its attacks connected.

Raphtalia was the one in danger.

I ran forward and blocked the thrashing tail before it could hit her.

"Ugh..."

"Mr. Naofumi!"

It was very heavy. I was able to hold it back for now, but if the tail was this strong then I'd never survive a bite from the jaw.

This wasn't good.

The monster was very large but slow enough that we'd been able to hold our own. Still, none of our attacks were strong enough to bring the dinosaur down.

Filo was getting a lot of good hits in, but if she wasn't strong enough to bring the monster down, then Raphtalia wasn't going to be able to do so either.

Melty's magic wasn't very powerful either. At the moment she was throwing out spells as a way to assist Filo, but they weren't strong enough to deal much damage on their own.

Had this been a game of some kind, it would be the kind of battle in which you just needed to run the clock down... too bad this wasn't a game.

If we figured out its weakness, it would run. Sure, that would be good for us, but then we'd have to worry about where it was running TO. A town full of people, no doubt.

Furthermore—I realized this when I blocked its thrashing tail—the thing had a lot of attack power. I was probably the only one with a defense rating high enough to survive an attack.

I might have to rely on the Shield of Rage. It was strong enough to block the beast's attacks, plus it had counter-attacks of its own.

The Shield of Rage was the strongest shield I had, but it was very dangerous.

It was formed from the hatred I had for this world. The first time I used it was in the battle with the Dragon Zombie, after it had eaten Filo.

When I use it, the rage takes over my body, and I get violent.

Because of that, I'd accidentally cursed Raphtalia, who'd been trying to help me.

It was the sort of shield that gave me a lot of strength but asked for something in return. It wasn't the sort of thing I could just whip out on a whim.

But it was also true that there were times when, had I not used it, we would have all ended up dead.

"It's okay."

"Then I'm going."

"Be careful!"

"Okay!"

Raphtalia brandished her sword and ran for the Tyrant Dragon Rex.

But her attack didn't seem to be very effective.

Filo was fighting well and holding her own, but she wouldn't be able to keep that up for very long. Her stamina had limits, after all.

I didn't know how much stamina the Tyrant Dragon Rex had, but it seemed reasonable to assume it was more than we did.

If we kept fighting as we were, this wasn't going to end well.

But what other choice did we have?

After I got the Dragon Zombie Core, my Shield of Rage grew stronger. Because of which, and because Filo had also eaten from the Dragon Zombie Core, whenever I used the Shield of Rage, Filo went crazy.

Was it worth the risk?

"Naofumi."

"What?"

Melty was yelling for me from the back line.

Was she able to see something from her vantage point at the back?

"Something strange is happening!"

"Huh?"

I looked around to see what she was talking about.

Off in the distance I heard some kind of animal call.

What was it?

The area started to fill with small floating lights, like fireflies.

"Huh?"

Filo held her wings against her head, like she was trying to concentrate.

"What is it?"

"I can hear someone talking. They're saying that they will be here soon, so we should wait."

"Who said that?"

"I dunno!"

What was happening? We were right in the middle of a battle here!

The Tyrant Dragon Rex seemed to sense that something was happening also. It raised its head and was looking around.

"Naofumi."

"What?"

"There's some kind of force field."

"Force field?"

"Yes. Can't you see it? It's like a mist hanging over us."

I tried to look far into the distance, but the air grew thick, and I couldn't see very far.

"That looks like a very powerful force field."

"What is it?"

"I've heard of a mysterious forest. There are legends about it. I heard that the old weapons of the Heroes from long ago are sleeping there, and that it's protected by a force field to keep people away."

"Sounds like you know all about it."

"My mother likes legends, and she took me to see the mysterious forest. The force field looked just like this."

What was that supposed to mean? Did it mean that we weren't going to be able to escape even if we tried?

"When you try to cross over it, it brings you back to where

you started. I think someone has cast a force field over us."

Someone was trapping us? That didn't sound good at all.

I imagined that Bitch or Trash had hired an assassin to do this to us. I imagined them reclining back and watching us to make sure we died at the hands of the Tyrant Dragon Rex.

What it meant was this: there was no way out.

I looked around. The grass and trees were filled with strange lights.

What the hell was going on?

Suddenly an enormous herd of Filolials appeared and came running straight for us.

The whole field was covered in Filolials. This was turning into a traumatic experience.

"Wow... Filolials!"

Melty's eyes were shining. She looked so happy.

Why did she like Filolials so much?! Whatever—this was not the time to entertain her hobbies.

"GYAOOOOOOOOOO!"

The dinosaur howled in anger at the new developments. Then he lowered his head to attack.

Dammit... We had no choice.

I prepared to switch to the Shield of Rage.

"Don't."

My shield arm flew back, struck with a sharp pain.

I looked down to find the shield itself glowing.

I was still able to change shields if I wanted though.
I tried, again, to switch to the Shield of Rage.
But…

—Due to interference, you may not change weapons.

A flashing icon appeared in my field of vision, and I was no longer able to switch shields.

There was also a small clock displaying the remaining time before I could make a switch. I could probably switch shields again when the timer ran out.

"Who's there?!"

A voice I'd never heard before had interjected and kept me from changing shields.

Why would they stop me? What were they after?

"You will be all right. Just wait. You do no need to turn to that power."

"Damn…"

"Hiya!"

Filo flipped through the air and delivered a solid kick to the dinosaur's jaw before landing deftly in the grass and dashing back, picking me and Raphtalia up, and taking us back to Melty.

"What's happening?"

"They said to stand back."

I didn't hear that. Or did she mean that strange voice?

THE RISING OF THE SHIELD HERO 4 119

We were completely surrounded by Filolials. There were too many to count.

Their eyes were shining in the dark. The sheer number of them was unbelievable.

What was happening?

My only idea was that they were somehow trying to trap the monster there. Could it be that they formed giant herds to hunt giant monsters?

Or maybe they were trying to get Filo to join their group?

The herd of Filolials split around the monster. It was just like the parting of the Red Sea.

"Gah!"

One of the Filolials stepped out of the group and started to walk in our direction.

It looked a lot like Filo when she was in her "normal" Filolial form, but this one was light blue.

It stood about two meters tall, and looked a lot like a large ostrich.

But it looked... fluffier than other Filolials. Like its feathers were softer. It also had a single feather that stuck vertically up from the crown of its head.

Most Filolials were pink, but this one was a light blue color. There were still white patches, but most of it was blue.

It was pulling a gorgeous carriage, and a large gemstone was set in the center of it.

The jewel reminded me of a gemstone I'd seen before… but I couldn't remember where.

I looked at my shield. Then I realized… It was the same shape as the jewel in the center of my shield.

"Hey! It's that Filolial from before!"

"You know this thing?"

"Yes. I met her before I ran into you guys."

"Really?"

She had a sense of authority about her. She was clearly the leader of the herd.

And she didn't seem as dull-witted as a typical Filolial.

The Tyrant Dragon Rex appeared to recognize these qualities in her as well. The beast seemed to be on guard.

It seemed ready to attack at any moment, but was holding back to see what the blue Filolial would do.

"Wow! What a cool carriage! I'm jealous…"

Filo's eyes sparkled when she caught sight of the carriage.

I didn't like it. The last thing I wanted was to parade around like new money.

Besides, I could imagine what the public would say if they saw me in that thing.

"Gah!"

The blue Filolial removed the reins herself and stepped forward.

Another Filolial swooped in behind her and removed the carriage.

"What's happening?"

"Gweeeeeeeeeeeh!"

The blue Filolial let out a sustained call. All the leaves on the trees and bushes began to shine a bright green, and a powerful wind blew through the area.

What was going on?

The blue Filolial began to grow. She expanded into a large, black silhouette.

She was huge...

The silhouette was big and puffy. She was transforming, but she was able to grow much larger than Filo could.

When she'd first stepped forward she stood about two meters tall, but she'd grown to at least six now.

She kept growing until she was the same size as the Tyrant Dragon Rex. Then she stopped growing.

"Wow! She's so big!"

Melty was unable to hide her joy. She whispered to herself like a giddy child.

Compared to the pink and white Filolials below, this Filolial Queen was clearly light blue.

The major difference was the vertical feather that stood from the crown of her head.

"I've kept you waiting, Shield Hero. And you too, little girl who likes Filolials."

The huge Filolial Queen finished greeting us and then

directed her gaze to the Tyrant Dragon Rex. Her voice sounded a lot like Filo's but was perhaps a bit deeper.

"She spoke!"

"Filo talks too."

"I know that!"

"Woooow! She's so big!"

"Uh… Uh…"

I stood there, mouth agape, as the huge Filolial Queen took a step towards the Tyrant Dragon Rex.

"Looks like the Dragon King Fragment has puffed you up a little. I think the Dragon King Fragment doesn't suit you. That's why you're so big. You might be big, but you're just an everyday monster. "

The enormous Filolial Queen spoke to the dinosaur.

"If you give me the fragment now, I will let you live. Hand it over and go."

The Tyrant Dragon Rex lowered his head and roared in response.

Attempting to scoop her into his jaws right then and there, he ran forward.

"No avoiding it then…"

The enormous Filolial Queen raised her foot and kicked the dinosaur.

But she seemed to have been holding back, as she didn't put much of her weight into it.

Regardless, when the kick connected, the Tyrant Dragon Rex went flying like a kickball.

The Tyrant Dragon Rex came crashing down in the dirt and then rose shakily to its feet.

Then it quickly turned and attempted to swing its powerful tail at the Filolial.

"Weak."

The Filolial raised a wing to block the tail easily. The Tyrant Dragon Rex roared in anger, bared its fangs and rushed at the Filolial Queen.

"Hiya!"

The Filolial Queen reared back and kicked the dinosaur's jaw hard.

Flipping backwards like a rag doll, the dinosaur crashed to the ground.

In a flash, the Filolial was beside it, kicking at its torso. The dinosaur flew into the air.

The huge beast was suspended in the air!

"Hiya! Hiya! Hiya!"

Without touching down, the Filolial delivered a series of kicks that kept them suspended. She was blindingly fast.

What the hell?! I considered myself an experienced gamer, but I'd never seen a combo like that.

It was like a fighting game. It was like an aerial combo. A counter indicating the number of successive hits appeared before my eyes. At the end it read 35 HITS!

The difference in strength was apparent—overwhelming.

With a final slam, the dinosaur came crashing down. The combo was over. The beast rose on unsteady legs.

Immediately afterwards, a large magical seal appeared in the air.

"Is it going to cast a spell?"

The Filolial Queen readied herself.

Then the beast leaned forward. I thought it was going to cast a spell, but instead it opened its mouth—and a massive pillar of flame came roaring out of it.

Whoa. I could feel the heat on my skin from across the field.

Had I been hit with an attack like that, I don't think even the Shield of Rage could have withstood it.

The Tyrant Dragon Rex was running at the Filolial and breathing fire. No matter how large she might have been, if the pillar of flame hit her she'd be roasted alive.

"Lukewarm."

The Filolial raised a wing, or I thought she did, and stopped the pillar of flame without blinking.

What was this? Some kind of monster battle? We were standing in the field and watching but didn't have anything to contribute.

"Let's end this."

The Filolial raised her wings and crossed them before her. I've seen something like that before.

The second I thought that, the massive Filolial Queen appeared to blur before immediately reappearing behind the Dinosaur.

Yup, that was Filo's trump card, a magic attack called Haikuikku.

"GYAAAAAAAAAAA!"

Her claws tore through the monster time and time again until, finally, the dinosaur fell to pieces and died.

Chapter Four: The Legendary Bird God

The felled Tyrant Dragon Rex lay in bloody strips, and there was something shining among them. It appeared to be some kind of glowing ore. The Filolial Queen picked it up and then turned to us.

"Sorry I kept you waiting."

"..."

We were all speechless.

Not even Filo had been able to deal damage to the massive monster, and this huge Filolial Queen had defeated it so easily!

"You're so big..."

Melty's eyes were shining as she looked up at the huge bird. She sure did switch moods quickly.

Whenever she spoke to me she bordered on hysterics, but she was polite when she spoke to others, and obsessively fawning when she spoke to Filo or other Filolials.

"You must be the Shield Hero."

"Oh... Yeah."

When something the size of a building speaks to you, you answer the best you can.

Had we been enemies, well, I don't think I could beat her in a fight... I couldn't see how that would be possible.

And if Melty had been right—if we really were enclosed in a force field—then we wouldn't be able to run either.

I even thought about trying to escape on Filo, but if this was a Filolial Queen, she'd be at least as fast as Filo. There was no escape.

"Do you need something from me?"

"I have many things I wish to discuss with you. But it's not polite to speak to you like this. Wait a moment please."

The huge Filolial Queen closed her eyes and seemed to be concentrating. As she did she began to shrink. Finally her large wings closed around her body completely.

When she opened them again, there was a young girl standing there, about the same height as Filo, with wings on her back.

Her hair was silver with thin streaks of light blue, and it was cut in a short bob.

But there were three tufts of hair standing up vertically from the crown of her head, like cowlicks.

Her eyes were red, and her gaze carried an air of authority about it.

Her face was small and well-composed. Quite beautiful, really.

She was dressed in a red and white gothic-style dress.

"Allow me to introduce myself. I am Fitoria, the Queen of the Filolials."

She flicked her head and smirked, a rather child-like movement that stood in opposition to the air of power and authority that hung about her.

It's hard to describe, but because she was in human form, I sort of got the impression that she was a small child trying to act like an adult.

"Fitoria?! But that's the name of the Filolial in the legends!" Melty was shocked.

"Really?"

"Yes. There is a legend saying that Fitoria was raised by four Legendary Heroes in the past... when they were summoned during a wave of destruction."

"The past... Well, I don't know how long ago you are referencing, but she might be the successor?"

I think I remembered that, back when Motoyasu and I were being summoned, they had said something about waves in the ancient past.

If we were talking about something that far back, then she couldn't be the Filolial of the legends, could she?

It must have been a name that the current leader of the Filolials inherited or something.

If not... just how old was this girl?

"My name has always been Fitoria, and there has only ever been one."

Fitoria turned her head to the side in confusion while she spoke.

She was very serious and powerful, but occasionally she displayed those very Filolial-like moments of animal stupidity.

"Are you saying that you've been alive since ancient times?"

"Yup."

She said it very matter-of-factly. I looked at Filo, then back at Fitoria. I guess I could believe it.

Just think how fast Filo had grown.

If Filo had gotten that big, I don't think we'd have been able to feed her though.

We had enough trouble feeding her as it was. I didn't want her getting any bigger. If she got too big to feed than we'd probably have to part ways.

But then I remembered how much money I'd invested in Filo. I couldn't let that go to waste.

"Master, you're thinking of weird stuff."

"You're right. That face he's making—it means he's thinking of something unrelated."

"You can read him so well. I have no idea."

"You'll figure it out."

Annoying brats. I wished they would stop trying to figure out what I was thinking.

"You were thinking that if Filo got that big, you'd have to abandon her."

"Boo!"

"Abandon her? How could you think such things?! To

think, only minutes ago you'd asked her to try and get bigger!"

"Oh relax. How would we feed something that big?!"

"Mr. Naofumi... I don't think she would get so large overnight..."

"Sure, but think about how fast she grew to this size. If she had another growth spurt, she might end up like that!"

"..."

"Ms. Raphtalia! Why aren't you saying anything?"

Melty grabbed onto Raphtalia's hands and shouted.

The scary part was that it could really happen. Maybe.

"It would take a long time to grow to that size, so don't worry about it."

Fitoria seemed hesitant to intrude, but she raised her hand and answered my concerns.

"Normal Filolials have fixed life spans of a few decades."

Well, that was a relief. I didn't want her to have a growth spurt and turn into a mountain or something.

But then I realized that Fitoria's phrasing implied that she had been alive for much longer.

"Now then, Shield Hero and friends, may I ask you to introduce yourselves?"

Well... she was right. If she had given us her name then I guess it was our turn.

"I'm Naofumi Iwatani. Iwatani is my last name, and Naofumi is my first name. It sounds like you already know I'm the Shield Hero."

"Yup."

Fitoria looked to Raphtalia next.

"My name is Raphtalia. Pleased to meet you."

"Pleasure."

"I'm Filo!"

Filo didn't wait to be addressed before jumping in.

Fitoria stared at Filo for a moment then directed her gaze to Melty.

"We've met before, haven't we? You love Filolials. You protected me then. Thank you for that."

"Yes. My name is Melty Melromarc."

"Okay. I'll call you Mel-tan."

Meltan? She didn't have good taste in nicknames.

Back in my own world, I had a friend that used to add "tan" to everything. That just reminded me of it.

Being an *Otaku* myself, I was probably in the same category as people that did that though…

"Meltan… Please to formally meet you."

See? Even Melty made a weird face when she heard it.

"Boo."

Filo shifted her weight and stepped forward. It almost looked like she was trying to protect Melty from Fitoria.

Was she jealous? She looked like a jealous friend who was mad that their friend was talking to someone else.

I pictured Fitoria saying something like, "Filo, behavior like that will not win you any friends."

Was I over thinking it? It reminded me of a traumatic scene from a famous game I'd once played.

If we all fell silent here, the conversation would take a weird turn. I decided to hurry things along.

"So? Of course I'll thank you for defeating that huge monster, the Tyrant Dragon Rex, for us… but… what can we do for you now?"

"I'll explain the details of it all, but this is not a good place to talk. I'll show you where to go, so please follow me."

Fitoria pointed to her carriage. Did she want us to ride in it while she took us somewhere?

"First, we should…"

"Should what?"

Fitoria turned her head to the side again.

I looked over at the Tyrant Dragon Rex's corpse.

In response, Fitoria furrowed her brow.

"I would rather the Heroes did not use things from dragons to improve their weapons."

Oh that's right, Filolials and dragons didn't get along. Apparently the Queen of the Filolials had the same way of thinking about them.

But that had nothing to do with me. I had to do whatever I could to get stronger.

Especially considering how powerful the Tyrant Dragon Rex had been… I couldn't afford to ignore materials like that.

"Too bad."

"Very well then. I'll have my tribe bring it after us then. Please get into the carriage.

"Will you bring the organs too? Filolials sometimes can't control their appetites, and I need more than the bones."

"As you like."

"Thank you."

"Naofumi, you're so petty."

"Whatever."

I went over to the shredded Tyrant Dragon Rex and let my shield absorb various parts of its body.

I let it absorb the flesh, bones, scales, horns, fangs, and organs. It unlocked a new shield.

…Or so I thought. Apparently I couldn't completely unlock the shield without reaching a higher level.

Compared to our own strength, the Tyrant Dragon Rex had been much more powerful, so I suppose it only made sense. My level still wasn't high enough to unlock the shield I'd gotten after defeating the Zombie Dragon anyway.

"Are you ready?"

Fitoria asked calmly.

"Sure…"

"Okay. And your name was Filo, right? Can you turn into a human and ride with them?"

"I could… but I'd rather pull the carriage."

"That is my carriage, so you can't pull it."

I didn't know if she really couldn't let someone else pull it, or if she was childishly rebuffing Filo.

Maybe she really was just like Filo but was pretending to be really important.

"Um…"

"Filo… don't be selfish. Respect what Fitoria says."

"Okay!"

Filo calmed down and turned into her human form.

What was with them? Whatever. We all climbed into Fitoria's strangely gorgeous carriage.

The interior was more spacious than I'd expected. But… I guess we were going to start traveling by carriage.

We were surrounded by a vast herd of Filolials. If we weren't careful, we'd be spotted soon enough.

I guess Fitoria had cast a force field over us though, so that should keep people away.

If Motoyasu realized that I was in the carriage, he'd come chasing after it—no doubt about that.

"Portal…"

Fitoria stepped in front of the carriage and took the reins before shouting something.

When she yelled, the scenery around us instantly changed.

"What?"

"Huh?!"

"Wh... What's happening?!"

"W... wow..."

What the hell? This girl clearly had some impressive powers.

"Did we move?"

Games often provide the player with a magical form of transport that will allow them to teleport to places they have already been.

Most famous games seem to have them... I guess they were part of this world too.

And yet... If I hadn't heard of it yet, then it must be pretty rare.

The Legendary Filolial... Yeah, maybe she did have reason to claim that title.

"We should be able to talk safely here."

We climbed down from the carriage and took in our surroundings. It was dark, which made it hard to pick out much, but we seemed to be in the forest.

Was it some kind of village in the forest? No... Ruins?

It appeared to be a destroyed castle.

There were stones laid out in lines and buried in the dirt, and here and there stone houses poked out of the gloom. Plants had grown over everything, and the size and extent of the root systems meant that these things must have been here for a while.

Further out, and the forest had taken over.

There was a thick white fog over everything, which limited how far we could see. Vines and shrubbery covered everything, as far as I could see. I couldn't discern a way out.

"Where are we?"

"This is the country that the original Heroes fought to protect, or the ruins of it anyway. That's what they say."

"That's a vague answer."

"Well, it's been here since before I was born. I try to watch over it."

"Do you live here, Fitoria?"

Melty's eyes were sparkling again.

"About half the time. My real home is… well… I don't take people there."

"Huh…"

"Probably the forest."

"Yup."

"It's so ooooold!"

"You can really feel the history."

"Tell me how you really feel."

Saying it's old, or that you feel the history here… Filo and Raphtalia were apparently really sharing the experience. As for me, the fog was so thick that I really didn't know.

She didn't really "lead" us here, after all. She'd just transported us. How convenient. How were we supposed to get back?

"Hey, since you just transported us here, I was wondering if you could teleport us to a specific place when it's time to leave."

With any luck we could get Motoyasu off our tail for good. Or even better, we could find asylum in the demi-human kingdom without needing to rely on Melty's mother.

"You just got here, and you're asking about how to leave?"

"It doesn't seem like the kind of place we should hang around."

"What?!"

Melty shouted in disappointment.

What was that all about? Did she want to hang out with the Filolials THAT badly?

I wanted to keep this as short as we could. We were just visiting. That's all.

"For the time being, you should try and get some rest."

Fitoria raised her hand, and a Filolial appeared from the fog tugging a carriage loaded down with firewood. She set it on fire, making a large bonfire.

That was a good idea, and we probably didn't need to worry about attracting enemies. The woods didn't seem to be populated by anything more vicious than a Filolial.

Since the Filolials had invited us here and asked us to rest, there was probably nothing worth worrying about.

Night was falling too. We should probably talk while we rested.

"Okay. It's definitely better to rest here than where we were before. C'mon everyone. Let's rest up."

"Okaaaay!"

"That was a long, tough day."

"Yes, it was… I sure hope that Keel and the others are all right."

"Worrying about it won't help them. If we try to go back to the town they'll catch us for sure."

"Yes…"

We all sat down before the campfire and relaxed.

We had piles of Tyrant Dragon Rex meat, and I started to prepare it for dinner.

Luckily enough, the well still seemed to be full of water. I checked to make sure it was safe then decided to prepare a stew.

"Let's get some food in our bellies."

I said to Raphtalia and the others as I cooked.

"…"

Filo stuck her index finger into her mouth and stared greedily at the bubbling pot.

There were less of them due to the teleportation, but the surrounding Filolials were looking on hungrily as well.

Dammit. It was hard to eat when everyone was staring at you.

"Um… Naofumi?"

"Mr. Naofumi. It's hard to eat with everyone looking at us."

"Yeah, me too."

"Huh? You think so?"

Raphtalia and Melty felt the same way I did. They cradled their bowls and looked around nervously.

Filo was just greedily slurping down her food without a thought.

"You want some food too?"

"May I?"

"Well, we don't have enough food to feed you at the size you were earlier."

"That's all right."

All I'd done is offer Fitoria some food, but the surrounding Filolials started gawking in response.

"Be quiet."

All of them fell silent at Fitoria's reproof but they kept staring on with oppressive determination.

"This is delicious!"

"It is."

Ugh. Now Filo was staring at me with that look in her eyes. She and Fitoria were like two peas in a pod.

They were different colors though, so I suppose that was proof they weren't related.

With Melty next to them, they could have all been sisters. They were pretty enough. I could have painted a picture of them.

"Very good."

Raphtalia had better manners than any of them. She was more dignified.

Melty was dignified too, but she shared something with the ravenous Filolials that made me want to lump them all together.

"What?"

Melty made a face and glared at me.

"Nothing."

"Were you thinking rude thoughts again?"

"No comment."

"That means yes, doesn't it?"

"I was thinking that those two make you look a little unrefined. You should pick your friends better."

"What was that?!"

There she went again. She could be so noisy.

"Now, now… I was…"

Raphtalia paused in the middle of her sentence to look around at all the Filolials. They stared back.

I couldn't ignore them either. I felt like the food was going to get caught in my throat. It was starting to get annoying.

"This is getting so annoying! Can't we just make a really big pot of it? I'll make whatever they want, just bring me some tools!"

In the end, I couldn't endure their incessant stares, so I made a giant pot of soup and let them go at it.

All in all, it took a few hours.

Before they'd all finished eating, Raphtalia, Filo, and Melty had all fallen asleep. I was exhausted from all the cooking.

"Whew…"

I was cleaning up the dishes and complaining to myself about why I had to spend my time feeding a bunch of birds when Fitoria came over to me.

"What do you want? There isn't any left."

"I know that."

"Oh. Okay then. What do you want? Can't it wait until morning?"

I wanted to get some rest.

Huh? Melty and Filo were leaning against some fluffy Filolials and sleeping soundly.

How convenient. It must be nice to get some sleep while someone else does all the work. She was clearly accustomed to living the royal life.

"I was thinking the same thing. But the timing is right, so I'd like to talk a little."

"What is it?"

"I'd like to know how the sealed monster came to be released."

"Huh? So you came without knowing that?"

"No… I came because I'd been given a report that a new queen candidate had appeared."

"A queen candidate? You mean Filo?"

Fitoria nodded.

"Can I ask you one thing?"

"What?"

It was a suspicion that had been growing on me ever since Filo had hatched.

"Why does Filo grow so differently than other Filolials?"

Fitoria had said that she was a queen candidate.

That's why I thought that she might have known the answer.

"Because she's being raised by a Hero."

I suspected as much. Filo clearly looked different from other Filolials, and she could even transform into a person. It was because I was raising her?

"I've answered your question. Now answer mine."

I don't know how much I can tell you. How much do you know about me?"

"I know that you are a Hero that was summoned here because of the waves. I know that you are considered the religious enemy of Melromarc, a human-supremacist nation."

"Oh…"

Had she learned all of that through word-of-mouth from the other Filolials?

I didn't know just how well Filolials were capable of communicating with one another, but I wouldn't have guessed that they were so good at gathering and transmitting information.

"I'm not all-powerful, you know. I forget things a lot."

"You said it, not me. So anyway…"

I explained everything about how the Tyrant Dragon Rex had come to be freed from the sealing stone.

Then I started telling her about myself. I told her how I'd been summoned, then framed and discriminated against. I told her about all the major events that had happened up until now.

"….Whew."

Fitoria sighed deeply.

"What?"

"I just get exhausted when I hear of the stupid things the Heroes are occupying themselves with, considering that the waves of destruction are what they should be focusing on."

"It's not me. It's them."

"I don't care about that. I just have to carry out the task entrusted to me by my old master… the Hero."

"Huh…"

"From my perspective, the little fights between humans and demi-humans are irrelevant. The world does not exist just for people. Even still, I cannot stand to see the Heroes quarrel. When the Heroes fight, I can't achieve what my master entrusted to me."

"And what is that?"

I guess she meant that a hero from the past had asked her to do something.

Based on what she'd just said, I guess I couldn't expect Fitoria to intervene in the battle between humans and demi-humans any time soon.

"It sounds like you're saying you don't plan on teaming up, but that you feel like you have to help me because I'm a hero."

"That's right. Both the humans and I are in the midst of a very long conflict. A long time ago I decided not to participate. I decided that I would only associate with my tribe, the Filolials."

What would a long-living monster like this Filolial think of humans? How would she use them?

For convenience? No—if there was a stronger power, a power they couldn't understand, they'd try to get rid of it.

At first they might try worshiping it or something.

Could it be that she'd grown tired of authority and renounced the world so that she could live with her Filolials in the woods? She might pretend to be a normal Filolial and just travel around.

Before Melty had fallen asleep, she kept talking about how she'd met Fitoria before. She was clearly very proud of herself.

It sounded like Fitoria was standing back to watch the way that normal Filolials interacted with humans—something like that anyway.

"Do the four Holy Heroes know? About the hourglasses? I've been covering the area entrusted to me, but the four Heroes aren't doing their part elsewhere."

"Hourglasses? I know about those."

"Then why aren't you participating in the waves?"

What was going on? I was getting a bad feeling. A strong one.

I knew that there were dragon hourglasses in other countries too.

Could it be… Was she saying that waves in other countries came at different times?

"What are you talking about?"

All I knew was that the waves came about once every month.

If they were happening all over the world, I don't think I'd be able to do much about that.

You'd think that the other countries would try to build up their defenses, so that they wouldn't need to depend on the heroes for protection. Oh well.

I assumed that one of the past heroes must have asked Fitoria to see to that.

But now she was upset that the summoned heroes weren't fully devoting their energies to battling the waves?

"I'm not like the other heroes. I may have been summoned here, but I don't know anything about anything. No one explained anything to me. I just found out there were hourglasses in other places the other day."

"Very well. I understand. I have another question."

"What?"

"I feel an ominous power coming from the Shield. Have you used the Curse Series?"

"You sure know your stuff."

She really was the stuff of legends. She even knew about the Curse Series. She knew about the Shield of Rage.

"I understand that the Curse Series is very powerful, but it asks for much in return. Eventually it will consume you. You mustn't use it."

"But there are battles I cannot win without using it. I've been able to control it so far, so I think I'm okay."

It was true. There had been a number of battles that I wouldn't have been able to win if I hadn't used the Shield of Rage. She was right that it asked for a lot in return, but I figured I'd be all right if I was able to control it.

As long as Raphtalia was with me, I should be able to fight off my rage.

"Are you sure?"

"Yeah."

Fitoria reached out and touched my shield. She shut her eyes.

"The cursed Shield will, one day, overpower the Shield Hero's strength. The dragon's consciousness entered the Shield when its core was absorbed. It must not be used near the person that killed a dragon—or the rage will become too powerful to control."

The Shield of Rage had grown stronger after absorbing the dragon's core.

Did that mean that it absorbed the dragon's anger too?

If that was why the shield had grown so powerful, then who was the person that it hated? Who was the person that had killed it?

Could it be Ren? The Sword Hero had killed the dragon.

So what Fitoria was saying was that I shouldn't use the Shield of Rage when Ren was around? That, if I did, the power would get out of control?

I had fought with Ren recently, but I'd maintained plenty of distance. And Ren hadn't really been trying to fight me anyway.

Was that why nothing had happened? Or could it be that the shield had tried to take over, but it wasn't powerful enough to control me?

"But if I want to survive the battles to come, I might have to use it."

I understood that it was dangerous. But if I wasn't able to protect people without using it, then what choice did I really have?

After the waves ended and the world was restored to peace, I planned on going back to my own world.

It was easy to say that the shield was dangerous and that I shouldn't use it—but there were times when I had no choice.

"Very well. Allow me to change the subject."

"It doesn't look like you agree with me."

She nodded. I guess she didn't agree but was ready to move the conversation to the next topic.

"The world is in great turmoil because of the waves. Why are the Heroes fighting among themselves?"

"It's not my fault. It's them—and the country. They framed me and are discriminating against me."

"I've heard the basics. They are irrelevant. The Heroes do not have time to spend on such trivial matters."

"Such high ideals."

"I've been charged with the protection of the world. But I cannot do it alone. I cannot do it without the Heroes."

After all the power she'd just showed off? Was she sure she couldn't save the world from the waves?

From what I'd seen, she was already much more powerful than Itsuki, Ren, or Motoyasu.

She still wasn't powerful enough to save the world.

Or maybe she was saying that she wouldn't be able to do so forever.

Did that mean that the heroes could still become much more powerful? More powerful than she already was?

I guess they were still heroes, even if they were rotten to the core. If the heroes weren't inherently useful, I supposed these countries wouldn't go through all the trouble of summoning them from another world.

"Honestly, the affairs of humans do not concern me. How they fight... what they fight... But the Heroes are different."

"Why?"

Fitoria silently shook her head.

"It happened... so long ago, so long ago that I can't really remember. All I remember is that I cannot permit the Heroes to fight among themselves."

She forgot the very thing she is so upset about?

Well, she was a Filolial, after all. I couldn't expect her to be some kind of genius with a photographic memory. Just look at Filo.

But she still remembered it. I couldn't put my finger on it, but something felt very wrong.

I had felt a strange pressure coming from Fitoria for a little while.

Something powerful, something... aggressive. It sent shivers down my spine.

"I remember. I was told... If the Heroes ever start to fight among themselves... then, for the good of the world I am to dispose of them so that new Heroes may be summoned."

There it was. That's what she'd wanted to tell me.

She was saying that if I didn't play nice with the other heroes, she'd kill us all. That was the only way to defeat the waves.

That's what the Legendary Filolial had to say. There must be a good reason.

It must have been an order from one of the heroes from the past.

But—

"It's not my fault. They refuse to listen to reason. They refuse to play nice. There's nothing I can do about it."

Yes. Bitch framed me. Trash arrested and discriminated against me, and the other heroes turned on me without even considering my side of the story. There was nothing I could do about any of them.

And now… after I'd raised all that money and earned so many people's trust… Now they framed me for the abduction of Princess Melty and sent assassins to murder us.

And Fitoria wants us to get along? All I could do was get Melty to her mother. That would deal a fatal blow to the Church of the Three Heroes, and then I'd find sanctuary in another country when it all blew over.

Be friends with the other heroes? Impossible.

"…Well."

Fitoria sighed, as if she were giving up. Then fire came into her eyes.

"Then I suppose there is no avoiding it."

She stepped back then walked off into the night. It was a strange way to end the conversation.

I didn't like where this was heading. I doubt she would just walk off and leave us alone.

But I... There was no way I could depend on the other heroes. It was impossible.

Chapter Five: Filo vs. Fitoria

It was hot...

"Gahhh!"

I could hear a bunch of Filolials calling out in unison, and my body felt warm and constricted.

When I opened my eyes I realized I was completely surrounded by Filolials vying to get near me.

"Wh... What's going on?!"

"Hey! Master is MINE!"

Filo was greedily pushing the other Filolials out of the way in an effort to keep me all to herself.

"Oh, come on..."

When I finally came to my senses I realized it was around noon.

If I started cooking and relaxing, would this day end up just like last night had?

"Hey, is it true that you fought with the legendary Griffin King?"

"Yup. I did. To be precise, it was actually a monster that a human made by changing normal griffins. He made so many of them that all the flying Filolials disappeared. The sky was filled with flocks of flying griffins."

"Okay, but did you defeat the Dragon King?"

"I did. I ripped him to shreds, but he kept regenerating. That made the fight difficult."

"Wow! Hey, is it true that the legendary Holy Sword rests in the Filolial sanctuary?"

"There's a holy sword, but I don't know about a legendary sword. I don't think there is anything like that. Though some of the old Heroes' weapons are still here."

Melty's eyes were sparkling again, and she was shooting questions like a machine gun at Fitoria.

At the same time, Filo stood back and watched. She was clearly jealous.

It was a funny scene. I hope their friendship could survive it.

"Okay. We're done resting now. What should we do?

I ate a light meal and turned to Fitoria. We really didn't have time to stand around and smell the flowers—or to eat them.

I figured that Fitoria was probably powerful enough to teleport us all to wherever the queen was. I'd have to find a way to convince her to help us though.

"Okay… now then."

Fitoria rose to her feet and began to cast a spell on Melty. The wind rose and formed a sort of cage around her.

"Wh…what's this?!"

Melty grabbed the bars and tried to escape, but they were

sharp and cut her hand. A little blood trickled over her finger.

"What are you doing?!"

Filo was glaring angrily at Fitoria.

"Mel-tan, you'll have to be my hostage for now."

"Why?"

"..."

Fitoria didn't answer but continued to glare at us. The air was crackling with tension.

Was this... Was this the continuation of what she'd been talking about last night? Was she going to kill us... and then go kill the other heroes too? We should probably assume so.

"Melty!"

Raphtalia shouted for Melty.

Damn... did we have to fight that giant Filolial here?

I couldn't imagine a way that we could win.

The area was filled with a threatening atmosphere, but it wasn't coming from me.

What choice did I have but to use the Shield of Rage?

"You mustn't use the cursed power."

Light appeared around my shield.

—**Due to interference, the shield may not be changed.**

...Appeared in my field of vision. It was the same thing that had occurred the day before.

"Please listen to me."

"Why should I listen to someone behaving as you are?"

"If you refuse to listen, I'll have no choice but to kill the rest of the Heroes."

"Wh…"

She probably could do it.

She was considerably more powerful than we were.

Considering that we hadn't been able to do any real damage to the Tyrant Dragon Rex.

Despite how powerful the beast had been, Fitoria had defeated it without breaking a sweat.

And now we had to fight her?"

We'd lose.

"There's no way we'll all just get along."

"What are you talking about?"

"Last night this girl said that she would kill us all if the Heroes didn't start working together."

"Reconcile with the other Heroes? I'm not sure that is possible."

Raphtalia knit her brow and thought for a moment. Did Fitoria even understand what we were saying? Wouldn't it be more rude to lie and say that we'd all just be friends?

"Very well then…"

Fitoria raised her index finger and leveled it at Filo.

"Then I demand a duel with the Filolial you raised. If she is strong enough then I will release Melty, and offer you a postponement."

"What's that supposed to mean?"

"You'll figure it out."

What did she want from me?

"I will battle in my current form. Filo, I ask that you also fight me in this form."

They had to fight in human form? Filo might stand a chance after all...

Had they fought in their true forms, Filo didn't stand a chance. But if they were both humans, maybe Filo could win. Luckily enough, we had a weapon that Filo could use when she was in human form.

"Okay!"

Filo reached behind the wings on her back and produced the power gloves.

The old guy who ran the weapon shop had originally made them for me so that I could pull the carriage if I needed to. But Filo's magic had turned them into something more like claws. They'd served us well the last time we'd gotten into a scuffle with Motoyasu. And yet...

"Hey! Don't just start whenever you want."

"Yes, Filo. You should do as Mr. Naofumi says."

"But Mel...!"

"If you don't fight, then everyone will die. We don't really have a choice."

"Damn…"

It sure seemed like Fitoria was planning on making the first move.

It made me very anxious to think that all I could do was stand back and watch. She might have been planning to defeat Filo, then turn to us and kill us next. I don't think I'd be able to stop her.

We didn't have any other choice.

"…Fine."

"Then let us begin."

Fitoria raised her hand, and a wall formed from wind appeared between them and the rest of us. Partitioned off on their own, Fitoria and Filo stood in a ring of sorts.

"You must remain in your human form inside this ring. The rules may not be broken."

"I'll save Mel! I won't lose to Fitoria!"

I was very anxious about standing back and watching the fight. If it looked like Filo was in trouble, I'd break the rules and interfere.

"Here I come!"

Filo raised her gloves and closed her eyes in concentration. The gloves morphed into claws, and she brandished them before rushing at Fitoria.

"Ya!"

Filo was the first to attack.

She jumped into the air and spun to kick Fitoria in the stomach.

"Dull."

Fitoria raised a hand and easily stopped the kick.

"Whoa!"

Filo spun back from the blocked attack, but Fitoria was there behind her, delivering punches, one after the other.

Filo was managing to avoid them. Then the ground shook. Fitoria had slammed the soles of her feet into the ground and formed a crater around herself. How powerful was this girl?

"You can do it, Filo!"

Melty shouted from the interior of her cage.

"I'm not losing!"

Filo turned back to Fitoria and swiped at her with the claws. At the same moment, Filo appeared to blur.

"Too slow!"

"Clang!"

There was a reverberating bang, but Filo had managed to dodge the attack with a deft backbend.

"W…What?!"

"Too slow."

"Ugh…"

Filo groaned in a voice she rarely used.

"She's so fast. But I'm not gonna lose."

Filo straightened her back and crossed her arms before rushing forward. Was she already using her best attack?

"Haikuikku!"

Suddenly Filo was a blur, and the air was filled with the reverberations of quick connecting attacks.

"I told you. Too slow."

Fitoria slowly raised and lowered her arms. Then she lightly spun one of them in a circle.

That was all she'd done, but…

"AHHHHHH!"

Filo was flipping backwards through the air.

Filo twisted, and the wings on her back opened. They filled with air, and she landed lightly on her feet.

"You blocked my best attack!"

"Mel is your friend, isn't she? If you don't give me all you've got…"

Fitoria stood there with both her hands on her hips, taunting Filo. She looked like she was disappointed in Filo's performance.

Suddenly Melty's cage shrunk. It was now pressing in on all sides.

"Wa!"

Melty squirmed and hunched her shoulders to keep the bars from cutting into her. Filo watched in horror, and something snapped.

"Mel! Uh…"

Filo's wings flew open, and she held her claws out at Fitoria. She attacked.

Fitoria did not move. She didn't dodge the attack or attempt to defend herself. Sparks flew when the attack connected, but she remained unharmed.

That was impressive. Was she strong enough to ignore Filo's attacks?

What could I say? Filo had the highest attack of anyone in our party, by far. If Fitoria could just play with her like this…

She must have had a great deal of experience. I wondered what level she was.

"Then take THIS!"

Fitoria curled her fingers into a fist and swung a counterattack at Filo. It didn't connect. It didn't even brush her. But Filo's clothes were apparently torn by it.

"I don't think magic clothing like that can protect you."

She went on pummeling, and now the attacks seemed to be connecting.

Dammit… I hated that I couldn't interfere.

What did she mean by magic clothing? That's right. Filo's clothing had been made at a magic shop. They'd formed Filo's own magic into threads, and then they used the material to make her clothing.

That must be what she meant. Magic clothing was clothing made of magic.

Fitoria raised her hands, and suddenly they were topped with glowing claws. She began to swipe at Filo with them.

They left trails of light as they moved through the air. Filo ducked under one of the glowing parabolas. It brushed the top of her head.

"That would have hit had you been in Filolial form."

Fitoria calmly explained.

The attack had been so quick that there had been no hope of dodging it. And it was a magic attack.

"I'm not losing!"

Filo once again began to move her arms up and down.

"I'm the source of all power. Hear my words and do as I SAY. Produce a tornado of wind and carry her away!"

"Zweite Tornado!"

A howling tornado erupted from Filo's hands and flew towards Fitoria. But...

"I'M the source of all power. Here my words and do as I SAY. Render her tornado ineffective!"

"Anti-Zweite Tornado!"

There was a loud clang, and something seemed to enclose Filo. The magic tornado that Filo had produced vanished as though it had never been there at all.

"Interruption magic..."

Let's see... Yeah, I think the beginning book on magic I had mentioned something like that.

Magic Interruption. Yes, I think it said that it was possible in theory, but that it depended on your ability to understand the nature of your opponent, which required great stores of strength.

Apparently it worked by analyzing and understanding the pattern inherent in the system of magic casing. Once the pattern was perceived, you had to send out the opposite pattern very quickly.

Higher-level spells took longer to cast, and therefore were easier to block. But using magic interruption on mid-level magic was supposed to be very difficult.

"I'm not losing!"

Resolute, Filo ran for Fitoria. But how could she expect this attack to be any different than her previous attempts? Fitoria had said that Filo's clothes were magic.

This was about defense. Defense was supposed to be my specialty.

Filo's clothes were originally made out of magic. Focusing magic could restore them.

If so, then that meant…

"Wait, Filo!"

"What is it, Master? I'm busy right now!"

"Use your magic to repair your clothing! Focus your magic on your clothes. It's the only way!"

"Okay!"

Filo jumped back to get some distance before holding out her hands and focusing on her clothes. They began to repair themselves.

Then they started to glow faintly.

I had a feeling that this would raise her defense while she was in human form.

Fitoria ran at Filo and started to punch at her.

"Ha!"

Fitoria's punch was strong enough to shake the earth, but Filo had blocked it with her outstretched hands.

"Ugh... So... strong... But..."

I wondered... would she have been able to bear the brunt of the attack if she hadn't focused her magic into her clothing?

Filo took the brunt of the attack then knocked Fitoria's arm away before rushing forward.

Fitoria was open. Filo lunged with the claws.

The wind seemed to vibrate. She must have been raising her speed.

"Hiya!"

She threw the weight of her whole body behind the attack, and it connected.

Or so I thought. But...

"Weak."

There was a small shower of sparks, but, other than that, Fitoria appeared unfazed.

I knew it. There was no way to get through her defenses.

This wasn't good. What if Filo lost? What should I do?

Filo kept looking over at me. I didn't have any more advice for her though.

That's what I thought anyway, but she was actually looking to Melty, then me, then back to Melty.

…So that was her plan…

I snuck over to Melty's cage and reached out to touch it.

There was a crashing sound as the blades of wind attempted to cut into me—but my defense was high enough to endure it.

Filo must have wanted me to break the cage and end the fight.

And she was right. If Fitoria was so much stronger than Filo, then there was no chance of victory.

"Melty."

"N…Naofumi?"

"Don't move."

I reached my arm inside of the case and tried to break it. But then…

An incredibly strong wind blew up from beneath me, and I went flying.

"I do not like cheaters."

Suddenly a tornado appeared and crashed into my torso. It felt like I'd been punched in the gut, and I flew backwards.

"Ugh…"

Did she just break through my defenses?

"Mr. Naofumi!"

"Ugh!"

I fell to the ground in pain, and my vision warped.

Damn... I looked down to see my armor dented. I was bleeding. If I didn't focus and cast some restorative magic, I'd be in real trouble. The armor could repair itself... but I... dammit...

"Master!"

"Stay focused."

"Muh..."

"Can you fight after you've used your magic?"

"I can!"

"Reckless. Let's finish this."

Fitoria's wings opened and pointed to the sky.

"Suuuuuuu..."

She paused and took a deliberate breath. Something was flying around us. It looked like she was gathering the magical elements to herself.

What couldn't she do?

I wished I could do the same thing... but I could barely manage to pull off a simple magic spell. Still, I guess the best way to improve was to copy someone that could do it.

It was something like stealing the contents of another person's brain. Though if you really wanted to take it far, what were schools, if not constantly copying people from the past?

Basically all of our accomplishments were nothing more than that: copying other people's successes.

Yeah. Someday I'd be strong enough to copy what Fitoria was doing. When I could, I'd make a point to learn it.

"I can do that too!"

Filo copied Fitoria, and she began to gather magic to herself.

"...Too slow."

The problem was that Fitoria had already gathered all the magic up.

Fitoria rushed Filo and pummeled her with her fists.

"U... Mu... Ku..."

But Filo's arms were crossed, and Fitoria hadn't yet broken through her defenses.

Fitoria jumped back and then twisted herself in the air, delivering an airborne kick.

"Can you stop this?"

"Mkyaaaaaaaaa!"

She wasn't able to block the kick, and she went spinning through the air before slamming into a wall of wind.

"I'm... I'm not losing..."

She rose to stand on shaky feet before, once again, gathering magic to herself.

"Mu..."

She seemed to have recovered enough of her magic. She broke her concentration and moved into her next attack.

"Hiya!"

Filo moved her wings up and down. She ducked down low, spread her wings, and held her claws forward.

She began to shoot forward, carried on a strong current of wind. It was readily apparent to any observer that her magic was greatly concentrated.

It must have been Filo's strongest attack.

There were too many preparations necessary. I didn't think she could use it in battle.

"Kuikku!"

Filo was flying at Fitoria like a bullet.

Her claws were out in front. She was flying just a hair over the ground, and spinning in the air. It was the fastest I'd ever seen her move.

How to describe it? It was like the final attack for a flying robot in a strategy game.

"Heh…."

Fitoria's eyes widened in surprise.

Fitoria's clothes were cut slightly, ever so slightly. They were covered in fine cuts.

Then Filo's claws connected with Fitoria's face. I couldn't believe it, but there was a scratch on Fitoria's cheek.

A drop of blood ran down Fitoria's cheek.

Fitoria looked at the blood that Filo had torn from her face. She looked at where it fell. She smiled.

That was when I noticed. I looked over at Raphtalia, and she nodded.

Fitoria was just playing with us. She wanted to see how Filo would react when faced with an opponent much stronger than herself. That's why she smiled when she was hit with such an unexpected attack.

The Legendary Filolial.

The description seemed to fit. Filo turned her nose up. She knew there was no way to win.

We'd known that the battle was not going to be simple, but we hadn't even decided the victor yet.

"Mu…"

Filo grunted. At first I thought she was dissatisfied, but now she looked irritated.

"Is it my turn now?"

Fitoria stepped forward and sent a series of quick attacks flying at Filo.

She was so fast! She'd been faster than Filo up until this point anyway, but now she was moving even quicker.

She wasn't moving so fast that she was invisible, like when using Haikuikku, but she was a blur—never where you looked for her.

"Uh… Ahhh!"

Filo couldn't block the attacks, and she flew through the air.

But before she landed, Fitoria was already there. She looked up at the falling Filo…

"Ha!"

And kicked her hard, sending her flying back to where she'd come from.

"Ugh…"

Then Fitoria settled herself. She looked at Filo, waiting for the next move.

Filo held her hand against where she ached, and magical light appeared there. She must have been using restorative magic, as her wounds were healing before our eyes. But she wasn't very powerful anymore. She wasn't able to heal herself back to normal, only until she wasn't in immediate danger.

"Ugh…"

Filo was very weak. She once again began to gather magic to herself.

"Look at me now."

Filo was done healing herself. Then she was on her feet and rushing at Fitoria.

Maybe I was imagining it. No, I wasn't. Filo was moving much faster than she had been up until now.

Filo gathered power into her claws then copied the attack that Fitoria had just used.

"Ha!"

After three attacks, the wall of wind that Fitoria had made appeared to grow weak. It was shaking.

"Is that all you've got?"

I'd noticed it for a little while now, but Filo seemed to be learning from, and copying exactly, all of Fitoria's attacks. No... Fitoria was TEACHING her. She just hadn't been holding back at all, so it took a while to notice.

Yes... It was all training. It felt like Fitoria wanted to train Filo... She wanted to train her so badly that she didn't care if Filo died in the process.

"Better hurry up. Meltan is in danger."

Fitoria held a hand out in Melty's direction.

The cage grew smaller around her, and the bars were slicing the ends of her hair.

"Kya!"

"Mel! Ugh!"

Filo opened her wings and used the bullet attack again. She flew at Fitoria, but she was even faster this time.

"HIYAAAAAAAAA!"

"Hm... Well, this is the end of the test. Do your best to stick it out."

Fitoria used both of her hands to block Filo's attack. When Filo spun away to recover, Fitoria planted a kick to her side.

"Ahhh!"

She went flying all the way to the cage made of wind, which she slammed into and kept flying.

Rolling along the ground, she came to rest finally, like a beaten rag doll.

I ran to where she fell.

But Filo held out her hand to stop me, and she rose on her shaking legs.

"I'm not… I'm not losing."

She didn't want my help, as if receiving help would disqualify her from the duel. She was shaking badly, but she took a step forward.

She looked so weak. It was like she could fall over at any moment. She wanted to win so badly that she refused to accept defeat.

"Filo! If you lose then we can't get Mel back!"

"Filo…"

"Filo! It's okay! It's okay."

"No… I… I'm going to protect you, Mel."

Filo tottered over to where Fitoria stood. The power gloves had lost their claws, but she curled them into fists and punched at Fitoria anyway.

"Yaaaaah!"

But the attack was very weak, but her willpower was strong. Filo's fist connected with Fitoria's stomach.

"…"

But it wasn't enough to hurt her.

"Yes. That's okay. That's enough."

Filo fell, but Fitoria rushed forward and hugged her. The cage of wind that had been holding Melty vanished.

"Filo!"

"Mel…"

"She's okay. She'll be all right."

Fitoria began to cast a spell on Filo.

Before our eyes, Filo's wounds began to heal, and all the tears in her clothing were mended.

"Huh?"

Filo quickly bat Fitoria's hand away and resumed her fighting posture.

"It's over."

"It is not over! I have to protect Mel!"

"I know. But Meltan is okay. Look."

Fitoria motioned for Melty to come over.

Melty looked very carefully at Fitoria before slinking over to stand by Filo.

"Do you understand? The test is over."

"Test?"

"Just a little one. I have my own situations to deal with also."

"Oh yeah?"

Filo didn't immediately trust her but turned her head to the side as she listened to Fitoria.

They'd just been locked in battle, but all the tension seemed to have evaporated.

"Filo, she was just testing you."

Raphtalia and I walked closer and tried to explain.

"Yes… It was a test. But I did truly intend to do as I'd said if she didn't come through."

Fitoria explained simply.

I didn't know why she felt like she had to do this. But, because of the fight with Fitoria, Filo had learned some great skills for fighting in human form.

"Filo, you have to think about your opponent. If you fight against humans when you are in Filolial form, it's like fighting with a giant target on your back."

"Really?"

It was true that Filo was very large in her Filolial form. Even if she could move very quickly, it made for a bigger target when facing a powerful enemy.

Also, when she fought in her Filolial form she basically had to make all of her attacks into kicks.

It wasn't that she couldn't use magic or rush attacks, but it would be best to think about what kind of opponent she was facing. Fitoria was trying to get Filo to notice that there were other ways to fight.

It would be useful to switch tactics in the middle of a fight anyway. It could confuse the enemy.

So basically, Fitoria told Filo that she should stay flexible about her options—and she taught her some new moves.

"This is proof that you have passed my test."

Fitoria said, and pulled out a tiara. She gave it to Filo.

"What? What's this?"

"It's your reward for passing my test. Now lower your head."

"Filo, you're supposed to go like this."

Melty grabbed Filo's sleeve and pulled her down into a bow.

Would you look at that? Melty was acting very princess-like for a change.

"Like this?"

"Yes, that's it."

Filo was bowing before Fitoria, who placed the tiara on her head.

"Filo, you will be my heir."

"What's that?"

"It means that you will be the next great Queen of the Filolials."

"Oh…"

"Filo! Good for you!"

Melty was so excited. She jumped up and down. Filo didn't seem so excited herself.

Suddenly the tiara on Filo's head twinkled and shined.

It sent light out in all directions, and then…

Ping! A single cowlick appeared on Filo's head. One strand of hair stuck straight up.

"..."

Raphtalia and I were both silent.

Was that some kind of prize?

"Huh?"

"Filo! You're so cute!"

Melty was very excited and was practically dancing in place... But Filo didn't seem to understand what was happening.

Melty hadn't noticed.

Wait a second. I considered myself a real *Otaku*. Did that mean I was supposed to get excited by this cowlick?

Nope... I wasn't feeling it.

"What happened?"

"Well..."

I pointed to Filo's head, and Filo herself followed my gaze. She reached up and...

"What's that? There's something weird on my head!"

Filo screamed and nearly jumped. She grabbed the clump of hair and...

Rip!

"Wh?!"

She pulled it right off.

Filo was really something. It looked like it must have really hurt.

"Ouch!"

It must have hurt, but Filo seemed proud of herself for getting rid of it.

Boing!

But after she'd torn it off, another strand of hair popped up to take its place.

"Another one?!"

"What?!"

Filo's eyes filled with tears as, time and time again, she ripped the cowlicks off of her head. A new one always popped up to take its place though, and so she eventually gave up and hung her head.

It was a weird little cowlick,

"It'll only keep growing back, so you'd better give up. The more you grow, the more cowlicks you'll have."

"What? But I don't want…"

Filo was looking at the cowlicks on Fitoria's head.

What did the Legendary Filolial have in mind by giving something like that to Filo?

I decided to have a look at Filo's status screen.

Her stats had improved.

It seemed like the tiara had conferred some abilities and status improvements.

Considering that, for the time being anyway, Filo had maxed out her level up potential, it was a good reward.

"And for the Shield Hero…"

"Huh? I get something too?"

Fitoria pointed in my direction, then curled her finger up and beckoned for me to come over.

Wait a second. If I walked over there, was she going to give me cowlicks too?

"I don't need a new hairstyle."

"Hairstyle?"

I didn't explain further. It would only cause a fuss if I did.

"It's better than that. And it will heal your wounds."

"Well, then…"

I didn't know what she was going to give me, but I hoped it wasn't anything too weird.

I probably couldn't have refused anyway, so I walked over to her. She reached out and touched my torso, healing my wounds. I hadn't been able to completely heal them, so there had been a dull pain in the area. She took the pain away.

"Show me your Shield."

She pointed to the shield and motioned for me to hold it up.

"Like this?"

I held the shield up. Fitoria pulled out her cowlick and held it up to the center of the shield.

The shield immediately reacted and absorbed the hair.

Filolial Series Forcibly Unlocked!

"Forcibly unlocked?"

I checked the tree, and there was a "Filolial Shield" glowing on it.

It had a bunch of equip bonuses that all seemed to benefit Filolials, like power and growth adjustment (large, medium, small), detailed growth stat adjustment (large, medium, small), and others.

One that immediately jumped out at me was called Ability While Riding (large, medium, small). It must have meant that Filo would fight better with someone riding on her back.

Still, my level wasn't high enough to use most of the shield's abilities. Luckily the shield was unlocked, so if I just met the requirements I'd be able to use its powers.

It looked like the requirements had been met to unlock any shield related to Filolials.

"Thank you."

"You are welcome. However I still have something I would like to discuss with you."

"What's that?"

"I'd rather talk in private."

This was becoming a rather strange reward.

Hey—did this mean that all of the Filolial's powers were concentrated into those cowlicks?

Filo couldn't level up anymore, at least for now. So I suppose it was a good thing.

"Um… Uh…"

Melty was hesitant, and somewhat embarrassed, to speak to Fitoria.

"What?"

"That was just to test Filo, right? You weren't…using me?"

"Of course not. Isn't there anything you want, Meltan?"

"Um… Can you become a really big Filolial and let me ride on your head?"

Oddly engaged and passionate, Melty made her request.

"…Very well."

Fitoria seemed a little put out, but as she pat Melty on the head, she started to grow larger. Then she smiled deeply.

"Wow…"

Then, just as she'd promised, she set Melty onto her head.

"It's so high up here!"

Melty was very excited.

"Shield Hero, please back up a little."

"Okay."

I stepped back as I was asked.

And… Fitoria soon grew to be about eighteen meters tall.

Just how big could she get? She was like a building.

"Wow! Wow!"

Melty's voice came down on the wind. Was it okay to take her so far from the ground?

But seriously, just how big could she get?

Or maybe that was her real size, and she had just transformed to match our size.

"Wow…"

Melty seemed very relaxed.

"It's like a dream…"

"Too bad it's not."

Filo was powerful enough to defeat a dragon, and that girl had used her like a toy… that wasn't a good sign.

"Now then. The day has only just started. I'd like for you all to get a little more rest."

"Sure—if you'll take us to where we want to go later."

"We'll talk about that later. For the time being, just try to relax. My friends here also extend their greetings."

"GAHHH!"

"What? Celebrate the birth of a new queen? You mean me?"

"Congratulations Filo! Ah, ha, ha! Look how happy the Filolials are!"

The other Filolials all crowded around Filo and lifted her up.

"M…Me?"

They had picked up Raphtalia as well.

What was going on? We were suddenly very popular.

We spent the rest of the day with the Filolials. It was a festival-like atmosphere.

So there we were in seclusion. But once we left, how long would it be until the rest of the world believed in us too?

Chapter Six: The Bird God's Peace

The whole day passed like a dream, and before long, night fell. Raphtalia, Filo, and Melty all fell asleep in a huge nest that the Filolials had prepared for them.

Just like the night before, Fitoria stayed up to speak with me privately.

"What is it?"

"About what we discussed last night…"

"Damn, you're persistent. What's impossible is impossible."

This morning she'd been serious about trying to kill us though. I realized that it was thanks to Filo's efforts that we made it out of that one.

But why was she so powerful? How did she get strong enough to fling Filo around like she was a doll? She was strong enough to take on all of the heroes at once.

"Did you really… try to be friends with them? Did you try?"

I didn't answer immediately. If I didn't think about my answer, she might kill me.

Motoyasu had made up his mind about me. I wasn't sure what Ren or Itsuki thought.

Since the run-in we had over Melty, we hadn't met again.

I had no way of knowing where they were, but I remember that when we last left them, they seemed to have some suspicions about what I'd been accused of.

"Did you try to clear your name?"

She had noticed that I hadn't really done anything.

Especially concerning the rape accusation Bitch had made, I had given priority to my anger because I really believed there was no chance of anyone believing me.

I told them that I had been framed, and they didn't believe me. That's why I didn't believe them.

But if I had been able to show them proof, would that have changed their minds?

We weren't close enough to sit down for a chat. They knew everything about this world, and they knew that I didn't—but they still sent me out on my own and made no attempt to help me. Why should I go to them?

All they wanted to do was play in their world and act all badass.

How was I supposed to know what they were thinking?

I'd thought about it before. I tried to imagine what Ren was thinking.

He knew that everyone was freaking out because I'd been accused of raping Bitch. Ren didn't know much about Bitch, but he knew that she was beautiful.

Who should he believe? The man accused of the crime, of

the woman who claims to be the victim?

If I were him, and I really didn't know anything about either of them, I'd have to side with the woman who claimed to be the victim.

It was similar to things I'd heard about back in my own world.

On a commuter train one day, a woman grabbed a man's arm and shouted, "This man touched me!"

Even if he hadn't touched her, everyone on the train would immediately look at him differently, suspiciously. Even if he could prove that he was being framed, the man's social position would be forever damaged.

What Bitch had done to me was similar to that.

"Sigh…"

My anger was starting to subside, ever so slightly.

Just as I didn't know anything about Ren or Itsuki, they didn't know anything about me. The same was true of Motoyasu.

Well, Motoyasu clearly only thought about women.

I felt like I had realized something important.

If Ren and the others were looking into what had happened, then it might be worth it to try and speak with them. If we ran into each other, that is.

If… Well, I'd try and talk the next time I saw them.

If everything went well, we might be able to make some superficial amends.

Of course, amends wouldn't be possible until Bitch and Trash had been punished.

"Do you remember our previous conversation? Where should I take you after we leave this place?"

"Yeah."

"I was planning on dropping you off somewhere near the Holy Heroes."

"You're coming too, right?

If she was as powerful as she seemed to be, she could probably help clear up the misunderstanding.

Her chief concern was that the heroes work together. Considering that, it seemed like a fair request.

"I will not intrude on your affairs any longer. Please show me that there is a reason for me to care about you."

"Very self-satisfied, aren't you?

"That's the problem. I haven't found a reason to value the current Heroes. The only one of you I've met that has potential is Filo. Prove me wrong."

She clearly considered herself above me, but if she thought that she was doing it for the good of the world, then she really might kill the heroes for their infighting.

I couldn't exactly say she was mistaken.

But I still had the feeling that she wasn't going to save the world by knocking off people that were fighting with each other.

Actually maybe I— or not I, but us... the heroes... maybe we were wrong about how serious the threat was.

"Besides, I have plenty of things to keep me busy."

"Like what?"

"Like saving the world from the waves. It's not like the waves only come to places where people live."

"Are there hourglasses outside of population centers?"

Fitoria nodded. I'd rather have not known that. So it wasn't just civilization that was threatened?

"I've been put in charge of those areas. I'd love for you to help me, but you need to grow stronger first."

So she meant that she'd gone out of her way to meet us and test us... while she had the time to do so.

She wanted to see if we were strong enough to face what was coming. If we weren't, she'd kill us.

"If you can, have a real conversation with them. The world doesn't have time for the petty squabbles of Heroes."

"You make it sound like the heroes are always fighting."

"I've seen it happen many times."

"Fine. I have to do all I can to patch up the relationship, right?"

"There's more."

"What?"

"If even one of the Heroes is missing when the waves come, the waves will grow stronger. If that is what's happening, then the Heroes must be killed so that new ones may be summoned. It must happen for the sake of the world."

Damn... I didn't want to know that either. That meant that the danger grew worse if any of the heroes died.

But if all the heroes died, then new ones could be summoned. What a situation.

She was telling us to kiss and make up. But if we didn't she'd kill us.

This Filolial Queen sure knew how to give an obnoxious order.

I was lost in my thoughts for a moment, so Fitoria stood up and turned back to me.

"I don't know how many waves it will take. But there will come a time when all the life in the world will be forced to sacrifice something great."

"..."

"The Heroes will then be forced to make a decision. I'll be waiting for you then."

"Decision?"

"Whether you'll fight for the world or for the people. If you can't play nicely with the other Heroes and just want to be rid of your purpose, then at least stay alive until then. If you choose to fight for the world, you'll have to make a great sacrifice, but you'll be able to fulfill your purpose."

"What happens if I choose to fight for people?"

"That's a thorny path. The past Heroes wished for it. But it's no longer possible. It is a path you cannot walk alone. You'd never make it."

"Hmm... Just how much do you know? Tell me everything."

"I've already forgotten so much. But I remember one thing. Saving the world and saving humanity are not the same thing."

The world and its people were different.

From the way she was speaking, it was clear that she was standing on the side of the world. She seemed mostly indifferent to what happened to its people. Then what did it mean to fight for the world? I knew she was referencing the waves, but I couldn't figure the rest out.

Regardless, there was a time when she wanted to see us again.

It might be after the final wave. I wondered... what WOULD I choose?

Even if it was on behalf of people, if I could do something to protect Raphtalia and the others, I'd probably choose to help people.

"So please, try to get along with the other Heroes."

"All I can say is that I will try. I can't say how they will react, but you did give us those rewards. The least I can do is make an effort."

She gave Filo a tiara, and me a shield. The least I could do was hear her out.

"You passed the trial. I have more hope for you than I do for the other Heroes."

"Why?"

"The Shield Hero who raised the new Filolial Queen can't be all bad."

"I am though. I'm bad."

I just said it without thinking.

I mean... I'd bought a little girl as a slave and forced her to fight for me.

I certainly wasn't a GOOD person.

"..."

Fitoria sent her gaze to the sky and sighed deeply.

"Think what you want for now. But don't forget that we are connected through Filo."

Had Filo not been able to pass her trial... she would have killed me.

She was powerful enough to do it. I'd even been wounded.

"Fine."

"Shield Hero, I think that you have the strength to fix things with the other Heroes. And honestly... they are all just too weak. With how things are now, I won't have to step in to take care of you all. You'll take care of yourselves."

"Will it be so hard?"

"It will be. And if you have to use that Shield..."

Fitoria reached a hand towards my armor.

I suddenly felt lighter.

The dragon core that had been imbedded into my barbarian armor somehow changed. It now appeared like a Taoist ying-yang symbol.

Barbarian Armor + 1 (Protection of the Bird God): defense up: impact resistance (medium): fire resistance (large): wind resistance (large): shadow resistance (large): HP recovery (very small): magic up (medium): agility up (medium): magic defense manufacturing: spiritual contamination resistance: automatic recovery

"What's this?

"It will help you resist the Cursed Series. Still, it won't keep you safe completely… Don't use the Shield if you can avoid it."

"I'll do what I can, but you shouldn't hold your breath. About this or about making up with the other Heroes."

"Please…"

Fitoria flashed the most sincere smile I'd seen yet as she walked over and leaned against me.

"You're heavy. Get off."

But Fitoria showed no signs of moving.

"…"

She kept leaning against me in silence.

What was she doing? She looked like a little kid about to burst into tears.

Why? It was my first thought. Why? What did she want?

Then I thought of reasons. She'd said that a hero had raised her.

Where was that hero now? He'd either gone back to his own world, or he'd died a long time ago.

Did she think I was like her new parent now? Did she see her old hero in me?

There was nothing I could do about it.

I ran my hand over her head. When I did, she buried her head against my shoulder and hugged me.

It seemed like the only reason she had to live was the promise she'd made to the hero in the past. Was that all she had?

She'd promised to protect the world. How many years had it been?

Thinking on how long she'd worked for the world, I felt like the least I could do was accept her request.

In all her years, how many people had she met and worked with? In THIS world? She must have fallen into disappointment and desperation many times. Was that why she didn't trust anyone but the heroes?

She was a rather clumsy girl. She seemed to be very powerful, but that was probably because she was trying so hard.

When a little girl asks you to do something, it's hard to say no.

I'd do what I could.

Eventually Fitoria's breath became deeper, and I realized she'd fallen asleep against my shoulder. Her snores sounded just like Filo's.

Someday, after I'd gone, would Filo lean on another hero's shoulder and fall asleep? As I thought about it, my eyelids grew heavy, and soon I was asleep too.

"Thank you so much!"

Melty and Filo were waving their arms energetically.

Morning came, and Fitoria declared that it was probably about time we hit the road. She motioned for us to ride in the carriage.

Once we were all in the carriage, Fitoria teleported us back to the field where we'd fought with the Tyrant Dragon Rex, and we all disembarked. Were the other heroes nearby?

"Are the other heroes somewhere nearby?"

"I sense some kind of reaction nearby…"

Fitoria was staring at the carriage. That wasn't a good sign.

A moment passed. Then Fitoria transformed into her normal Filolial form before raising her wings and running away.

"That was an interesting experience, wasn't it, Mr. Naofumi?"

"Sure was. Okay, Filo…"

"Uh huh?"

Oh, I forgot to mention that Fitoria had given Filo a parting gift.

It was a new carriage. It was made of wood, though it wasn't of exceptional quality.

Everything was getting really complicated. Why had she put so much on my shoulders?

Filo had preferred the carriage that I'd bought, but there was really no choice but to compromise.

Filo turned into her Filolial Queen form and started to pull the carriage.

"Let's go!"

"Okay!"

"Yeah!"

"We can do it, right, Filo?!"

We'd gotten far off course, but we were back on it now. We headed for the southwestern border.

"I didn't think it was going to be this far..."

We'd arrived at the border. From where we stood we could see a small fort-like structure where guards watched the border from their patrol along the roof.

There weren't very many people crossing the border, and there were guards inspecting the contents of large luggage carts.

"Damn. They're keeping a close watch."

"Because they are looking for us, right? At least there are fewer guards here than there were up at the northeastern border."

"That's true…"

Motoyasu was standing near the border crossing. The fire-spewing demon was with him.

I wished he'd go somewhere else. He'd never really listened to me.

Or so I was thinking when Fitoria's words came back to me. Could it be that my own assumptions were preventing us from reconciling?

Regardless, Bitch was there too—and there was no way that she would hear me out.

Anyway, there didn't seem any way to cross without just charging head-on.

I held on to a small hope that maybe they would listen to Filo, Melty, or Raphtalia.

If we looked for another crossing now, we'd wander for a few days at least. And besides, our goal was right there before us.

The main problem was Motoyasu. We'd made it out of all of our scuffles so far. If he wouldn't listen to what we had to say, then we would just have to push through.

Right—we'd just have to force our way through.

"Melty, the goal is right there. We have to push through,

whatever happens. Still, I'm going to try talking to Motoyasu."

I figured she was throwing some kind of hysteric fit, but it was important to make sure we were all on the same page.

"Okay."

"Huh? What's that?"

"What's what?"

"I thought you'd tell me not to because it would make us look bad."

"..."

She turned away and sighed in frustration.

"If the country is behaving so rashly, then a rash treatment is necessary."

I knew what she meant. She was thinking of the nobleman that had wanted us dead so badly he'd release the seal on an ancient monster. He'd burn the country down to get at us.

Melty was decisive. That was good.

Forcing our way over the border would probably result in less destruction than continuing to run.

"Okay. Let's move! Are you all ready?"

"Completely."

"Yup!"

"I'll give it my all."

"All right!"

I raised my hand, and Filo threw her weight forward, running full-tilt with the carriage.

We ran right up to the border crossing.

"It's the Shield Demon!"

Some greeting…

I'd been planning on compromising and trying to talk things over. And this is how they said hello?

I'd reconsidered my approach after talking through it with Fitoria. But had I been wrong?

"Stop right there!"

Before the actual crossing there was some kind of mat laid out. It was covered with protruding nails. We'd never get the carriage over it.

But Filo didn't show any signs of slowing down.

"Here they come!"

Motoyasu leveled his spear in our direction.

He was a feminist. He wouldn't raise his spear to Filo… would he?

His spear began to glow.

"Myne!"

"Okay!"

Bitch started to cast a spell.

"Zweite Fire!"

"Air Strike Javelin! And…"

As Myne finished casting her spell, Motoyasu raised his shining spear and threw it at us.

"Combo Skill, Air Strike Fire Lance!"

A spear made of fire was flying straight for us.

Shit!

I immediately jumped up onto Filo's back and began to cast my own spell.

"Air Strike Shield! Second Shield!"

The two Air Strike Shields appeared in the air and stopped Motoyasu's burning lance.

But the shields were not able to stop the lance completely. It ricocheted and kept flying for the cart. Filo jumped away from the cart to dodge it. I turned back to see Raphtalia and Melty hold hands and leap from the cart just in time.

Was Motoyasu flinging skills at us without hesitation now?

Besides, what WAS that? Magic and skills could be combined into combo skills?

I guess so. It was like the magic sword.

Had he been holding back this whole time? Is that why they hadn't used it up until now?

"What are you doing?!"

I was planning on trying to talk to him before we ran away, but he'd just run up and started attacking.

"Myne!"

"I know!"

Bitch, the princess, shot a look over at the soldiers.

When she did, a magic cage, rippling and crackling with energy, appeared around us.

"What?!"

"What the… What is this?!"

"What's happening?"

It was very large, about forty meters across. It appeared to be made out of lightning.

Was it… magic? Or was it made from something else?

"We finally found you, Naofumi. You won't get away this time."

"Motoyasu…"

He was looking at us, unmistakably gloating.

What was that supposed to mean? His normal nonchalance was gone.

"Naofumi, this is a magical device called a Lightning Cage."

Melty looked at the cage and explained its purpose.

"It is a trap installed over a specific area. It is designed to trap wizards and magic users."

"For wizards? What's the point of it?"

"It's supposed to keep the targets trapped inside."

Now it made sense. They'd seen us escape on Filo's quick feet before, so they wanted to fight in an area that would circumvent that entirely.

"I can break it, but it will take a little time."

"What's the normal way to get out?"

"You need the key from the person who set it up."

I climbed down from Filo's back and glared at Motoyasu.

"Are you going to fight?"

"Well I wanted to discuss things before it came to that. But it's looking like a fight is more likely."

Raphtalia unsheathed her sword and readied it.

"Raphtalia, you should focus on defense. Stay back if you can."

"But I..."

"Am I fighting?"

"Yes. If it comes to that."

Motoyasu was weak when it came to pretty girls. He had just attacked without hesitation, but I was going to assume that he thought we'd dodge it.

"Melty, can you focus on breaking the cage?"

"I can try… but I can't make any promises."

"Okay then—Raphtalia, you focus on protecting Melty as she works to break the cage."

"All right!"

After I finished assigning everyone their roles, I walked over in Motoyasu's direction.

"Motoyasu, listen to me."

It might have been because of the chat I'd had with Fitoria, but I was starting to suspect that Motoyasu really was just being deceived by Bitch.

If that wasn't the case, then he wouldn't have tried to go out of his way to save Raphtalia from me.

He might have been a little slow on the uptake, but for the time being I was going to assume that he had never really intended to frame me.

"You think you can brain wash me with your Brain Washing Shield?!"

Oh man... He was already convinced that the Brain Washing Shield was a real thing.

Honestly though, it was his complete lack of critical thought that reeked of brain washing.

But he was the Spear Hero. If I could trust what I'd been reading in *The Records of the Four Holy Warriors,* then the Spear Hero was supposed to have a loyal heart.

Loyalty, in this case, clearly meant that he did not doubt those that he considered his friends.

And Bitch, the princess, and Trash, the king, were right behind him. If he'd believe his so-called friends without a second thought, then he was just an idiot.

"Mr. Motoyasu! We have to hurry and save Melty and the other brain washed victims of the Shield Demon!"

Bitch was always ready to add fuel to the fire. How rotten was this woman?

"I'm not going to hold back anymore."

"...Me neither."

After I was summoned here, I had to endure Motoyasu's absurdity on the second day, then on the first day of the second month.

The thought of ending all that seemed reasonable enough.

Dammit! There I was, falling into the same pattern again. Why didn't I learn?!

"Anyway, listen to me. Is this really the time for heroes to squabble among themselves? Where are Ren and Itsuki? If you don't think of a good reason for just you to devote all your time to chasing me, then you're acting like a fool!"

If he were convinced I was evil, then I would turn the conversation to Ren and Itsuki—because they weren't chasing me.

If we talked about them enough, maybe Motoyasu would wake up to his own suspicions.

"Even though they're dead, I won't believe anything you say!"

"Huh?"

Dead? What was he talking about?

Ren and Itsuki? Us? Who? What?

"Hey, Motoyasu. What are you talking about? Who's dead?"

"That's how you tricked Ren and Itsuki too! That's how you killed them!"

"What? What are you talking about? Explain yourself!"

"You're trying to trick me! I won't listen! I know all about it! After that monster was released from a town YOU were at, you snuck up behind Ren and Itsuki and killed them!"

What the hell happened in Melromarc while we were with Fitoria?

The only idea I could come up with was that Ren and Itsuki had gone looking into the broken seal. They were getting too close to the truth, so someone had them killed.

I don't know if it was Trash or the Church, but someone was trying to pin the whole thing on me, and they were whispering to Motoyasu about it!

"You're wrong! Think about it! I don't have a reason to kill Ren or Itsuki!"

"Shut up. I don't believe you. I'm done holding back! Even if a girl has to be the new Shield, I'll have to dirty my hands to avenge Ren and Itsuki!"

It wasn't working. Motoyasu had made up his mind that I had murdered the other heroes.

Damn. Someone had beaten me to it.

Fitoria, I'm sorry. The heroes didn't seem to care about saving the world at all.

Of all the heroes needed to somehow stand up to the crisis bearing down on the world… somehow… there were only two left.

And looking at Motoyasu's behavior, he wasn't going to be satisfied until I was dead too.

But I couldn't die there.

I changed my shield into the Chimera Viper Shield and turned to face Motoyasu.

Motoyasu had Bitch and two other girls in his party. There

were soldiers pouring from the border crossing. The cage kept them from interfering directly—but it also prevented our escape.

As for my side of things, Filo and I stood at the front lines. Melty was in the back trying to break the cage while Raphtalia protected her.

"Everyone, let us have our revenge!"

"Motoyasu, you're crazy. It's time you realized that."

Fine. Things were different now.

Melty couldn't fight, but I still had Filo and Raphtalia.

If I really used my shield, we wouldn't lose.

Finally, we were going to settle this whole matter once and for all.

"AAAAHHHHHHHH!"

We ran headfirst into the battle for the future.

Chapter Seven: The Battle of Shield and Spear

"Filo, you go for Motoyasu, and…"

As the battle began, I gave Filo orders.

Motoyasu said that he wouldn't hold back—even against women. His eyes were burning with hatred. He readied his spear.

"I, the next princess, am the source of all power. May the entire universe hear my words and heed them. Rain fire on the enemy!"

"Zweite Fire Squall!"

When Bitch's pompous chanting came to an end, it was followed by magical fire raining from the sky.

"Naofumi! Filo!"

"I am the source of all power! Hear my words and heed them! Stop the rain that falls on them!"

"Anti-Zweite Fire Squall!"

Melty stopped trying to break the Lightning Cage so that she could cast an interference spell on the raining fire.

But she wasn't able to completely negate the effects of Bitch's spell, and fire continued to fall on us.

The whole area burst into flames. It looked like a sea of fire. Luckily, it was only large enough to affect Filo and me on the front line.

"That's right. I'm not letting you kick at Mr. Motoyasu this time."

Bitch was running for us now, casting spells without hesitation.

But Melty was good with magic too.

Still, Bitch's level was higher.

"Filo! Are you okay?!"

"Yup! I'm fine!"

Filo hadn't taken any significant damage from the fire.

As for me… I'd been fine the last time the Crown's wizards decided to subject me to baptism by fire. It didn't bother me this time either.

"I am the source of all power. Hear my words and heed them! Bring the rain of mercy!"

"Zweite Squall!"

Melty summoned a powerful rain to protect her and Raphtalia.

"Ha! Mr. Motoyasu, you just stay focused on the Shield Demon! I'll take care of this bird with my magic!"

Bitch and the other girls in Motoyasu's party all began to chant spells.

"I'm going!"

Filo didn't bother to pay attention to the chanting. She rushed straight for Motoyasu.

"Wait, Filo!"

She shouldn't just run in—we had no idea what was waiting for us!

"Wing Tackle!"

A huge ball of wind appeared and flew straight for Filo, who was still running at Motoyasu.

"Hoh!"

With a puff, Filo transformed into human form in mid-stride. In a flash she slipped on the power gloves and ran to slice at Motoyasu.

"Ugh…"

Motoyasu turned his spear vertical and blocked Filo's attack.

Now I see. Fitoria taught Filo how to fight in human form, and Filo had used that to dodge the attack!

"Here I cooooooome!"

Filo's claws were slicing at Motoyasu in an instant. It was like a catfight. Filo's high agility rendered her attacks so quick that they were hard to follow. Sure, she had already been really fast, but the tricks Fitoria had taught her had an apparent effect. She was stronger.

"Sorry, Filo!"

Motoyasu readied his spear and sent a skill at Filo.

"Shooting Star Spear!"

I wouldn't let him get that skill off so easily! I jumped between him and Filo and blocked the attack with my shield.

Motoyasu's spear began to glow brightly, and it formed into a spear of light. He threw it at us.

The energy spear split and rained down from above.

"Ugh?!"

I used the hardest part of my shield to block the attack.

The shock of the attack was very powerful. I felt it reverberate through my shield.

My bones rattled. I felt like I could hear them. Was he using his most powerful attacks already? What did he want?

Well, if it was a real fight, I guess there was no reason for him to hold back.

"How'd you like THAT? I've got more where that came from! Chaos Spear! Rising Dragon Spear!"

Motoyasu sent out skill after skill. My Chimera Viper Shield didn't even have a chance to trigger its Snake Fang counterattack.

Dammit! He was so confident! His level must have been very high.

"Myne! Everyone!"

"I know! Zweite Fire!"

"Zweite Air Shot!"

"Fire and wind—and my skills combine. Combo skill! Air Strike Burst Flare Lance!"

"Ugh!"

Every place on my body that I hadn't covered with my shield shouted out in pain.

I didn't even want to think about what would have happened if my Barbarian Armor hadn't come with fire and wind resistance. Had I only survived because of Fitoria's protection?

I didn't want to see it, to accept it... but I couldn't ignore the blood seeping through the cracks of my armor.

I needed recovery magic... But Motoyasu wasn't going to give me the time to cast it.

"Shield Prison!"

A cage of shields appeared around Motoyasu.

"Windmill!"

Motoyasu spun his spear in wide circles very quickly. The shields composing the cage all flew away.

Damn... His attack power had clearly outgrown my ability to defend against it.

The cool down time for his skills had expired, and he began to send skills at us again, one after the other.

There was no way to win this fight if we had to be on the defensive the whole time.

"Master!"

Filo crossed her arms and ran at Motoyasu.

"Don't interfere!"

Motoyasu spun his spear around and jabbed Filo in the gut with the handle.

But before the hit connected, I was able to cast a spell.

"I am the Shield Hero and the source of all power. Hear my words and heed them. Protect her!"

"First Guard!"

There was a crashing sound, and it looked like I got the spell cast just in time. The handle of Motoyasu's spear clattered away from Filo before the hit could connect.

Luckily we'd found out, in the course of the battle with Fitoria, that Filo's human clothes had an excellent defense rating.

Combined with my defense spell, her defense had become impressively high.

"Dammit!"

"I'm not losing!"

Too alert to let the chance slip by, Filo flashed her claws at Motoyasu while he recovered.

"Damn! I won't let you get me!"

Motoyasu dodged her attack. He moved to counter attack, but Filo had already jumped back and was chanting a spell.

"I'm the source of all power. Hear my words! Attack him with a fierce tornado!"

"Zweite Tornado!"

"I'm the source of all power—may the whole universe hear my words and heed them! Disperse the tornado!"

"We are the source of all power. Hear our words and heed them! Disperse the tornado!"

"Anti-Zweite Tornado!"

Because of the interference magic from the other three, Filo's tornado became nothing more than a refreshing breeze.

Filo began to concentrate even harder. I grabbed Motoyasu's arm to keep him from moving.

"Let me go!"

"Why should I? Filo!"

"Yup! Haikuikku!"

Filo was a blur, moving very quickly. She was suddenly behind Motoyasu. I still had a grip on him.

"Ugh…"

There was a ripping sound, and Filo's claws bit into him again and again.

"Don't think that's enough to beat me!"

Motoyasu tore himself free of my grip and spun his spear, readying it. He thrust it straight at my eyes.

He was fast. I tipped my head to the side just in time for the spear tip to graze my ear.

"Ha!"

"Waahh!"

A soldier had been trapped in the cage with us, and Raphtalia took him out.

The soldiers were trying to rush in any time they thought that Melty or Raphtalia had let their guard down. They were always wrong. Those two weren't to be trifled with. They could certainly protect themselves… But how long was it going to take to finish?

What should we do? If we could defeat Motoyasu, we'd get an opportunity to escape. Of course we'd still have to deal with Bitch and the others.

Things were looking bad. It was going to be a matter of what would run out sooner: my endurance or Bitch's magic.

"Huh?!"

Bitch and her friends were drinking magic water to replenish their lost magic!

That wasn't good. Did that mean that I'd have to somehow hold on until they ran out of magic potions?!

"You're pretty good, Naofumi. Is this how you managed to kill Ren and Itsuki?!"

"I already told you I didn't do that! Listen to me!"

Motoyasu was using skills so quickly that he was running out of breath. Still, I was starting to take a lot of damage!

I felt blood dripping from my body.

"Besides, I'm not powerful because of the reasons you think. I've had a hard time of it here! I'm not like you, Mr. 'I know everything about the world.' I'm not trying to be badass!"

Since I was summoned to the world, I'd spent so much time trying out so many different things, battling so many different monsters.

I hadn't pulled any punches when it came to methods that

might make me stronger. I'd tried to unlock as many shields and abilities as I could. But... but in the end... Did a shielder really stand no chance?

"Fool!"

"What?"

Motoyasu was distracted. Bitch was screaming his name. I followed his gaze to see what he was looking at.

The magic sword was protruding from the shoulder of one of his party members.

Hey now—that should make it harder for them to keep up the magic barrage.

Raphtalia had been paying attention. Noticing that we were in trouble, she'd broken from her post at the back and come to assist us.

As for Melty... she was still working to destroy the Lightning Cage. Any time a soldier got too close for comfort she used a spell to send him flying.

But there were still soldiers trying to get close.

"Princess! Watch out!"

"Mel!"

"Ugh!"

Seeing that Melty was about to be overwhelmed, Filo immediately transformed into her Filolial Queen form and rushed to help. She tossed the soldiers away as if they were toys.

She wasn't using Haikuikku, but she still moved very quickly. It was thanks to the battle with Fitoria.

"Mr. Naofumi! Stop watching Filo—you're leaving yourself wide open!"

"Damn!"

Bitch was furious that she'd lost a party member. She drew her sword and swung it at Raphtalia.

"We've crossed swords before. You cannot defeat me!"

The clashing of their swords was loud and sharp. But Raphtalia was parrying all of Bitch's attacks.

Yes—it was a good fight. I was just praying that Melty would find a way to destroy the cage.

"Myne! Damn!"

Motoyasu turned to run to Bitch, but I stopped him.

"Motoyasu, listen to me. Everything that is happening is because of a conspiracy perpetrated by Bitch, the princess, and the Church of the Three Heroes. We did NOT kill Ren or Itsuki."

"I don't believe you! Out of my way!"

I tried, again and again, to reason with him. But Motoyasu wouldn't listen. This wasn't loyalty. It was blind faith! He was too stubborn to listen.

What should we do? I couldn't attack, and if Filo started attacking there would be no one to protect Melty. Sure, she'd come if I called her…

"Mr. Naofumi!"

Raphtalia shouted my name. Her tail was all puffed up. She had something she really wanted to tell me.

That's it—Motoyasu had just shown me the way.

Motoyasu was watching for Myne to leave herself open. I brushed past him and synchronized my breathing with Raphtalia's.

"I am the source of all power. Hear my words and heed them. Hide us!"

"First Hiding!"

I was concentrating and focusing on Raphtalia, and just as she cast her spell, a new skill name appeared in my field of view.

So that's how you do it…

"Hiding Shield! Change Shield!"

"What are you doing to Myne? Paralyze Spear!"

Motoyasu turned and sent a skill flying at Raphtalia. But… "What?!"

A shield appeared immediately before Raphtalia's eyes.

Yes, that was our combo skill.

Hiding Shield. It was a skill that made an invisible magic shield.

I used Change Shield to turn it into a shield with a counter effect.

I decided to use the Soul Eater Shield, with its counter effect of soul eat.

"Ugh!"

The Soul Eater Shield bit into Motoyasu, turned into a ball of magic, and flew towards me.

"It stole my SP!"

I had hoped for that effect. The soul eat effect stole his SP.

I had no way of knowing how much SP Motoyasu had, but this should make things a little easier on us.

"Don't underestimate Mr. Naofumi."

Raphtalia said before disappearing with Hide Mirage and moving away unseen.

"Where is she?!"

"Mr. Motoyasu! Leave her to me!"

Bitch tried to cancel Raphtalia's magic, but Raphtalia was already too far away.

"It won't be that easy!"

Motoyasu lowered his spear and came charging at me like a boar.

"Take that!"

Motoyasu saw that I was relieved by Raphtalia's escape. He sent a skill flying at me. From the way he moved, I assumed it was a Shooting Star Spear.

My new and improved armor had made my vision better… but could I do it?

I reached out… and grabbed the handle of the glowing spear.

"You idiot! Did you just grab my Shooting Star Spear?!"

"You're the idiot, using the same skills over and over! I can follow your every movement, Dumbass!"

The Chimera Viper Shield's counter effect, Snake Bite (medium), activated and bit into Motoyasu.

"Ugh… My body…"

Finally, he was poisoned.

Motoyasu made a convoluted gesture and somehow produced medicine from his spear.

How did he do that?

"I won't let you!"

"Ha! Try and stop me!"

I reached out to stop him from taking the medicine, but I was too late. He'd managed to drink it while I was trying to figure out where it had come from.

"Heh… Don't think that poison is such a big deal."

Okay, but how do you get an antidote out of a spear? I didn't understand.

"Poison doesn't work? Is that what you said? I hate to tell you that I've seen it work plenty of times."

Filo was attacking so quickly that Motoyasu was having trouble coming up with an answer.

"Seriously, calm down and listen to me! We didn't do anything to Ren or Itsuki! How many times do I have to tell you that it's all a conspiracy—and the woman behind you is the one pulling the strings!"

"Why should I listen to you? I believe in my friends!"

Friends? I think he meant to say "women."

Regardless—I'd tried. It was fair to say I'd been true to my promise to Fitoria.

And I hadn't tried to use the Shield of Rage yet.

"Okay, well, I tried to be fair to you. I tried to talk it out. I didn't want to do this."

I made a show of holding my shield out. If I didn't do something, the situation would only get worse.

If Melty wasn't able to break the cage, then support troops would keep showing up until they overwhelmed us. If we didn't escape before that happened, that would be the end of us.

"Don't forget Filo!"

I called out to Raphtalia for her support.

"Judging from how you've been attacking, you've got reason to be cautious."

"Ugh…"

"Melty."

"What?"

"You understand?"

"…Yes."

I only had one idea.

I'd use Raphtalia's magic to make an invisible shield, and I'd set it where Motoyasu was moving. It would have a counter effect, and Filo and Melty would combine their magic to damage him.

If we just kept using magic, they'd interfere and stop it. But would they be able to stop this?

"Your friends sure do like using fire and wind magic. I'm sure you realize that neither of those are very effective against me, right?"

I wasn't sure what to be grateful for, but it seemed like Fitoria's protection was giving us an edge over Motoyasu.

"And certainly you realize that I still have a trump card I haven't used yet?"

Motoyasu had seen the Shield of Rage once before.

He was having a difficult enough fight as things were—and he knew I wasn't using the shield yet.

So what would happen if I pulled out the Shield of Rage now?

Well, Filo would go crazy... but that wasn't such a big problem.

"Not yet!"

Motoyasu quickly leveled his spear at me.

"Air Strike Javelin!"

The spear was whistling through the air at me.

"Yeah, right!"

I snatched it out of the air. There was a metallic clang when it hit my fingers, and I felt a little pain.

I was holding the spear, but the second I loosened my grip it flew back into Motoyasu's hand.

"Mel."

"Right. Filo, breathe with me!"

"Okay!"

Melty and Filo synchronized their breathing and began to chant a spell.

"We are the source of all power. Hear our words and heed them…"

"Combo Magic?!"

The Bitch and her friends all went pale.

What was that? Wait… I'd read about it in the magic book.

Some very advanced magic required the cooperation of another wizard or witch.

Combo magic was one of those types.

At the very least it required two people, but they could combine their powers to make more complicated spells.

The level above combo magic was called ceremony magic. Apparently it was very large-scale magic that was used in wars. It could be very powerful… or so I'd heard.

"Destroy them with a swirling storm!"

"Typhoon!"

Melty and Filo moved their hands together, and a small tornado emerged from the point where they met. It was small, but looked very powerful, and it was filled with rain and hail. It howled at Motoyasu and his party.

They wouldn't be able to stop it. They'd have to endure it.

"Damn! I'll protect you!"

Motoyasu dashed to stand before his party. He held his spear out horizontal and took the brunt of the tornado head-on.

"Arghhhhhhh!"

He wasn't able to bear the force, and he went flipping through the air.

But then the tornado dissipated. Maybe Melty and Filo's magic wasn't strong enough to keep it sustained.

Motoyasu collapsed heavily, but then he was back on his feet in a second.

"I... I can't lose here. Not to you... If I lose, then Princess Melty, Raphtalia... Filo... they'll all belong to you."

The thought of him truly believing in his justice, fighting all this way, made me feel like he had some qualities that might actually be commendable.

But hey... how come I was the bad guy?

Motoyasu wasn't so stupid as to think I was the mid-level boss in his little game, was he?

It pissed me off just to think about it. Who did he think he was?

"I'll save them. For Ren and Itsuki!"

"You womanizing clown... It's pathetic to see you like this."

Why wouldn't he just believe me? Wasn't it an easier

explanation than all of this brain washing business?

If only he'd dedicate that fanatical resolve to something more important... What a waste.

"Ugh..."

We couldn't deliver the final blow. His friends were standing in the way.

But to think that he fought this whole way and wasn't giving up even though he was on the verge of collapse... I guess he really was a hero in that regard.

But he couldn't just blindly believe in himself and continue to insist on his own personal version of justice.

"Give it up. You can't beat us. All I want is for you to listen to me."

We were at a crossroads. I had to find some way to get him to listen, or this was the end of the line.

...Unless we could run away.

"Melty, I appreciate your help with the fighting. But please go back to breaking the cage."

"I already am!"

"Mr. Motoyasu! If we don't defeat the Shield Demon now, he'll escape! We have to take care of them now, or we won't get another chance to save Melty!"

"I know that!"

I guess Motoyasu and his party members had no way of knowing that it was all a conspiracy. They really wanted to kill Melty.

It was kind of sad. The real enemy was standing right next to him, and he didn't know it.

But Bitch didn't know how to give up.

I looked over to Raphtalia, and she nodded back at me.

I wanted her to use Hide Mirage to vanish and shut Bitch up once and for all.

She still had the magic sword. If she could use it to knock Bitch out, we might still have a chance of escape.

But I couldn't pretend that I'd be satisfied with that. A part of me wanted her dead.

Still, if I ever wanted to clear my name, I couldn't go around killing people.

If I wanted to take care of Bitch, I'd have to make sure that Trash had been dealt with first.

If I didn't, I wouldn't be any better than he was.

But if I wanted to get rid of someone that was standing in my way—I'd just have to sacrifice them and power through.

Was that right? No! I had to prove my innocence!

"I'm not losing… I'm not!!"

I couldn't tell if that was some kind of kamikaze thing, but Motoyasu was running right for me with his spear out.

"Filo!"

"Yup!"

The next attack would put an end to this… Or so I thought. Before they could clash, the whole area was filled with a bizarre sound.

I looked around and discovered that all the soldiers that had been standing around were gone. Something was happening, but what?

I heard rhythmic slaps… like someone was… clapping?

"Ah… I'd expect no less from the Spear. You've demonstrated excellent resolve. Thank you for your efforts."

The whole area was filled with a presence so powerful it was nearly suffocating… but what was it?

Chapter Eight: Judgment

Filo's wings were standing up straight. She quickly reverted to her Filolial Queen form and ran back down the path she'd come up. She plucked Melty up and set her on her back. Raphtalia was about to duck to the ground, but Filo reached out for her.

"What?!"

"Me!"

"Wh… What's happening, Filo?!"

"AHHHHHHH!"

"I… I'm the princess. I don't care what your emotions might be doing to you. You cannot just pick me up and…"

She must have used Haikuikku, because she was just a blur. She ran through Motoyasu and Bitch, kicking them left and right as she ran for me.

Huh? Who would have thought Motoyasu would be so easily defeated?

Then I noticed that I was clearly out of breath.

Furthermore, it looked like neither Motoyasu nor Bitch had taken any damage.

"Hey, Filo…. Ugh!"

Suddenly Filo, and everyone else, friend and foe alike, were lying in a pile at my feet.

"Master! Prepare to defend! Switch to that black Shield! If you don't, we'll never survive!"

"W…What are you talking about?"

"Just do it! Put a lot of Shield in the air over us."

"Ugh… Fine!"

Persuaded by Filo's panic, I switched to the Shield of Rage. I used Shield Prison and followed it with Air Strike Shield and Second Shield.

At nearly the same time as the Shield Prison's deployment, a massive pillar of light appeared in the sky directly over us.

"Ugh…"

I was rocked to my very core by an intense shock.

The pillar of light immediately blasted through the Second Shield and Air Strike Shield, but the Shield Prison seemed to be holding.

"Filo! Are you okay?"

"Yup! I think I'm fine!"

The standing feather on her head was glowing. Had it saved her?

Normally Filo went insane whenever I used the Shield of Rage because she'd eaten the dragon core that had caused it to become stronger. This time, however, she seemed to be able to control it.

It seemed I had a lot of things I needed to thank Fitoria for.

She really did seem to know what she was talking about, and she was certainly powerful enough to command the heroes to cooperate.

There was a cracking, splintering sound, and I raised my shield skyward to protect everyone from what was coming next.

The Shield Prison broke, and light filtered down on us. I could see the light around the edges of my shield, so it was apparently covering a very wide area.

Filo stretched out her wings to cover the pile of people around us.

"Uuuuuuuggghhhhhh!"

I felt my strength being chipped away by the light. I felt like I was being erased.

"Just a little more... There! Done!"

The light vanished as quickly as it had appeared. I kept my shield at the ready.

Filo also hopped to her feet and pulled her wings back, freeing everyone from her stifling feathers.

The entire field around us was black... scorched.

The fort that had originally been built to defend the border had been reduced to a pile of rubble, and we were standing in the middle of a crater. It looked like an asteroid had hit us. There were a few soldiers standing around. They were looking at us and smiling.

Had Motoyasu and Bitch tried to end the fight with some

kind of powerful spell? What was going on?

"Could it be…?"

"The Shield Demon remains calm after being hit with the highest ceremonial magic, 'Judgment.' Very impressive."

I looked in the direction of the voice and saw the same high priest that had met with us at the church back in Melromarc castle town. He was smiling. A large crowd of attendants stood behind him. There were knights among them.

"You…!"

The high priest looked over at us all. He stared at Motoyasu.

Were these support troops? No… That attack had definitely included Motoyasu among its targets. But if it wasn't support troops, then…

We must have only survived the power of that attack because of the Shield of Rage. But hey, Filo… Why did she go out of her way to save Motoyasu and Bitch? We were so close to being free of them. They could have tasted some real pain for once.

The other heroes had apparently already died. So why did I care if we lost one more? He didn't listen to reason anyway.

She really should have just protected Raphtalia and Melty.

Whatever. Putting that aside for the moment, what was this high priest up to?

"What are you thinking? How could you use an attack that might have killed both the Spear Hero and the princess?"

"The Spear Hero… was it?"

These guys were supposed to worship the Sword, Bow, and Spear. I wouldn't have expected him to behave in a way that would put one of them in danger. But there he was, still smiling at us.

What was happening? I was starting to get a bad feeling about it. He looked like he'd go right on smiling the same way had his attack left behind a pile of corpses. It was like a half smile. It contained a secret. I don't know what it was, maybe the color in his cheeks. Anyway, something wasn't right there.

That made me think. What had happened to Ren and Itsuki? Someone had killed them.

Motoyasu obviously thought that I was responsible, but I wasn't. That meant that the real criminal was still out there somewhere.

It seemed reasonable to assume that this was the guy behind it all.

"The objects of our devotion are the Heroes that save the world from destruction, from the waves. Heroes that travel the world stirring up trouble are not the true Heroes. They are a mockery of our faith."

The high priest was speaking casually, as if this were just a normal conversation.

"What was that?!"

Motoyasu was shocked. He stared at the high priest with intensity.

"For the justice of the people, an adjustment must be made regarding the ascendancy of the crown. The princess you see here is already dead—murdered by the Shield Demon. Do not waste your time worrying about a corpse."

"How could...? Whatever."

Raphtalia started to voice her disagreement but gave up.

The last time we'd met the high priest, he'd seemed peaceful, equitable, and fair. That must have been a misunderstanding on my part.

"One must be grateful for the mercy and power of the holy water one has received, yet the Shield Demon has continued to behave aggressively. I have come as the representative of God to purify him."

His logic was something to behold. It sounded like he had given us the Holy Water at the proper price because he hadn't considered us a threat. But now that he had something to lose, he was going to kill us. So I guess he hadn't really understood the big picture back then.

Either that, or he'd kept his head down to avoid suspicion.

"Give me a break! I'M the princess here! I haven't been killed by the Shield!"

"Actually, Princess Malty, all this has already been decided. Do not worry. We have already made preparations for your successor. The country will be in safe hands. Everything proceeds according to the will of God."

Bitch… She would do anything, anything at all to get what she wanted. Now that the high priest was explaining the conspiracy to everyone, she didn't see the need to butt in on the conversation. Her face seemed to grow paler by the second.

"You're… lying, right?"

"Ahahaha! No. If the world is to be saved, it must be cleansed of vulgar people like you."

"Shut up! Do you mean to say you tricked us?!"

Motoyasu was blubbering. His face streaked with tears, he pointed his spear at the high priest.

"We've been fighting to save Princess Melty… to save this very country! Has that been a lie?!"

"Not exactly. All of this has been for the good of the country, for the good of the very world. The Shield Demon has been abducting and leading people, and the other three Heroes have been behaving in a way that leads our countrymen to doubt the truth of our teachings. This has been a fight to correct these injustices. The Crown must be secured."

"You hypocrite…"

I whispered, but the high priest heard me. He twisted his face up and spoke with apparent consternation.

"Yes… False Heroes causing problems throughout the land has caused people to question their faith. The false Sword Hero caused a virulent disease to break out and spread. It brought chaos to the ecosystem. The false Spear Hero released a powerful, sealed monster, and the false Bow Hero has been hiding his powers, bringing pain and confusion to my disciples."

I was the one that cleaned up all of those issues.

I wasn't sure what Itsuki had done, but the governor he'd ousted for fraudulent taxes must have been very wealthy. Maybe he was donating that money to charity?

And besides, the crazy nobleman who'd released the sealed monster had been a fanatical devotee of the Church.

"Furthermore, the false Sword and Bow Heroes had launched unnecessary investigations into these matters. They had to be taken care of, so we did so."

The high priest was still speaking as if all this were the most obvious thing in the world.

"What?!"

Hey, Motoyasu—what are you so surprised for? If only you'd listened…

"We called the Sword and Bow, and they came to the designated meeting place, whereby they were erased through the same magic you just witnessed, 'Judgment.' This, too, is according to the will of God."

Ren and Itsuki… Just as I'd suspected. They hadn't been chasing me because they'd found the whole situation suspicious. They'd launched their own investigations.

Itsuki… Well, he'd believed in Ren and listened to what he'd said.

How could they do such a thing? If Itsuki found out about all this, his sense of justice would have compelled him to put a stop to it.

But they'd beat him to it, and killed him without warning.

"You killed them? They were fighting for this world! Ren! Itsuki!"

Motoyasu was furious. He was screaming.

Give me a break. It's not like they were best friends or anything. Apologies to Ren and Itsuki, but I wasn't really feeling anything emotional at the news of their deaths.

To be honest, I was remembering what Fitoria had said, about how the waves would get worse if any of the heroes died...

"Please don't put it that way. I'd rather you said that we purified the world of the demons who were trying to take advantage of us."

"You..."

"As for the king and queen, we'll tell them that the country nearly fell into the hands of the false Heroes. We were able to save the world from them, but in the process the princesses..."

Ha! Who would believe that? Or... actually Trash would probably accept it without a second thought—anything to pin his troubles on me.

Actually, back in my world, there were probably plenty of powerful people that looked pathetic after the truth came to the surface—people that had been executed for scheming to instigate wars.

I guess I didn't know the truth either, but at the very least I could say one thing. They were going to execute us based on their own selfish theories.

"Naofumi. Let's call a truce. I need your help."

Motoyasu turned to look me in the eyes.

"How convenient for you. Don't think I'll let you forget how you were treating me up until five minutes ago. Do you even understand why you ignored me when I asked you to listen? How many times did I ask?"

I wouldn't let him off that easily. I asked him to listen to me, and he answered with attacks. I couldn't let that slide.

Besides, the fool had honestly believed in the stupid Brain Washing Shield.

"Please! I... I have to give them a funeral! I cannot forgive this!"

"Sure, sure. I'm sure you can beat him on your own."

I wouldn't let him off the line. Did he understand how miserable he'd made me all these months?

"You won't help me? Don't you feel anything for Ren and Itsuki?"

"I feel plenty of things. I plan to end this with a bloodbath. But Motoyasu, I don't feel any responsibility to help you."

The cage was broken. If we all jumped on Filo we might be able to escape.

I was sorry for Fitoria, but even if we reconciled, I'd never be able to trust him.

I didn't plan on fighting him for forever, but I wanted him to know how I felt.

"By the way…"

I extended my index finger and pointed at Motoyasu. Then I lowered it to the ground and smiled.

"Do me a favor and die. All you think about is what's in your pants."

"You bastard!"

Motoyasu stumbled, weak on his feet. He made a fist and swung it at me.

"You sure you want to punch me?"

I had the Shield of Rage equipped. That meant that if he punched me, self-curse burning would activate—and that would probably kill him.

"Damn…"

Still, it would have hit Raphtalia, Filo, and Melty—so I'd have to control it.

"What a fight you two have going! I'd expect no less from the false Spear Hero and the Shield Demon."

"Shut up!"

"Yeah, shut up! I don't need you anyway. I'll take him out on my own!"

"Ahaha! You think you can defeat me? How quaint."

The high priest laughed and called for an underling to bring him a weapon.

What was it? It looked like a giant sword…

It was shining silver and inlaid with complicated designs. Honestly, it was really cool. The center of it held a square-shaped jewel of some kind that gave me a bad feeling. It looked like the sort of weapon that started showing up in the latter half of a game… like the Sword of God?

"Wh… what's that…?"

Bitch and Melty both went pale.

"Naofumi! Be careful! That thing is…"

"I'll begin with the Shield Demon. Accept the judgment of God."

The high priest raised the sword into the air. Despite that he was standing quite a distance from us, he brought it down.

And a powerful shockwave came flying straight at me. I quickly raised my shield and took the hit.

"Ugh!"

It was so powerful that I nearly went flying. It was much, much more powerful than Motoyasu's Shooting Star Spear, and I was nearly knocked unconscious.

The ground before me split, and the split grew wider.

Hold on a second. I had the Shield of Rage equipped!

I'd used that shield to block the most powerful skills that Motoyasu and the other's were capable of, and it hadn't been a problem. If he was able to hurt me that easily… just what was that weapon?

"Naofumi… That's a relic from the past! It's a replica of the weapon used by a Legendary Hero…"

Chapter Nine: Replica

"That's a replica?"

It sure looked more powerful than the original.

Or should I say that I was comparing it to Ren's weapon because it was a sword. It was certainly more powerful than Motoyasu's spear. It was probably at least fifteen times more powerful. If it was only fifteen times more powerful, then I should be able to use the Shield of Rage to defend against it.

But judging from the strength of its last attack, it must have been more powerful than that.

"But how could…. That was supposed to have been destroyed hundreds of years ago."

"Not destroyed… stolen. And the organization behind the theft must have been the Church of the Three Heroes."

It was like the various conspiracy theories about bombs back in my world. They must have been produced in vast quantities, but some are missing. So where did they go?

But more importantly, if that was a replica of the legendary weapon, then did that mean that Ren's sword would have become something like that?

Granted, I had more reasons to be suspicious than most did, but was it really okay to entrust that much power to a single person? If that thing was just a replica, then who knows what the real thing would be capable of? If they had that, did they really need to bother with summoning new heroes?

But why think about such things? I could just ask the high priest directly.

"If you had something like that, why bother to summon us at all? If you made more of those you could handle the waves on your own."

Melty shook her head.

"If it were that simple to copy the Legendary Weapons then we would have already done so… To make something like that requires vast resources that we simply don't have."

"Really?"

"Yes. To swing it even once requires the accumulation of hundreds of people's magic over the course of a month. And mass production is out of the question. That thing has been around since ancient times. It's a legend in and of itself."

"Wow."

I'd seen something like it in an anime. It was a story about a giant robot that needed to use all the electricity in Japan to make a single shot. Maybe this sword was like that? If it could scatter-shoot, like buckshot, it would be a real terror.

"Yes, our disciples have risked their very lives, day and night, to imbue this with their magic. I had to use it for the sake of our holy battle. The holy battle we face right this moment!"

Holy battle, huh? Well at least he was prepared.

The Legendary Hero… So this was a copy of his sword or something? They said it had been stolen hundreds of years ago, and they'd spent a long time filling it with magic. And he used it right from the get-go?

Damn! That thing could prove to be a real problem.

No, it was proof that he was in a real tough spot. If we could just get over this, there would be ample opportunity to counterattack. We just had to see it through.

"Now that I've used it once to get a feel for it, perhaps we should proceed to battle?"

The high priest held the sword out. When he did, it suddenly changed shapes to resemble a spear. The shape changed, but the quality had not. If they said it was a weapon used by the same person, I'd believe it.

"It transforms?!"

"Yes, because it is a Legendary Weapon. Sword, Spear, Bow… We must purify them all."

Escape was looking like a good option, but would we be able to get away with someone using a weapon like that?

When he'd sent out that shockwave, it had moved so quickly that dodging it would have been difficult.

Apparently he'd been holding back too. But if he had used a bow-like skill with that weapon, I don't think that Filo would have been able to outrun the attack.

"There is a limit to what my disciples can do, so I'd like to end this as quickly as possible."

The high priest shouldered the hopes of his disciples and knights as he turned the weapon on us.

The spear-shaped replica weapon began to glow then split into three spears of light.

"High-Skill, Brionac?!"

Motoyasu, the Spear Hero, shouted. It must have been a skill he knew from his game.

If he was screaming, then it must have been a powerful skill.

A simple swing of the sword had been damaging enough. What would its skills be capable of?

We couldn't run, but could we endure? According to Motoyasu and the other heroes, the shield wouldn't stand a chance.

No way out... is that what this was? I wasn't ready to give up yet.

"Filo!"

"Yup!"

Filo knew what I wanted in an instant. She picked me up and threw me at the high priest.

The second the high priest was within my skill range, I shouted.

"Shield Prison!"

A cage of shields appeared and enclosed the high priest.

If I could use Change Shield (attack) and then Iron Maiden…

"What are you up to?"

He didn't even have to do anything. The latent energy from his skill alone was enough to shatter the Shield Prison.

What?! No, wait… I had to stay calm.

I wasn't going to be able to use Iron Maiden. That meant I only had one other attack option.

I had to hit him with Self Curse Burning.

But to do that, I'd have to be in his attack range and get his spear attack to…

No—that wasn't it. I could still take the initiative.

"Filo! Throw Motoyasu over here!"

"What?!"

"Yup!"

Just as I'd asked, Filo threw Motoyasu in my direction before I'd even hit the ground.

"Ahhhhhhhhh!"

I could hear Motoyasu's scream get louder as he flew closer to me.

"Motoyasu, attack me!"

"What?! Ah, okay!"

Motoyasu was an idiot, but at least he figured out what I was after.

I turned to face him, and Motoyasu thrust his spear at me. There was a metallic clash as the tip clattered against my shield.

Yes—that was perfect.

"Shooting Star Spear!"

Immediately after hitting me, Motoyasu turned and sent a skill flying for the high priest.

"Fool."

Motoyasu's skill broke in mid air. It failed to penetrate a mysterious force field that the high priest must have had around himself.

"What?!"

"My turn!"

Self curse burning activated, and a huge vortex appeared centered on myself. The cursed flames spread to enclose the high priest.

The force field around him vanished, and the flames...

"That won't work!"

The high priest's disciples were all singing...

"Our God is the source of all power. Hear the truth and head it. Miraculously purify the curse!"

"High-level ceremonial magic, Sanctuary!"

The area was suddenly filled with white light, and my self curse burning was blown away.

Was I stupid? Of course, I should have known that "holy" power would have a negative effect on my "curse" power.

Could it be that the holy water I'd bought to cure Raphtalia's curse had just been a trick? Maybe.

But to heal her, I'd needed the best holy water there was. I thought the curse was powerful, and yet he'd destroyed it in an instant...

"Air Strike Shield! Second Shield!"

Before Motoyasu and I could hit the high priest, I conjured up some shields that we could use to move back.

"Hey, Motoyasu's friends! Can we get some restorative magic?! If you treat us like enemies, we aren't going to make it out of this!"

"Oh! Um... Zweite Heal!"

Motoyasu and my wounds healed. That was good and necessary.

Ugh... I had to fight with Motoyasu. I couldn't think of a worse situation. But if we didn't do something about the enemy in front of us, we wouldn't survive.

"Master! I'm coming too!"

"Be careful!"

"Okay!"

Filo turned into her human form and ran for the high priest. So did I, and so did Raphtalia and Motoyasu too.

There was no reason to stand there and let him play with us.

Just because the self curse burning hadn't worked didn't

mean that we should just stand there twiddling our thumbs.

Luckily enough, and maybe just because the powerful skill took a while to charge, the high priest was still pointing the spear at us. He wasn't moving.

"Hai....kuikku!"

Filo shouted as she ran, and turned in to a blur. Then she was behind the high priest.

But everything stopped for a minute. Filo was cradling her fist.

"Ugh... It's so HARD!"

Whatever sort of force field that replica weapon had produced had stopped her punch.

"Shooting Star Spear!"

A thousand lights flew at the high priest, but they didn't seem to reach him.

"Use Fire Lance or something!"

"Hey, yeah! Myne!"

"I'll punish you for defying the future queen!"

Bitch was furious as she cast her spell. Her friends were casting too.

"Mr. Motoyasu. This is support magic! Zweite Power!"

Hey, couldn't they cast that kind of thing on Filo too? Couldn't they try and be a little more helpful?

"Thanks! Come on!"

Motoyasu flashed a smile at his party and then obnoxiously

winked. Then he used a skill, but it was slower than before.

"Fire-Storm Shooting Star Spear!"

It was basically the Shooting Star Spear imbued with wind and fire magic. It took a little longer to activate than his basic skill.

The flames flickered in the wind. The blade blazed like a shooting star. The winds came up, and the fires blazed all the more as the spear accelerated.

There was no snap, no flash. Motoyasu heaved the spear at the high priest.

Had it been me, I wouldn't have even tried to block it. It was easy enough to dodge.

The attack wouldn't work on anything but a completely immobile enemy. Unless, that is, it had some kind of effects I didn't know about.

Besides, they'd just cast support magic on Motoyasu. Maybe that would do something?

And yet... with a disappointing clang, the spear clattered against the high priest's defensive barrier, accomplishing nothing.

"Ugh..."

Motoyasu moved to put distance between the high priest and himself. Then he held his head in his hands as though he was suddenly dizzy.

"Mr. Motoyasu, are you all right?!"

"Yeah, but… I need SP. And the cool down time…"

Apparently he had to pay a price for using a high-level skill.

It took a while to pull the skill off, and it had been too slow to hit its mark. If it took so long, you'd think it was powerful, but it hadn't been enough to make it through the barrier. How hard was that thing?

It had rendered my self curse burning useless, and neither Filo nor Motoyasu's attacks had been able to penetrate it.

"Your Holiness!"

"We're about to use defensive magic!"

"Our God is the source of all power. Hear the truth and head it. Protect the holy one!"

"High-level ceremonial magic, Castle Wall!"

Three of the disciples standing behind the high priest cast support magic on him, but there was no way for us to interfere before it was effective.

What the hell was a castle wall? A wall of light appeared around the high priest, and it looked a lot like a fort.

"Hiyaaaa!"

Raphtalia and Filo attacked the wall, but it simply repelled them.

"Filo! Raphtalia! I'll help too!"

Melty used her preferred spell, Aqua Shot, but it was as ineffective as I expected. Nothing made it through the barrier.

I started to think that it might be better to focus on

attacking the disciples in the back. But before I could give voice to my concerns…

"Well, I think that's enough playing around. I'm ready to put an end to this."

The spear in the high priest's hands began to spark, perhaps indicating that it was ready to use a skill.

"All right, we have reached the end. Farewell, Demon and false Hero."

The spear burst into light, and the high priest smiled at us. He looked like a satisfied exorcist.

"Mel!"

In a flash, Filo was protecting Melty. Raphtalia took my hand.

"Is this it…?"

Motoyasu muttered. It sounded like an admission of defeat.

"I…I'm going to be the queen! If you treat me this way then I—"

Bitch was screaming whatever came into her head.

The other girls in Motoyasu's party had lost their composure entirely and were sobbing hysterically.

The only one of us that might be able to survive the attack was me…

Which meant that all I could do was run to the front and hold up my shield.

Obviously, I wouldn't do it to protect the likes of these jerks.

But I'd do it to protect Raphtalia. To protect Melty—and Filo. I'd do it to protect the people that believed in me.

I readied my shield and stepped forward.

"I'm with you."

Raphtalia stepped forward at the same time as me. She held my hand.

She stayed with me this whole time.

Even if she hadn't been aware of it, she'd been bought as a slave by the Shield Demon and forced into the world of battles and violence.

"I'm sorry. I'm sorry I brought you into all this."

"Don't be, Mr. Naofumi. I believe you can still protect us."

"You're right. I don't know what the past Spear Hero was like, but this is still a skill from the Spear Hero."

There was still more to do. This couldn't be the end.

Finally all the conspiracies, and my chance to right them, were standing right before me.

Brionac... It was the name of a spear from Celtic mythology. And I was about to block it.

The high priest raised his spear to the sky...

"Hand Red Sword!"

"Shooting Star Bow!"

A shower of swords appeared directly above the high priest, and one huge arrow. They came streaming down from the sky.

"What's this?!"

The high priest immediately stopped using the skill and used another one, which I think had been called Windmill Spear, to block the sudden shower of weapons.

I turned to find the source of the voices, and I saw...

"What's this? I thought that the two of you had been purified by the judgment of God. What are you doing here?"

Ren, Itsuki, and their respective parties were standing there. I thought they were dead! But there they were anyway—alive.

"Don't just go imagining us dead! Did you bother to check for bodies?"

"Just on the edge of a crisis, glad we made it."

Ren and Itsuki were standing in their battle poses and calling out to us.

"I'm sure that you wouldn't even think to check for bodies after using magic on the scale you did But these are the consequences of your oversight."

I looked at the crater that remained from the high priest's original attack.

Fair enough... If the attack was powerful enough to leave a crater of this size, you wouldn't expect there to be anything remaining of its victims. Still—we'd all survived it.

I was looking over at Ren when I suddenly realized how heavy my body felt.

The Shield of Rage was screaming in my head as though it

had finally found the enemy worthy of all its hated.

It was just like Fitoria had said. The shield had found the person it hated. Ren was filling the shield with rage.

I had to contain it… This was no time to lose control.

"How did you…"

Motoyasu was talking to them as if he'd seen a ghost.

I didn't share the same suspicions, but it was a little odd that all of the heroes suddenly found themselves together way out in the middle of nowhere.

"Shadows… or something like that, came out of nowhere and saved us."

"Yes, it was very close."

"Huh? Shadows are the ones that told us where we could find Naofumi. I thought they were on the Church's side?"

I had been wondering if Motoyasu had some way of figuring out where we were going. After he disappeared I wondered if he had only "vanished" to head us off. It was sounding like I was right.

What did it mean? It meant that shadows working for the Church had been slipping Motoyasu information about our whereabouts.

Which reminded me…

"You said that the shadows weren't a monolithic organization, didn't you?"

"That's right. The shadows that helped us said that they were under orders from the queen."

Okay then. So I guess that meant that there were still shadows looking out for us.

That meant that it was probably safe to assume that the queen and the Church were enemies. At the very least, now that all four of the heroes were enemies of the Church, there wasn't much of a chance that she would be working with them.

Still… Why did they have to just show up like that? It was so over-dramatic. It reminded me of a weekly, serialized manga or something.

It made me wonder if they had been holding back and watching for the best time to show up and save the day.

If it were a manga, I guess that would make Motoyasu the protagonist, and I'd be… what? Some kind of mini-boss? Give me a break.

Nah, I'd be the kind of character that was chronically misunderstood but actually a good guy at heart. If all this were a manga, I mean.

Not to disappoint, but I couldn't picture Motoyasu and I embracing in an emotional reconciliation.

"Backup is coming to help us arrest you, High Priest! Give it up!"

Ren pontificated, very authoritative. But the high priest didn't seem very concerned.

"How many troops arrive is irrelevant. Victory is mine. That simple fact will not be changed. All your efforts are meaningless!"

The high priest slipped back into skill summoning.

"You think?"

"Yeah."

The two heroes and their parties formed a line and began flinging skills at the high priest.

"Shooting Star Sword!"

"Shooting Star Bow!"

Arcs of light flew from Ren's sword, lightning arrows from Itsuki's bow. They flew straight for the high priest.

But they broke against the replica weapon's force field. The high priest just smiled.

Ren and Itsuki didn't give up though. They continued casting spells and summoning skills.

But the force field around the high priest expanded, and none of their attacks were able to make it through.

"I should have expected such disappointing efforts from false Heroes."

"Wha…?"

"This is tough. I didn't think he had a force field like that!"

"I thought you were going to take him out! You can't?! Why did you bother coming?!"

Did they just want to make a good entrance?

"You showed up without a plan?"

"Don't you think you could be a little more polite?"

Ren and Itsuki's weapons burst into light. But it would take time for them to activate their skills.

"Thunder Sword!"

"Thunder Shoot!"

With a loud clap, the high priest's force field shattered.

"We were just buying time to activate these skills."

Whoa. They'd broken through the field that my self curse burning had been useless against. They might have been assholes, but they really were heroes. Nothing at all like Motoyasu. Did we stand a chance?

"I could have done that if only I'd had SP…"

"Oh, get over yourself!"

Or hey—if he had access to such powerful skills, why hadn't he used them against me?

I guess the skills took a while to activate, and I hadn't given him a window of opportunity. Although his Shooting Star Spear had been a little sluggish…

Whatever. If we were going to attack, the time had come!

"C'mon everyone. Let's go!"

Ren shouted, and we all started to attack.

"I'm first!"

Filo had dashed to the front of the line. Judging on speed alone, she was by far the fastest one of us.

"Hiya!"

Motoyasu ran at the high priest and thrust his spear at him.

"Take that!"

Ren followed him, his sword cutting arcs left and right.

"Everyone, I'm right behind you!"

Itsuki drew back the string of his bow and shot an arrow.

"Mr. Naofumi. I'm going too."

"I am too!"

Raphtalia and Melty both ran to attack.

The high priest held his weapon out and took the brunt of everyone's attacks. They didn't seem to faze him at all.

A barrage of attacks from heroes didn't bother him at all?

"Fools. You think you can defeat me when I have a Legendary Weapon like this? Ha!"

The high priest's disciples immediately cast restorative magic on him, and the small wounds he had received vanished.

Things weren't looking good. If we could manage to get a single hit in, the disciples healed it instantly.

"Now then… Let us move into the casting of Judgment."

The disciples all nodded, and a moment later they all began chanting in unison.

"All those that would pretend to be Heroes are evil."

This guy was really something. He was obviously a fanatic. Didn't he notice that?

"This will take care of you all."

The high priest was really planning to kill everyone.

He was charging up for something, probably for the Brionac attack…

"Naofumi."

"What?"

Ren was speaking to me.

"Work with me. Let's take him out."

"You're really the last person I want to work with. But, oh well…"

We weren't going to be able to escape the high priest's attack. And it looked like he was planning on using the Judgment spell at the same time. Not even I could survive both of them.

"First take out the people in the back. Until they're taken care of, we don't stand a chance."

"Yeah."

Ren and his party were already running for the group of disciples.

Unfortunately the disciples weren't mere underlings. They seemed to be pretty damn powerful, actually.

More than any other time, all the heroes, Raphtalia, Filo— all of us were fighting together.

And the high priest was charging up for a major attack. And the disciples were preparing to use Judgment.

"Friends, this is a holy war! Fight for justice! Your deaths will not be forgotten."

"Yes, Your Holiness!"

The fanatics behind him all responded in unison.

The high priest was taking the attacks of the sword, spear, bow, and all of their party members. He was bleeding, but he didn't seem to notice or care.

He'd move until he lost his legs. Then he'd use his arms. Then when he lost them, he'd use magic.

His fanatical devotees also seemed ready to fight to the death.

They were positively insane!

"Damn... I can't get an attack in."

There were too many of them. It looked like a scene from the *Battle of the Three Kingdoms*, or from *Dynasty Warriors*.

Of course the real enemy was the high priest himself, but he was surrounded by so many people it was hard to get a hit in.

It was easy enough to take one or two of them down, but the second a hit connected, another person was there to cast recovery spells on them.

Had this been a game, it would have been enough just to defeat them. But this wasn't a game.

Of course I didn't have some moral reason to avoid killing them. I WANTED to kill them, but it took time to do so.

"I'll run into the crowd. Then one of you needs to attack me. Think of how much you hate me. Then attack. My counterattack will flare up and hit everyone, so make sure you're not in the area. Keep your distance."

Self curse burning was my only real chance to attack. I'd have to rush into the crowd and try and interfere with their casting of Judgment.

If I was in a good spot when it happened, I could take a lot of them out with self curse burning.

"Okay."

"Okay, I'm going in!"

I told everyone that could use magic to focus on support. Anyone else who remained and wasn't a good melee fighter was supposed to stay back and use magic to protect the supporters.

The heroes were the attackers; the supporters were the magic users, and everyone else was to focus on defense. Yeah... I didn't have a ton of faith in the plan.

"Here we go!"

I took the lead and ran for the crowd of disciples.

I wasn't able to attack, so if I wanted to deal any damage, I only had one option.

"Naofumi!"

Motoyasu swung his spear into my shield, and self curse burning activated.

"AAARRRRHHHHHH!"

Any disciples that weren't summoning Judgment turned to use holy magic to counter my self curse burning. But they weren't able to nullify it completely, and the dark flames consumed a good number of them.

"AAAARRRRRHHHHHH!"

The cursed flames would also delay any recovery spells they cast. If we got our attacks in before they recovered, we might stand a chance.

I used Air Strike Shield and then Change Shield to call up

the Rope Shield. Then I used the grappling hook to swing back to where the other heroes were.

The hook had a special effect that produced a string I could manipulate. I wrapped it around my arm and used it to pull me back to everyone else—and it worked well.

"Thunder Sword!"

"Thunder Shoot!"

At the same time, the other heroes all used their strongest skills against the crowd of disciples.

All the skills looked like they were formed from lightning.

A bolt of lightning shot straight through the high priest before exploding in the midst of the disciples gathered behind him.

"AAARRRRHHHHHHH!"

The disciples went flying like leaves from a tree, but the high priest himself didn't seem to have suffered any severe damage.

How strong was this guy? How powerful was his weapon?

"That's enough toying around."

A smile spread over his face, very victorious, and the high priest leveled his spear at us.

"Everyone get together! Wait! Everyone use Naofumi as a shield!"

In an instant everyone was clumped together behind me. Did they have a meeting about all this beforehand or something?

"That skill he's about to use covers a very wide area. It splits into thousands of spears and pierces through crowds of enemies. If you want to defend against it, it's better to gather in one spot."

"Uh huh…"

"Well, if you really know how to use it, you can set the number of targets…"

It was sounding like the sort of skill that could lock on to its enemies. That could be pretty annoying.

"Brionac!"

The high priest's skill activated and came flying for us.

A blazing white light filled the area and drew near.

"We can take this!"

"Yes!"

"Everyone, help me!"

"Shooting Star Sword!"

"Shooting Star Bow!"

"Shooting Star Spear!"

Ren, Itsuki, and Motoyasu all sent out flashing skills.

Their three shining skills converged and merged into a large beam of light.

Their party members all used their attack magic too in an attempt to raise the power of the attack.

"Filo! Melty! You two help too!"

"Okay!"

"Naofumi! You should help too!"

"All I can do is defend! What do you want from me?! What about Raphtalia?!"

"I, um… I still don't know any attack magic!"

Raphtalia nodded apologetically.

That was the problem with having an unconventional skill set. All I could do was defend. Raphtalia's magic was only good for manipulating light and shadow. Melty's face was scrunched up in annoyance, but she added her attack power to the heroes'.

"Here it comes!"

There was a loud crackling sound as the energy forms slammed into each other.

"Here we gooooooooo!"

"ARRRhhhhh!"

"Hiyaaaaaaaa!"

The huge beam formed from the heroes' skills held against the high priest's attack.

The support magic started flowing in too, and slowly, slowly, the beam appeared to overpower the high priest's skill.

"Heh… Is that all you've got?"

The high priest was still smiling.

Was he holding back?

"You idiot! We're not beaten yet!"

"Yeah! We're still going strong!"

"Yes, everyone—more power!"

The three heroes all focused and gave all their power to the attack beam.

I could barely tell, but it looked like the beam grew a little stronger. Was it pushing back the high priest's attack?

And yet... What was this feeling I had? I felt something... ominous.

"All right. Here I come."

The high priest spoke calmly then began to focus.

When he closed his eyes, his weapon turned black, then white, then began to slowly flicker.

It looked like he was ready to use a powerful attack.

"Watch out!"

Shit! If they all died, I'd be in trouble!

Couldn't we have all teamed up some other time? Did we have to try this now?

I pushed the other heroes to the ground, canceling their skill, and I ran to the front.

A beam of light shot thorough my body. Along with the pain came a roaring, unbelievably loud sound. I thought I'd go crazy.

The beam did not make it through me. I'd protected everyone.

"Huff... Huff..."

"Mr. Naofumi!"

"Naofumi..."

Ren looked down at me, speechless. The other heroes and their party members were silent too.

"Ha… I never expected you to survive that. You really are the Shield Demon."

The high priest pompously spun his spear as he spoke."

"Are you all… okay?"

My eyes were blurry, but I turned around. I saw a huge "V" cut into the ground around me. If I hadn't blocked the attack, people would have died. Luckily everyone had been able to get behind me in time.

"Zweite Heal!"

They cast strong restorative magic on me, and my wounds healed before my eyes.

To think he'd been able to use such a powerful skill while taking the brunt of the heroes' attacks… How powerful was he?

"Ugh… My SP…"

"Me too."

"And me."

The three of them had used all their SP and were reaching for bottles of Soul Healing Water to replenish it.

It would take a little while to recover enough SP to use another attack.

I heard shouting. Just as Ren had said, support troops were showing up behind us. A large crowd was forming. With any luck, they'd take care of the high priest's disciples.

"I suppose I'll just have to deal with them too."

"Stay back!!"

Ren shouted, but it was too late. The high priest turned his spear into a sword and stuck it into the ground.

A huge earthquake occurred, and the ground split apart here and there. Behind us, where the support troops were gathering, the ground split and magma came rushing out.

"AAAAAAHHHHHH!!"

Nearly all of the support troops were on fire, flying through the air.

That must have been most of them. The high priest was too powerful.

"Ahahaha! Well, that was simple. As long as I have this weapon, I'm just like God. If I am God, who needs the Heroes?! I am God! Everyone! Let us judge those who oppose me here and now!"

"YES!"

And I thought that our situation was improving. With the support troops defeated, it seemed like nothing had changed at all.

The blade of the high priest's sword began to turn and warp before reforming into the shape of a phoenix.

I bet he was about to use a skill even more powerful than Brionac.

This wasn't good. The surviving support troops probably

had no idea that the high priest was so powerful.

If we weren't careful, he'd kill them all with one shot.

"Are we ready with Judgment? Let's go together."

The high priest indicated that he wanted to use his skill at the same time as the Judgment spell.

It seemed like we'd gained a second or two to collect ourselves, but who knew what sort of attack he was preparing?

"Is this it?"

The other heroes were looking very pale. I guess we had a chance at winning, but it was too late... We were too reckless...

Or I should say that if Ren and Itsuki hadn't shown up, Motoyasu and I would have already died. From that perspective, it was reasonable to say that we'd done our best.

But had I done MY best? Was there anything I could still do?

If I used the Shield of Rage... Wasn't there still some way out of this?

Fitoria had warned me time and time again... but what choice did I have? If we didn't make it out of this fight, there was nothing left for us. We'd all die here. If that were true, then why hold back?

"Ren, get over here."

"What? You have a plan?"

I asked him to come over, and so he did—but he was suspicious.

I felt the shield throbbing. It was shaking.

I'd intentionally sealed it away, but inside the Shield of Rage lay the core of the dragon that Ren killed.

My vision was filled with its memories, with its desires… It had found its enemy, and it begged for slaughter.

That's it… More. Explode with rage!

I'd been restraining the power of the shield for Raphtalia. Now I tried to draw out all of its power.

"Raphtalia… Your hand…"

"Yes."

I took Raphtalia's hand, and then held my shield arm out towards Ren.

Then I looked over at Bitch and Motoyasu and called for all the rage within me that I'd spent these months learning to control.

I hated everything, I forgot everything. My vision tunneled and went black. I was filled with black emotion.

Released emotions have triggered its strength!

Curse Series, Shield of Rage abilities up! Transforming into Wrath Shield!

Wrath Shield III: abilities locked: equip bonus: skill "Change Shield (attack)," "Iron Maiden," "Blood Sacrifice": equip effect: dark curse burning: power up: dragon rage: roar: familial violence: magic sharing rage robe (medium)

In an instant, I was filled to the brim with darkness.

Chapter Ten: Shield of Wrath

"!!"

I turned to the sky and screamed, but no noise came from my throat.

I hate it! What did I hate? The whole world! Everything!

I hated everything so much I thought I was going to lose my mind.

Everything was red and black, and everything I looked at caused more hatred to bubble up from within.

"!"

I heard someone speaking to me. For a second, it felt like I'd been doused with water. But even that was meaningless.

"!"

Everything I touched was irritating. I wanted to burn it all!

"Master, do you really hate everything?"

"Everything tried to trick me, to hurt me, to kill me! I hate everything!"

"Really? Really? Do you really mean it?"

Yeah... so what?!

"Did you hate all the time you spent with me and Raphtalia?"

I... remembered that voice.

I remembered a young girl that stayed by my side through

everything. She was loyal through everything. She protected me even when she was hurt. It filled my mind.

There was one that hatched from an egg, grew up, and said that she loved me.

"That…"

"I knew you didn't. I knew you didn't because, Master, you always tried to do things for us!"

The black and red were giving way. Everything was clearing. It was like they'd thrown water on the fire. I felt the water seeping into my heart.

"So, Master, I'll eat your anger! I'll eat your hatred!"

Suddenly everything was clear. I looked around.

"Mr. Naofumi!"

"Are you okay?!"

It looked like only a few seconds had passed since I screamed at the sky.

Raphtalia was speaking to me. She was worried. Ren put his hand on my shoulder.

"Master, are you okay?"

"You… You held me back?"

"Yup. It was hard on you, wasn't it?"

Filo was in her Filolial Queen form. She hugged me from behind. Her wings and legs were burned. They were black. She must not have been able to endure the power of the shield once it grew stronger. It must have been very painful. And yet…

And yet she was worried about me.

"I'm… Raphtalia and I… and Mel, and everyone! We all believe in you. We believe in you, so… do your best!"

"…Yeah. You're right… You're right."

I couldn't afford to be swallowed by hatred.

All I had to do was crush the source of my pain. If I could just kill him, what happened later didn't matter.

I'd… for Melty, for the heroes… I'd kill him!

"…I'm going."

"What are you going to do?"

"I'm going to use my strongest shield's strongest skill."

"What's with that Shield? It's always been ominous, but it looks even worse now."

The Shield of Rage II had an angry dragon shape on it, but when it became the Shield of Wrath it looked even scarier. The dragon's face had twisted into a demon's, and its corners were bent and warped.

"It's a skill I'll probably use on you some day. Attack him and give me a chance to use it."

"You… Oh well. I guess we don't have any choice but to rely on you."

"That's correct. You're a hard guy to trust, but it's our only chance."

"Whatever."

"We'll use our magic to support you."

The heroes all nodded and turned to face the high priest.

"Now, now… What a useless resistance. Let's end this. Our preparations are complete. Your end is at hand."

The air seemed to be filled with magic. The sky was filled with light, growing denser, ready to fall on us at any moment.

"Let's go!"

When I shouted, all the heroes ran towards the high priest.

"Filo, put me on your back and fly!"

"Ooo-kay!"

Filo flipped me onto her back and leapt high into the air.

"High-level ceremonial magic, Judgment!"

The baptismal light in the sky came shooting down!

"Goooooo!"

I held my shield up.

A sound like breaking glass filled my ears, and the light fell on me.

But it wasn't powerful enough to break through the Shield of Wrath III. Not a single photon made it past me.

"He's not hurt by Judgment?! Could it be?!"

The high priest was shocked. Half of his smile melted away.

I'd paid a heavy price to use that shield. I hoped it was as powerful as it felt.

"You fool! You won't survive this!"

The high priest raised his sword and brought it down in my direction.

"Phoenix Blade!"

A bird made of fire erupted from the blade and flew straight for me.

"I don't think so!"

I readied my shield. Filo was chanting a spell, forming some kind of connection with me. I suddenly knew what to do.

The words appeared in my head. Rage Robe (medium) activation requirements?

"The Shield Hero and his tribe are the source of power. Hear my words and heed them. Turn these flames into strength!"

"Wrath Fire!"

My rage would be my power.

The bird of fire flew straight into me. The flames spread to try and burn me, but all the fire turned into power for me.

"What?! He ate my skill?!"

The attacks of the heroes and Filo's powerful kicks cracked and then destroyed the high priest's force field.

"Here I come!"

Filo used her best attack!

She was in her Filolial Queen form, but she was moving her wings in the same way as she had when she'd attacked Fitoria.

She had enough power to use it now, in a real battle. She was moving towards the high priest very quickly.

The high priest turned his weapon into a spear and readied it to block her.

He started to spin the spear in front of him. I was getting a bad feeling.

"State of Selflessness!?"

Motoyasu shouted in surprise. It must have been a powerful spear skill.

"You cannot resist the will of God! I am God himself!"

Everything but Filo's attack flew back. The spear was filled with light.

"Ugh!"

"Ouch!"

The light from the spear reached me. It felt like it was trying to rip me open from the inside. It was very painful.

A counter skill?! How obnoxious was he?!

"But you can't stop us!"

"Can't I?"

Then his weapon turned into a bow and he jumped backwards.

"Don't let him escape! Filo!"

"Yup! Haikuikku!"

She was on him in a flash, kicking.

But the high priest vanished the second her kick connected.

He couldn't get away. He had to die.

Where… Where was he? The minute I started to wonder, a large number of high priests suddenly appeared!

What now? All the disciples had suddenly switched form.

They looked just like the high priest!

"Mirage Arrow?!"

Itsuki shouted.

"That skill forms illusions and confuses the enemy! Be careful!"

Damn… how were we supposed to find the real high priest?

The field was filled with high priests, and there seemed to be more and more by the second.

"Heh, heh, heh… That was interesting, but it's time we ended this."

All of the high priests raised their bows and pulled back the string. He was ready to use a skill.

"This is the most powerful single skill. Shield Demon, I hope you enjoy it."

The bows were shining. Shit! I could probably survive it, but how would we get a counter attack in?

"I am the queen and the source of all power. Hear my words and heed them. Restrain them in a cage of ice!"

"All Drifa Icicle Prison!"

All of the high priests suddenly realized that their legs were encased in ice.

Then, one by one, the fake high priests all reverted to the original forms.

"Now."

Who was that? No, I didn't have time to worry about that now. I had to focus on defeating him. I had to take down the only real enemy.

Blood Sacrifice!

The moment I thought of it, the necessary words appeared in my vision. I spoke them.

"Let this foolish criminal be punished as I see fit. The sacrificial shout to heaven! Let his fool's scream piece the sky! May dragon jaws born from my flesh erase him from this world!"

"Blood Sacrifice…. Ugh!"

Wh… Wha?!

The second I finished summoning the skill, blood bubbled out of my mouth and pumped from my pores, my flesh ripped, and my bones screamed out in agony.

Was it a suicidal skill?!

The high priest saw me howl in pain and smiled.

But a second later… a large, bear trap-like set of rusty claws appeared directly beneath the high priest's feet.

No… I should call it a dragon's jaw made from metal.

Unlike a normal bear trap, this had rows upon rows of sharp metal prongs… It really looked like a dragon had opened its mouth from underground, and like a shark, it had many rows of teeth.

"Wh…"

A loud, metallic snap echoed over the field, and the jaws sprung shut on the high priest.

"UGAHHHH!"

His screams filled the air.

There was a flash, a spray of red blood, and a dark shadow.

"What is this?!"

The jaws snapped shut, but all they did was heavily damage the high priest, who quickly summoned a skill to break the jaws. However, his attacks were not effective.

The jaws snapped shut twice, three times, and the replica legendary weapon was covered in cracks. The jaws snapped again, and with them came the sound of metal clattering and breaking. Again and again, like they were smiling, the jaws snapped shut.

It was… gruesome.

"Ugh… I… bl… God…"

Finally, the high priest was little more than a bloody clump. The jaw snapped shut a final time and sunk down into the earth—vanishing.

"…"

We all watched on in silence.

All the skills that came from the Curse Series were gory things. It was a soul-eating Shield, after all.

After watching that, I could agree with Fitoria's warnings.

I realized, and agreed, that it was not the sort of thing to use normally.

The remaining disciples were whispering to each other in desperation.

"...And that's the end of you all."

The support troops charged into the crowd of disciples and began to restrain and then tie them up.

So I guess we won.

I was watching the support troops, but then I slumped forward and fell off of Filo.

The Shield of Wrath had unlocked a new skill, Blood Sacrifice.

It was very powerful, but asked for so much...

"Master?!"

Filo was covered in my blood. She was holding me, and she looked worried.

My shield had reverted back to the Chimera Viper Shield.

"You're badly hurt! Someone! Someone help!"

A woman officer came running when Filo shouted.

"Mother?!"

Melty shouted when she saw the woman.

That was right... The officer who'd been leading the support troops... She looked exactly like the queen's doppelgänger.

Her mouth was hidden with a folding fan, but I was pretty sure.

"Your performance was very impressive, Shield Hero."

She must have been the one who'd shouted and stopped the high priest in his tracks.

"Everyone! Treating the Shield Hero's wounds is our highest priority! That's a royal order. Whatever happens, the Shield Hero must live!"

"Yes!"

The medical team from the support troops ran over to where I lay and began to cast spells over me.

"Drifa Heal."

I was surrounded by light, but my pain didn't go away at all.

"This… This is a curse. But I've never seen one so powerful."

The medics exchanged shocked glances. They began casting anti-curse magic. They sprinkled me with holy water. But nothing was working.

"We must investigate this further! Everyone please hurry! Yes, you too!"

The queen gave Filo and the medics orders, and they all ran off.

"Uh…"

My entire body was screaming in pain. But I couldn't lose consciousness… not here.

Because I still didn't know if the queen was a friend or an enemy.

"Y… You're the queen?"

"Yes, I am the Queen of Melromarc, Mirellia Q. Melromarc. I apologize that it took us so long to get here."

"Yeah... that was really... slow."

Slow, slow to do anything and everything. Did she have power, or not? Did she run the country, or not?

Didn't she have a grasp of everything that had happened?

I had so much I wanted to say to her.

I wanted to tell her just how terrible her daughter and husband were... I had so much resentment.

"It's true... All of this was my fault."

"Mother..."

"Mama, why are you apologizing to the likes of him?!"

Bitch was pointing at me and screaming hysterically. Veins were standing out on her forehead.

"Malty... There are things we must discuss when we get back to the castle. I suggest you prepare yourself."

The whole scene seemed to rumble and shake.

No one was mad at me, but I still felt my nerves tense up and my blood run cold.

The queen snapped her fingers, and two shadows appeared behind Bitch. They tied her up.

"But, Mama!"

"Shut that fool up."

"Ha!"

They stuffed a gag in her mouth and led her off.

"What are you doing to Myne?!"

Motoyasu was standing there, unable to believe his eyes.

"I am Myne... Malty's mother. I have simply exercised my authority to have her transported back to the castle. Now then, Heroes, the battle is over. Let us return to the castle in peace."

The queen had a powerful aura that shut Motoyasu and the others up immediately.

As for myself, I didn't have the energy left to complain. It had been a hard battle.

"As for you, Shield Hero, or should I say Mr. Naofumi Iwatani? The treatment of your wounds is my highest priority, so please try to get some rest. I will make all the necessary preparations."

Medics appeared with a variety of medicines, tools, and holy waters.

It felt a lot like being in an ambulance back in my own world.

"But... But I..."

What are you doing here? Aren't you supposed to be in the country to the southwest? I had so many questions.

"I understand. Why have I been away this whole time? Why didn't I help you? If I was supposed to be in another country, why am I here, leading an army? There is so much for us to talk about, but for now please just focus on getting better."

"Mr. Naofumi!"

Raphtalia looked very worried. She was crying as she walked up to my side.

"I thought my heart had stopped! Please tell me you're all right!"

"Well… I…"

I really did feel like I was seriously injured. Everything pulsed with pain, and I was exhausted.

Filo seemed to understand that everything was going to be okay. She transformed into human form, and she and Melty came over to the carriage they were loading me into.

"Your wounds are serious. Hurry, this way."

Filo was also hurt. Her limbs were all burned black with cursed flames. The medics called to her.

"No! I have to stay with Master!"

Maybe she was just too concerned with my wounds? I could only guess why, but she refused to go with them.

"Filo, it will be okay. All these people are here to heal your Naofumi."

Melty was very worried. She held Filo and ran her fingers through her hair.

"But Master…"

"You know that Naofumi would want you to have your own wounds treated. He wouldn't want to see you like this, would he?"

Perhaps wondering if that were true or not, Filo cocked her head and looked at me.

I swear. She was so selfish all the time, but now she was worried?

"It's fine. Go get treatment."

My words came out almost as a whisper. Then Filo nodded, and she went over to receive treatment from medics. They began to chant spells that were supposed to be effective against curses.

"This curse is very powerful…"

The medics were whispering to each other. I guess it really was a powerful curse.

The Curse Series suddenly seemed aptly named.

The shield was powerful, so I'd been careful to only use it when I really needed to. Still though, this Blood Sacrifice was an entirely new matter altogether. It asked of so much from me, just as Fitoria had said. It invited my own destruction.

"Hurry with the 'Sanctuary' preparations!"

Was that the magic that had nullified my self curse burning?

The people gathered around were not only from the Church of the Three Heroes…. but they seemed to be part of some other religion… but what? Maybe it was the Church of the Shield? That seemed like something I could get behind…

I was thinking it all over when my eyes began to feel very heavy.

"Mr. Naofumi!"

"Naofumi!"

Raphtalia and Melty shook me awake.

"Huh? What?"

"You have to stay awake."

"What are you talking about? You're acting like I'm dying or something. But I'm not. I'm fine."

Though I couldn't fault them for thinking that. I really could have died.

I certainly wasn't going to die in a place like that... but I was very tired.

I wanted to sleep... even if only a little.

But I couldn't yet. I wasn't safe yet. We weren't in a safe place yet, but I couldn't even move.

And so...

"Raphtalia, if anything seems strange, you take Melty, jump on Filo, and run."

"All right. But if it comes to that, I'm taking you with us."

"Sorry. I don't think I can make breakfast for you tomorrow. I need to... rest."

As I spoke, I felt my vision fading. A moment later, and I was in a deep sleep.

"Mr. Naofumi! You can't sleep. You can't! Mr. Naofumi—"

Chapter Eleven: The Queen

Two days passed.

"Ugh… I'm so tired."

"Snore… Snore…"

"Munya… Master!"

"I… ca… Fi….lo?"

When I finally got my eyes opened I realized that I was in a giant bed with Raphtalia, Filo, and Melty.

"What the hell?! Get off me!"

I threw them all off the bed and proceeded to berate them. The three of them stood there, strangely smiling.

I'd been carried off in the medical cart and was being treated in a town near the castle.

The Blood Sacrifice curse was very powerful, and they'd taken me to a specialized treatment facility—but not even they had been able to completely get rid of it.

I asked what I could do to heal it, but apparently it was the sort of curse that couldn't be removed with medicines or magic. I had to treat it like a wound, and it would slowly heal over time… or so they said.

The actual wounds and burns had been healed. I had the majority of my strength back, but they said that I would probably continue to feel sluggish for a while.

I checked my status magic, and all of my stats aside from defense had fallen by about thirty percent.

Apparently the Blood Sacrifice curse would lower my stats until it was completely healed.

It had been effective enough to warrant its use, but I had to admit that it came with a heavy price tag.

"How long will it take to heal?"

"Our best guess is that it will take about a month."

A month… That was a pretty long time. That would mean I'd be back on my feet just in time for the next wave.

"And how are you feeling?"

The whole world was in the middle of an absurd crisis, but the queen came to speak with me before my treatment.

She seemed to be expressing concern for my well-being.

"…"

I still didn't know if I could trust her. Besides, she'd given the medics orders the whole time I'd been unconscious.

The queen turned to a doctor, and they discussed my condition.

"Really? Then he'll be able to accompany us?

"Where are you going?

"Back to the castle, of course."

She covered her mouth with her folding fan, but a vein was popping out from her forehead. She had a strange, oppressive sense of authority about her.

"Mother is very angry…"

Melty was shaking and hiding behind me.

She did seem to be a little on edge, but I guess that's what her anger looked like.

"I hope you're not planning on executing me or something like that."

"I would never do something so foolish. But I would very much like you to be there when… *my plans* are enacted, Mr. Iwatani."

"What are you talking about?"

"You'll just have to wait until we arrive at the castle. And I have so many questions I'd like to ask you. We'll have the opportunity to talk soon."

The damn queen was making it impossible for me to refuse. Would she say anything to get me to the castle?

Sure, I suppose I could refuse—but that wouldn't help me. My highest priority was to prove my innocence, and I was going to need her to make that happen.

Melty had said so before.

The queen was apparently furious with Trash and Bitch. She said that the queen had been ripping up their portraits, that she'd been setting them on fire.

It made me wonder what she was thinking… Could it be?

Regardless, I didn't have a good reason to refuse her.

Although, in time, I could imagine that the fact that she

was Trash's wife and Bitch's mother might drive a wedge of sorts between us.

"Hm..."

Melty was still standing behind me.

"Oh come on... I guess I have to take you with us?"

"Mr. Naofumi?"

Raphtalia sounded very worried.

"I don't think I can refuse, so what choice do I have but to go? They've been taking care of me this whole time, so I doubt that we have anything to worry about."

"Yes, indeed, I would like it if you would come as well."

I could see what she was getting at. She was waiting to see how closely our interests aligned.

I didn't know what her plan was. But no matter—if she were going to hand me off to the enemy, then I would just have to use the Shield of Wrath again.

"We're taking care of the bird god's carriage too. Let's return it along with its luggage."

"Really?"

Filo jumped forward when the queen mentioned the carriage.

"Yes. It's parked in front of the hospital. You can go see it yourselves."

"Okay! Yay! Mel, let's go!"

"Okay!"

Filo and Melty went running out of the room.

That girl really liked carriages. After they left, I turned back to the queen.

"Something bothers me."

I didn't know what she wanted, but I got the impression that there was something else she wasn't telling me, something behind her supposed good intentions.

If there was a good reason for her to not only defy the Church but treat the shield demon nicely, then I wanted to know what it was.

And I wouldn't accept any pretentious explanations like, "for the good of the world," either. In trying to figure out her true intentions, I began to look at her face carefully. When I did, her hand started shaking. The fan was swaying in her hand. What was happening?

"Aultcray… Malty… This isn't the end…"

There was no doubt about it… She was furious.

Suddenly, a shadow appeared. He was holding portraits of Trash and Bitch, and he quickly pasted them up on the wall.

In a flash, the queen summoned magical icicles. She threw them at the portraits, pinning them to the wall before summoning flames to burn them to ash.

"That's not enough… not enough. I want to see their faces twisted in fear."

I wished she would find somewhere else to have a private

freak out. She looked a little unstable. She must have really been harboring some intense emotions about them—her own husband and daughter.

I knew how she felt. Yup, I'd believe her—for now.

"I'll do what you say."

"Thank you, Mr. Iwatani."

The queen smiled. As the corners of her mouth turned up, I could sense her willpower.

"Well, well! If it isn't Malty and Melty! I'm so glad you were able to defeat the Shield and return to me safely. But why is Malty tied up? And is that a gag in her mouth?"

On our way to the castle, the queen ordered that Bitch and Melty lead the line, and the rest of us would follow well behind.

The other heroes were with us in the back. I didn't like that I'd been ordered to be at the front of the heroes. The queen was insistent though, saying that I had done all the work and suffered the most. So I relented.

By the way, after all this was over, the remaining disciples from the Church filled me in on some of the stuff that was going on.

Word of the high priest's death hadn't yet reached the general population, and so the Church was still acting as though nothing had happened. Or at least that's what it looked like. The truth was that members of the Church that had been complicit in the conspiracy had been arrested.

"Because she doesn't know how to shut her mouth, that's why."

The queen's footsteps echoed off the stone walls as she walked forward and approached the throne. Trash noticed that I was following her into the room also, and his face contorted in anger.

"What is HE doing here? Seize him! He must be put to death!"

"I will not allow it!"

The knights ignored the king's orders—probably because the queen technically had more power than Trash. They still seemed a little confused though. The knights around the queen were glaring at me.

"She's... That's not the real queen! Arrest her!"

"You... you would mistake ME? I cannot tolerate this behavior any longer!"

"I am the queen and the source of all power...."

"That spell... Can it be?!"

"Hear the truth and heed it. Restrain him with a cage of ice!"

"Drifa Icicle Prison!"

A cage of ice appeared around Trash.

It seemed like Trash was shouting from inside it, but his voice didn't make it out of the cage.

"I cannot believe how low you have sunk."

The queen snapped her folding fan shut, and the cage vanished at the same time.

"Such powerful magic! Indeed, you are truly my wife! What has happened to you?!"

Trash was looking at her up and down like he couldn't believe his own eyes.

"...And with the Shield!"

Seriously, any time something happened he didn't like, he blamed it on me.

He needed to calm down. He was making it very clear why I never wanted to visit the castle again.

"You're wrong. I swear. Do you really believe that the Shield Hero has the sort of powers you ascribed to him?"

She walked up to the throne and slapped him hard across the face.

Trash was knocked speechless. He was shaking as he stared at me.

"None of this is Mr. Iwatani's fault! Have you been listening to me?!"

"Ugh!"

She slapped him again.

Trash opened his mouth to speak, but before he was able to get a word out she slapped him again.

"I told you that you were to have authority over Melromarc

while I was in other lands. I told you, time and time again, not to treat the Heroes poorly. But you ignored me! Are you TRYING to start a war?"

"But I…"

"I don't want to hear your excuses! The very world is threatened by the waves. And now… during this time when we all must band together… you… you!"

The queen continued to berate him, and he never got a word in.

Watching the scene unfold, I couldn't ignore the distinct sense I got that she was doing all this so that the other heroes would understand that she was the one in charge.

"Now, with that out of the way, allow me to re-introduce myself. I am the ruling queen of this land, Mirellia Q. Melromarc. Aultcray may seem to carry authority, but he does not—not any longer. Do not believe what he says."

"Um… Uh…"

"Pleased to… meet you?"

"Whoa…"

The other heroes all expressed their emotions in turn. They all had trouble finding the right words.

"Heroes, I would very much like a little of your time today."

"What's happening?"

"Let's discuss it during the feast."

"Um… Myne?"

Motoyasu seemed to be a little concerned for Bitch, since she was still gagged and couldn't speak.

"She has no reason to speak, so I've silenced her for now. Understand?"

"Yes, but... Isn't this a little much?"

"No, it isn't. But if you'd like to hear her protests then I suppose I have no choice..."

The queen snapped her fingers and the ropes restraining Bitch loosened. Bitch immediately moved to pull the gag from her mouth.

"Sniffle..."

She must have been embarrassed to be seen so powerless. Trash seemed to sympathize. He looked on with sad eyes.

"What's this 'sniffle' supposed to mean? We're not done talking!"

"It's not my fault! All of this is the Shield's fault!"

"Yeah! He's right!"

Bitch chimed in.

"Mama! This wretched demon tried to rape me!"

"And...?"

"What do you mean? Mama... I've never... What are you saying?!"

"It's not like you were a virgin, were you? Did you think I didn't know? I knew..."

"What?!"

Motoyasu shouted like he couldn't believe his own ears.

"No… Mother… My first was Mr. Motoyasu!"

"How presumptuous of you. You really thought I didn't know? Now, if you really did have relations with the Shield Hero then there might have been a way to save you…"

The queen glanced at me.

ME? With Bitch?

"Don't make me throw up!"

"Well, that's the end of you. I suppose I'll just have to hold out hope for Melty. It will be hard, but I'm sure there are plenty of reasons to remain hopeful."

The queen was now making important pronouncements as if they were nothing.

"What are you saying? Melty is just a little girl!"

"Silence!"

I certainly never thought that I'd be on the same side of an argument with Trash, but why did I have to have a relationship with Melty?

Huh? What was that? Ren and Itsuki were both looking at me with strange expressions on their faces.

I didn't need this. I didn't have a Lolita complex. I wasn't so perverted that a little girl turned me on!

"Yeah! What are you saying?!"

"What are you talking about?"

"Nothing you need to worry about, Filo!"

I'd have to let this one go.

"I'm sorry! But it's only natural that Melty should marry Mr. Iwatani."

"What?!"

"Don't you understand? There is no better way to defeat our old enemy."

"What's that supposed to mean?"

"What do you mean?"

"Yeah... We're getting curious too."

Trash was clearly upset, and Ren and Itsuki followed his questions with their own.

"Well..."

I understood though. The queen began to explain, and confirmed my suspicions.

Siltvelt worshiped the Shield Hero. And Siltvelt was also Melromarc's enemy. If the royal family of Melromarc adopted me into their lineage, that would make Melromarc into a holy nation from the perspective of Siltvelt. I wasn't able to read much more into her plans, but at the very least the common people of Siltvelt would think more positively about Melromarc. It was a plan that would flatter the Shield Hero, and if they ended up giving birth, that would cement everything.

Then they would just have to maintain a friendly relationship. If they pulled that off, they'd be true allies.

"Have you no shame? You would use your own daughter that way?"

Itsuki stepped forward and shouted with rage.

"Use her? Very well… Are you saying that in your own world there are no politically arranged marriages?"

"I've heard that they used to happen, but that doesn't mean they aren't problematic."

"There's no problem. I see that Melty and Mr. Iwatani are already on good terms. Melty, do what you can to get along with Mr. Iwatani."

"N…No!"

Melty's face was bright red. She seemed to really hate the idea.

Which was only fair. Who would want to be used for political purposes, especially at that age?

And, of course, I didn't feel like doing anything that would benefit Melromarc.

"Is that so? The shadows led me to believe that there was still hope for you."

"Bummer."

"What's that? Are you saying I'm not attractive?! Wa…"

"What's the problem? Are you saying I shouldn't look at you as a child?!"

She was at that obnoxious age.

"Very well. If that's all there is to it, then I suppose I cannot interfere."

For some reason, Itsuki was satisfied and stepped back into line.

"Bow Hero! Why are you giving up?!"

"I see that she has a point, and that there is hope for you. What are you supposed to do? You're going to be the queen."

"I don't plan on laying my bones to rest in this shitty world."

"That won't be necessary. As long as Melty becomes pregnant with your child."

I didn't like where this was going.

Basically, she meant that if I married into the Melromarc royal family and gave Melty a child, then I would be free to go back to my own world.

I guess it did make a little sense. I'd heard that the queen was an experienced diplomat—and she sure wasn't pulling any punches.

Where did these ideas come from? Was she reading too much manga?

"All of this is because my foolish husband and daughter destroyed our other opportunities. Everything was fine when you left to be in Iwatani's party. You could have brought more people into the party and domesticated him—kept him for yourself. Had you done so, the throne would be as good as yours."

"Who would do that with someone as ugly as him? He tried to rape me!"

Ugh… there goes Bitch again.

I couldn't let that one slide… I'd have to help her understand her position…

"He's not ugly!"

Raphtalia, Filo, and for some reason Melty all shouted out in unison.

What's that all about? Especially Melty.

"What's the problem? I'm just telling the truth. If you get upset about it, that proves that you agree!"

"It does prove something. It proves that you no longer have even a drop of purity left in you."

"What proof are you talking about? Ask Mr. Motoyasu. I was a virgin!"

"Malty, if you're going to lie, you'd better be prepared to lie all the way until the end. You might be able to fool the Spear Hero, but you cannot fool me. I've known you for a long time, and you've always had the nasty habit of taking joy in the misery of others. Furthermore…"

The queen was really shouting at Bitch now. It was clear to everyone that Bitch wasn't listening anymore though. She'd tuned out and was just waiting for her mother's speech to end.

I wondered how many times she'd been lectured by her mother up until now.

"You heard that your sister had been swept up in the conspiracy, but instead of trying to protect her, you took advantage of the situation, going too far as to turn her over to the Church yourself!"

Huh? So Bitch had just taken advantage of the situation

with the Church? I'd thought that she was working with them.

Could it be that the two of them were just really stupid?

"You probably thought that you'd be the next person to sit on the throne."

"I… I did not!"

I thought back on all we had been through. How many times had she referred to herself as "the future queen?" We'd all heard it come from her lips, time and time again. If she hadn't thought that she really was going to be the future queen, she wouldn't have said things like that—would she? Besides, she had stuttered when the queen pointed it out.

"Yeah! Myne's not like that!"

Motoyasu shouted out in support, but the queen wasn't listening.

"You're lying!"

"No, it's true!"

"If it's true, then you'll show us proof."

The queen snapped her fingers, and knights clapped their hands down on Bitch's shoulders. Some wizards appeared, carrying an item I was familiar with. It was the ink pot used in slave registration magic.

"What are you doing?!"

Motoyasu noticed that something was up, and he started to shout.

Soldiers came to control Motoyasu and Bitch. The wizards

turned to Bitch and began a ceremony.

The queen produced a needle, pricked her own finger, and dropped a little of her blood into the ink pot.

I... I knew what she was doing.

"N... No! Release me!"

"I will release you once I've verified your innocence. I hope the Heroes understand."

No, they wouldn't. Or so I thought. Itsuki and Ren were watching on in silence.

Even dumb Bitch had figured out what was going on. She tried to wrestle herself free from the soldiers, but they wouldn't let her escape. I was more concerned with how Motoyasu would react. Perhaps seeing that there was no way out, he readied his spear.

"Stop that!!"

I wouldn't let him interfere.

"Shield Prison!"

I turned my shield into the Shield of Wrath and, repressing my anger—or should I say controlling it, I shut him inside a Shield Prison.

Ren and Itsuki nearly stepped in to stop me, but noticing the crowd of soldiers in the room, they held back.

"N...No! Stay back! Who do you think I am?!"

"The older princess. That is... if you can prove your innocence."

The queen dropped a hand and gave an order.

They poured ink from the pot onto Bitch's chest. The slave seal appeared there, burning into her.

"NOOOOOOOOOOO!"

Bitch screamed like that for a minute or so, but once she calmed down the seal disappeared as if nothing had happened.

It was different than what Raphtalia had gone through. Raphtalia's seal remained like a tattoo, but Bitch's disappeared completely.

"This is a powerful slave seal. It is normally invisible, but when certain conditions are met, it will return, punishing the subject."

In that regard, it was more like Filo's control magic.

"The condition is that you must not attack Mr. Iwatani. Do not raise your hand against him!"

Bitch glared at the queen. There were tears in her eyes.

"Now then, Malty. Here is the question: were you raped by Mr. Iwatani?"

It was a good plan to wring a confession out of her. I'd done the same thing to Raphtalia once.

Because she couldn't lie if the slave seal was on her.

If she tried to lie, the seal would activate and punish her.

Of course it would only work if the queen and the seal were real.

"Yes!"

Bitch arched her eyebrows and nodded.

At nearly the same time, the slave seal came burning back into view and exerted a powerful pressure on her chest.

"OUCH! It hurts!"

Bitch couldn't handle the pain, and she fell to the floor.

"M…Myne!"

Motoyasu ran to her and helped her sit up, but the effects of the slave seal didn't go away.

"The effects won't go away until you tell the truth."

"Fine… Fine! The Shield Hero didn't rape me. It was all a lie!"

The second Bitch admitted her lie, the seal vanished.

"See? Everyone have a look. It was a lie."

"How can you say that when YOU forced her to say it!?"

Motoyasu was furious with the queen. I could see where he was coming from. From his perspective, she was most definitely an enemy.

"I don't know what kind of magic that was, but you forced her to lie!"

"If you think so, Spear Hero, then why not temporarily register Malty as your slave as well? If you do, then you'll quickly understand how the slave seal works."

"Yeah! Fine! I'll prove her innocence!"

Just as the queen had done, Motoyasu let a drop of his blood fall into the ink pot. They spilled the ink over Bitch again, and she was registered as his slave.

"Now you can see for yourself how the slave magic works. Look at your status screens to see."

Motoyasu's eyes moved as though he were reading something. Then he nodded and turned to Bitch.

"Myne… You were almost raped by Naofumi, weren't you?"

"Ye… Ouch! OW!"

She was about to lie again when the slave seal activated. She fell to the floor again.

"B…But…"

All the color left Motoyasu's face.

"There's more though, isn't there? You stole all of Mr. Iwatani's possessions, didn't you?"

"I did NOT! OW! OOOOWWWW!"

The woman really couldn't lie…

A little speechless, I stood there and watched Bitch roll around on the ground in pain.   "And you were the one who set fire to the forest while you were chasing Mr. Iwatani, weren't you?!"

She knew. Of course she knew. If she knew what kind of person Bitch was, it was an easy assumption to make.

"I didn't, I… AAAAHHHHH!"

Her screams were growing panicked. If she didn't start telling the truth, she'd die.

She must have known that, and yet she went on lying...
What a woman.

"YOU set those fires?!"

Motoyasu was shaking.

"It can't be true! Myne would never do something like that!"

"Mr. Kitamura, you must understand this. This girl has always been a liar. She always hid in the shadows and tried to get others in trouble. She's been this way from childhood."

"No, she isn't like that! It's HIM. It's HIS fault."

Motoyasu was thrusting his finger at me.

He didn't understand the difference between belief and blind faith. Eventually that would knock him off of his feet.

"All of this is because of my daughter Malty. She pulled the strings and tricked my husband, Aultcray, into persecuting Mr. Iwatani."

Motoyasu was still furiously jabbing his finger at me, but Ren and Itsuki were nodding. They seemed to understand.

"You know..."

"Is there no other proof?"

"There is plenty of proof. If you want to know something, just ask."

"Are you so confident? It is true that some of Myne's behavior during the last incident cause me to wonder. We were supposed to protect Melty, but she attacked her. What was her intention there?"

"Melty is the first in line to inherit the throne of Melromarc. Therefore, if Melty were to disappear, Malty would become first in line."

"Now I understand."

Ren was nodding too. He'd been paying attention for a while now.

Even Itsuki, who liked to pretend he was a shining knight of justice, was nodding.

"Should we support Naofumi?"

"Yes. Even back when Motoyasu was dueling him, Naofumi had been hit from behind by magic. What was that? It's very strange to think back on it, even now."

"Yeah, and the next day when we were supposed to receive our funds for the next month, she had his funding taken away. It's very hard to not harbor doubts in a situation like that."

It had taken a long time, but her true colors were finally plain for everyone to see.

It felt like the winds of fate were finally blowing in my direction. I could assume that I'd proved my innocence now.

"Aultcray is next."

The queen cast her gaze at Trash, and he seemed to flinch on the throne.

"What were you doing? You made no attempt to discover the truth. We were supposed to be taking special care of the Shield Hero, but you threw him out into the world naked. I don't even know what to say. In the past, no matter what my private feelings about you may have been I'd been able to keep you domesticated, but…"

"It's all the Shield's fault!"

"Malty was not raped. Her lies have been shown for what they are. What do you have to say about it?"

"Urg… It's the Shield! He's to blame!"

Was that all he could say? Just how much did he think he could pin on me?! Trash…

He was just adding fuel to the fire at that point.

"I swear… You would have been smarter about this in the past. You used to be smarter than this!"

The queen held a palm to her forehead—clearly she couldn't handle much more of it all.

"It seems like you are not going to be able to defend yourself."

Like a breeze had blown through, both Bitch and Trash turned their eyes to the floor.

Still, I didn't get the feeling that they were going to apologize to me. That didn't seem possible.

They were so irritating. Why did the queen force me to stand there before them? Ideally, I wanted to spend as little of my time with them as I could.

It's not like I could expect them to revaluate their behavior in any sort of meaningful way.

I wondered why she didn't make Trash into a slave. Was there some kind of reason behind it?

Well… I guess he wasn't lying the way that Bitch was.

"I thought, for a long time, of ways to get around having to say this—but I now believe there is no other way."

The queen was absentmindedly opening and closing her fan as she spoke, but now she authoritatively clapped it shut and pointed it at them.

"I officially disown you both. From this time until eternity, neither of you will be considered part of the royal family."

"What?!"

"Mama?!"

Bitch and Trash both shouted in shock and protest. They weren't able to accept the severity of their transgressions.

It wasn't so bad. I was starting to enjoy it! I hoped she'd come up with more things to show me.

"Mr. Naofumi, what are you smiling about?"

"Come on… You know."

"I know where you are coming from, but…"

"Mother… She's serious."

"Huh?"

Filo turned her head to the side. She didn't seem to understand what was happening.

She could be pretty stupid when she wanted to be. All she understood was food, carriages, and Melty.

Wait. Why was I thinking about Filo? There was so much other exciting stuff going on!

"Why?!"

"Both of you have behaved in unforgivable ways. Had you been truly repentant, I could have found some way to petition Mr. Iwatani for forgiveness. And yet…"

"You think I'd forgive them?"

"I thought of various ways to earn your trust after these two admitted their crimes and apologized…"

Trust… apologies, ha! I'd rather just watch to see how this all played out.

"What will happen to Melromarc if you remove me from the royal lineage?!"

"Nothing bad. To be honest, you're garbage—the scum of this country."

"Wah…"

"How can you speak to your own child that way?!"

Motoyasu was screaming in anger.

"Don't you understand? You reap what you sow. And it is now more than clear that Melty is the only one here capable of running the county. Malty, you've lost."

She was right—the country would be in much better hands with Melty.

She could be a little hysterical, but she'd grown up a lot with all we'd been through.

Besides, she only really ran her mouth off at me.

"If you remove me from the throne, there are many people and organizations that will be upset."

"I've already silenced them. Did you think I was just sitting back and watching in silence for these last three months? If so, you're mistaken."

"Bu…"

Trash was so shocked he couldn't speak. He just kept flapping his lips without saying anything.

"Besides, why did you summon the Heroes on your own! We needed to discuss this."

"What do you mean?"

"Certainly the Heroes found it odd that they would be summoned to this world without the approval or appearance of this nation's highest authority?"

"Naturally."

Like she said, she really didn't seem like the kind of person that would leave such important matters up to her subordinates.

Besides, if they had summoned us and been a bit more diplomatic, if they had really made the effort to win us over to their side, then they could have put us to better use.

I didn't want to admit it, but that went double for myself—considering how little I'd known about the world when they summoned me.

They could have gotten me to fall in love and arranged any

political marriage that was convenient.

"Before we take this any further, we need to get one thing very clear. Our country was supposed to be the fourth country to summon the Heroes. This was decided at an international diplomatic meeting."

"Wait just a second!"

Now she was blurting out some serious stuff.

Different countries could summon the heroes? There was an agreed-upon order?

What was Melromarc up to?

"Explain."

"All right."

The queen began to explain things.

The waves had come, and many different countries had suffered heavy losses. To discuss their options, the kings and queens of various nations all agreed to a meeting.

Certainly, there were different interests expressed, and some of the countries were natural enemies (like Melromarc and Siltvelt), but no one could avoid the truth: the world was sliding closer to complete destruction. If any of the countries had squabbles, they agreed to put them aside until the relative safety of the world was secured.

At that meeting, it was agreed that Melromarc would be the fourth nation to summon the heroes.

It also sounded like the typical procedure was to summon

one hero at a time. Most of the time when they attempted to summon heroes, no one showed up.

Also, and this was supposed to go without saying, the heroes were expected to travel around to all the different countries.

"So why did this country summon them?"

"The Heroes are normally summoned using pieces of ancient holy relics. The ceremony can only be performed at a specified time, but…"

It meant that they had summoned all the heroes while the queen was out of the country.

"The Church of the Three Heroes had been around for a long time, and its roots run deep in these lands. As far as I know, they are a very conservative organization. Still, it appears they had unexpected ambitious plans."

"That sounds like a big problem to me."

The heroes were supposed to save the whole world, but we'd all been summoned to the same spot.

"Yes, that is why we have been so heavily criticized."

"Why would you leave the country in the hands of a war hawk like this?"

That was a big problem. She gave him way too much authority.

Ren and Itsuki seemed to agree. They nodded. Their party members looked like they had something to say though.

I'd heard a little about it from Melty. She had said that some really nice members of the nobility, the ones who had been in charge of Raphtalia's village, had been killed in the wave.

"What are you saying?!"

"Shut up!"

The queen shouted for silence.

"Myne's father isn't that bad!"

Motoyasu still had wisdom to contribute, apparently.

"Motoyasu, you only feel that way because of the special treatment you received. This all makes sense to us."

"Yeah. I felt like things were unfair this whole time."

"That's the precise problem. The first wave came while I was away on diplomacy. I had appointed someone I trust, my right hand, to take care of the kingdom in my absences... but..."

"...But?"

"They died in the wave... And they had spent so much time earning the trust of the demi-humans..."

"May I ask a question?"

"What is it, Mr. Amaki?"

"Why did this human-supremacist country harbor nobility that wanted to work with the demi-humans?"

The queen opened her fan and hid her mouth when she answered Ren's question.

"We wanted to avoid war with Siltvelt, and so it was part of our strategy to fix our relations with demi-humans. Siltvelt was aware of this, and they were doing the same thing for humans in their country."

I was starting to understand. The nobility had been kind to the demi-humans as a sign of good faith to avoid war with Siltvelt.

"It's odd how open you are being about this."

Itsuki said this to the queen, expressing his suspicions.

"After we forcibly summoned your here, take it as a sign of my sincerity that I, the highest authority in these lands, would speak honestly with you like this. If I don't go out of my way to earn your trust, how could I ask for your cooperation?"

Ren and Itsuki looked at each other then nodded.

"However… Aultcray has already shown a great deal of preferential treatment for the Spear Hero. The Bow and Sword Heroes have also demonstrated their loyalty. But, from this point on, if it seems like I am showing the Shield Hero preferential treatment, please understand that I am simply trying to balance and correct the past misdeeds here."

"All right."

"You're right. If Naofumi really was innocent of everything, then the scales must be balanced. I understand."

"Back to the topic at hand… It seems that Aultcray's incompetence has led to the destruction of our demi-human protected district."

The queen reared back and stomped on Trash's foot with all her might.

"Owwww."

"And I found this out at the exact same time that I discovered your secretive summoning ceremony!"

The queen slapped Trash time and time again.

"Ugh..."

"This is what I get for allowing a fool like this to rule in my stead! A never-ending series of ridiculous events in my absence! Even if the true enemy WAS the Church..."

"Ugh!"

"And the very next day after the Heroes begin their quest, you call in the Shield and deem him a criminal!"

"UGH!"

"Then you continue to discriminate against him! Do you have any idea how close you brought us to war?!"

"UGH!"

"And then, immediately following the second wave, you tried to steal his slave from him? What were you thinking?!"

She was really worked up...

"Because of your foolish behavior, Siltvelt and Shieldfreeden are infuriated. They could attack at any time!"

I was starting to sympathize with the queen's position.

Everyone she'd entrusted the kingdom to had died or disappeared, and she had to keep the world from war all by herself.

I was impressed. She must have been a véry skilled diplomat.

Even if she just looked like a hysterical woman in her twenties exploding at her husband.

And she was Melty and Bitch's mother? She certainly looked young for her age.

"Then, on top of everything, you write to say that you want to see Melty? How selfish can you be?!"

"Ugh!"

"And the people that would use you and your red face to accomplish their own goals… They were right there before you, and you didn't notice? All of this is your fault!"

She was fuming with anger. She went on.

"I hereby declare the Church of the Three Heroes heretical! Melromarc will follow the Church of the Four Holy Warriors from now on!"

"W…What?! You would abandon the very traditions that gave rise to our kingdom?!"

"There is no reason to maintain a tradition that causes nothing but trouble!"

The Church of the Four Holy Warriors?

"What's that?"

"A religion that worships the four Holy Heroes equally."

Melty explained.

I guess that was only natural. If there were four people that saved the world, you'd expect a religion to crop up about them sooner or later.

"The Church of the Three Heroes originally branched off from the Church of the Four Holy Warriors. But to explain why, we'd have to go all the way back to the founding of Melromarc."

"Huh…"

If Siltvelt worshiped the Shield Hero, then it was only logical to assume that other countries worshiped the heroes in different ways. It was easy enough to imagine the reason. If Melromarc and Siltvelt were not on good terms, and Siltvelt worshiped the Shield Hero…

It was only natural that they'd come up with a way to say that the other country's religion was false, that their god was a demon, etc. That would explain the start of the Church of the Three Heroes.

"Sigh…"

The queen finished scolding Trash. Refreshed from slapping him so many times, she opened her fan, hid her mouth, and turned to me. Too bad I hadn't gotten the chance to slap Trash.

"There is much more to discuss, Mr. Iwatani. But it will have to wait until later."

"I'd rather not hear about all that."

"Myne and the king are not bad people! This is all a misunderstanding!"

Motoyasu had been standing in silence for a little while, but he finally stepped forward and stated screaming again.

What did he want?

"But everything makes sense, doesn't it? We were nearly killed, and the facts behind all these events have come to light and been proven."

"Yeah. We looked into all sorts of things. I got suspicious. It really does seem like Naofumi has been discriminated against. It's actually very impressive that he was able to earn the trust of anyone at all. None of that was due to anything like a Brain Washing Shield. It is all because of Naofumi and his friends. They earned people's trust."

Itsuki and Ren both spoke up on my behalf.

"When I accidentally unleashed an epidemic on that village in the mountains, it was Naofumi that cleaned it up. That is plenty of reason to trust him."

"Yes, and if you saw the weapon that the high priest was using against us, it's clear enough who was behind all of this."

"Ugh…."

Motoyasu's fingers were curled into a shaking fist. He was still glaring at me.

"Mr. Kitamura, if you wish to protest further, you will have to do so after you are able to provide some proof of your assertions."

"Fine. I'll be right back with proof. Myne! Let's go.

"Unfortunately, I haven't finished speaking with Malty. You will have to wait until we are finished here."

When the queen finished speaking, a large number of castle knights appeared behind the throne and began walking towards him.

"Bu…But! But Myne!"

"Spear Hero, please step outside."

They were very polite as they motioned for him to leave the throne room.

I hoped he wasn't so stupid as to cause a ruckus in the throne room.

"Stop changing the subject."

"I'm very sorry."

"It's really Motoyasu's fault, so I wouldn't worry about it."

Itsuki seemed to have some suspicions that Motoyasu was receiving preferential treatment. I didn't see a reason to correct him.

"Anyway… There are still many punishments I need to heap upon my husband and daughter."

Bitch and Trash were both pale. It was time to pay the piper.

"Are you disappointed?"

"Of course!"

"Yes! Mama! I'm not bad!"

"I believe I already disowned you, so please stop calling me mother. As for what to do with you… Ah, yes, perhaps I'll have you pay off some of the country's debts. Here you are."

The queen paused for a beat.

She handed Bitch of sheet of paper with a number written on it. Bitch's face went even paler.

Bitch was true to her nature. Apparently she'd been loose with the country's purse strings too. I can't say I'm surprised though.

"How am I supposed to pay this?!"

"That is the amount of money you asked the guild for. You cannot just take what you want from the treasury and not be expected to return it. I also took the liberty of adding the funds that were necessary to put out the forest fires you started. Just as that paper says, you will now work like a slave to pay off your debts to the Crown."

"But that's impossible!"

"If you don't like it, then work with the Heroes to save the world. If you actually contribute, then I'll think about it."

Bitch finally shut up, so the queen turned to Trash.

"And look at you, feeling so safe that your daughter is the only one in trouble! All this goes for you too, Aultcray."

Trash was so shocked he stumbled forward. The damn fool couldn't even raise his head to the queen.

Couldn't he behave a little more kingly?

"You will either fight for the future of our country on the frontlines against the waves, or abandon your responsibilities and become a normal adventurer. Make your choice."

"Ugh… My wife… My QUEEN. I was deceived. That is all. Please have mercy."

And who deceived him? The Church? Or me? Was he about to throw Bitch under the bus?

"Yes, Mama, forgive me…"

"I'm all out of mercy and forgiveness… Ah, I have an idea."

The queen beckoned for me. I quickly stepped forward.

"Mr. Iwatani. How should we punish these two? I give you the right to decide."

"Death! Put them to death!"

Chapter Twelve: Paying the Piper

I said it without even stopping to think. My subconscious must have hated them as much as I did—seemed natural enough.

Honestly though, there wasn't really another option besides death. What else could finally rid me of my hate for them?

"Death, hmm? Well, considering all the trouble they've caused, it does seem appropriate."

"Yeah, and they really mucked things up for Melromarc on the international scene."

Ren and Itsuki were coldly calculating.

It was easy to be calculating about other people's business. As long as they didn't have to be held responsible for what they said, they could say whatever they wanted.

"But you! You…"

"You better be joking!"

The queen raised a hand, and they shut up.

"If we have them executed, will you truly be satisfied?"

I had the strange feeling that the queen's magic was flowing towards me.

This is what people mean when they say that shivers go up

and down their spine. "Ominous…" The word came to me and described the feeling perfectly.

"Of course they may be killed. However, there are other options as well. We could torture them, let them think they will be freed, and once their freedom seems secured, and a smile crosses their faces, THEN we kill them."

"You're… actually—go on."

"I'm saying that simply executing them is boring. We could also give them simple jobs, and when they learn to make themselves useful, we could keep them around like pets… domesticating them to death. I'd enjoy that."

To think that she could consider the disposal of her own family members without emotion… The queen might be the darkest person in the whole country.

"Do you think that she's really been behind all of this? She looks capable of it."

"You're right. That was seriously cold."

The stupid heroes kept changing the subject!

"Anyway, these are simply suggestions. I'll say no more about the matter. Those were my final emotions."

"Oh, I think I follow you."

She was saying that I could do whatever I wanted, but that she didn't want them killed. She'd punish them in some other way.

"After all the evil actions of the Church, it would cause

quite a stir if the queen were to exercise her authority to kill off members of her own royal lineage. I believe it would have an effect on our standing in the international community."

"On the other hand, after all the trouble these worthless cretins caused, maybe crucifying them would send a message to the community that we are serious."

"Shield… You bastard!"

Trash was screaming, but the queen ignored him and spoke.

"Normally I would agree with you. But I don't think that is applicable in Aultcray's case."

"Why not?

"This fool used to be quite impressive. In the past his deeds won acclaim all over the world. He was, and may still be, respected by others. If we were to kill him…"

I don't know what Trash had done to distinguish himself— but whatever. I understood what she was saying.

He was too famous.

Besides, he'd been exercising royal authority this whole time. He was too well known.

Apparently he'd been a respected warrior in the past and had proved himself in many battles. The people that had worked with him and fought with him wouldn't stay quiet if they discovered he'd been executed.

It might be interesting to see how it all developed. If Trash used to be a hero, then he dirtied his hands and still had to go on living without the respect that he used to bathe in, it might be interesting to watch it all unfold from above.

"Understood. We'll go with your idea then."

"Thank you."

"—On one condition. They can live, but they have to suffer."

"Naturally… Now then, what should their first punishment be?"

Yeah… I could do anything except kill them…

"We could start by ripping off their hands and feet…"

"Mr. Naofumi…"

Raphtalia was looking at me like she wanted to say something.

She was probably thinking that, while I had the authority to order such a thing, and while they deserved it, I should probably hold back a little.

What to do…

Besides, if I let them off the hook now, how could I be sure I'd get another chance?

"…Mr. NaoFUMI."

Bitch wiped away her tears and pleaded with me. The way she'd pronounced my name was different than Raphtalia or Melty's intonation. What was she trying to say?

Her eyes were filled with tears. They were sparkling. Her cheeks flushed red. It really did look like the depth of her sins was beginning to sink in.

She was a real actress when she needed to be. If I didn't already know who she was, I'd have been fooled.

She probably used this routine on Motoyasu.

I suddenly realized that was the first time she'd ever called me by name.

"Please don't do anything as foolish as to look for revenge. Revenge only breeds further revenge. If you, Mr. NaoFUMI, could bear to show mercy, then I'm sure the queen would be grateful…"

"Whoa…"

Ren was looking at Bitch like he couldn't believe his ears. Itsuki was shocked too. He scratched his head in confusion. Melty held her head in her hands and stared at the floor. Raphtalia rolled her eyes in disbelief. Filo was… Filo cocked her head to the side in bewilderment.

As for myself…

…hm.

"Well…"

Later that day, soldiers mounted their horses, Filolials, and dragons. They rode whatever they had and were dispatched to all the villages and towns in the kingdom to deliver a message.

"To take responsibility for all the terrible things that have happened in Melromarc, from now until infinity, King Aultcray and Princess Malty shall be known by the names 'Trash' and

'Bitch.' Anyone who calls them by their previous names, for whatever reason, will be swiftly punished!"

They printed this on signs and fliers and bulletins and had them distributed and posted in all the cities, towns, and villages of Melromarc.

The citizens, irrespective of their place in society, all stood before the announcements and said the same thing:

"What?"

"What kind of idiot could put up with such a thing? You idiot!"

"What are you doing? You demon!"

Bitch's face was all twisted up in rage.

From now on, when people spoke of these two they'd say things like, "So Bitch was…," or "How about Trash…?"

It felt great. I never thought I'd get to see this.

"You earned it…"

"I think so too. It's true that the punishment is terrible, but it also seems just."

Ren and Itsuki couldn't keep themselves from commenting.

"You bastard!"

Trash's red race grew even redder, and he shouted in anger.

"Ahahaha! Now THAT's the face I wanted to see this whole time!"

Finally, the whole world would call him by my private nickname for him: Trash.

"'Revenge only breeds more revenge… bear it?' Such beautiful worlds—I suggest you take your own advice, Princess Ma…. I mean, Bitch."

"Shut up! I'll never forgive you!"

She looked like she was ready to come swinging punches at me, but the queen's guards wouldn't let that happen.

"Don't forget that Bitch also had a fake name for adventuring. What shall we do about that name?"

"Whore."

"Whore…?"

Ren and Itsuki said nothing. They seemed to be a little offended. Guess I couldn't blame them.

"Very well, I will register the new name as her adventurer's title. She'll no longer be able to use the name 'Myne' to register for quests or stay at inns."

"I'll kill you! If you turn your back, I'll kill you!"

She was furious—seething. But I felt so good. Her little outburst couldn't bother me.

"You're welcome to try. If you attack me, you'll be put to death."

"Yes, she has lost all of her rights. If she acts out, the slave seal will kill her."

I saw what she was saying. It would cause issues if the queen were to execute a member of the royal family. That is why she disowned Bitch first and changed her name. Then she would be free to kill her without worrying about the backlash. It was smart, efficient. I liked it.

Not only that, but it came with a rule that Bitch wasn't allowed to attack me. She must have wanted Bitch to know how it felt to be me—unable to attack.

"Now, now... don't you think you've taken this too far?"

Itsuki spoke up. I didn't care.

"Nope! It feels great!"

"Now then, to fully earn Mr. Iwatani's cooperation, we'll have to fulfill his old request, won't we?

"What do you mean?"

"Before all this happened you told Trash to crawl down before you on his hands and knees, did you not?"

The queen clapped her hands, and shadows and knights appeared behind Trash. They seized him by the shoulders and forced him and Bitch to their knees.

"Hey now, wait just a second! Just who do you think I am?!"

"Yes, I am the ki...."

"An adventurer and a soldier, am I right?"

The queen spoke down to them where they kneeled on the floor. She made them understand their new positions.

"Now bow to us. Of course, you too, Bitch. If you disobey, the slave seal will hurt you."

"But... My Queen! I... No... I won't bow! I wonnnnnnn't!"

"You must be joking. Why would I bow to him?

I….AHHHHHHH! OUCH!"

The knight grabbed the back of their heads and forced them down until their foreheads scraped the ground.

Bitch was furious. Even though the slave seal was burning into her, she still resisted.

They kneeled with their heads on the floor, surrounded by shadows, and continued to scream.

"Please…"

"AAARRRRHRHHH!"

"AAAAAHHHHH!"

Trash and Bitch were screaming to keep anyone else from talking.

"Shut up!"

The queen snapped, and Trash and Bitch were immediately gagged.

"MMMMGHHMMMM!"

"MMMMUUUUUHHHH!"

They used all their remaining strength to resist, but they weren't able to put up much of a fight.

"'Please! Shield Hero! Please help us!' Just like that."

"'Shield Hero! Please fight for our country!'"

There were some excellent impressions of those two happening.

"How's this?"

"What do you mean you were…?"

It felt so good to see the two of them forced to bow to me. It felt great, but…

I mean it REALLY felt good, but it wasn't exactly what I wanted.

"They don't seem repentant, do they? I guess there's no choice…"

"Are you sure this isn't taking it too far?"

Ren and Itsuki were whispering to each other.

I didn't see a reason to stop it. Everyone needed to see who the real bad guys were here. They needed to understand.

Bitch and Trash were screaming and protesting so violently. It almost looked like they were going to have heart attacks and die right there.

Eventually they calmed down and shut up. Their gags were removed.

Bitch looked like… she looked like she'd been raped. Her eyes were just staring off absentmindedly, and thin streams of tears fell down her cheeks.

Did she hate me that much? Did she hate to kneel so much?

Ren walked over to Trash and waved his hand before his face. Trash didn't react because he wasn't able to see. Having confirmed this, Ren returned to where he had been standing. Bitch was still whining.

"Perhaps this is enough torture for these two."

The queen raised a hand and shouted an order.

"Remove them from the throne room!"

"Yes!"

The two of them were taken out of the room.

After they were gone, I turned to see Raphtalia looking at me disappointedly. Melty seemed upset too. Filo was smiling and having a good time. But it seemed like they had revised their opinions on me.

They didn't say anything, but they looked like they thought I'd taken it all too far.

"And that will end their punishment for the time being. Mr. Amaki, Mr. Kawasumi, and their parties will find rooms prepared for them in the castle. Please rest. I still have some matters I would like to discuss with Mr. Iwatani, so I request that he remains behind."

"Ah… ah."

"I would rather not put my faith in people that behave that way but…"

"Wait. Compared to the state they put this country in, this punishment is too mild. It might seem like a lot, but that is only because you were standing here to witness it."

"That might be true."

Ren and Itsuki were discussing the day's events as they left the room with their parties.

"Now that we have punished them in this way, I would like to ask for your cooperation, Mr. Iwatani."

"Well…"

I couldn't think of a good reason to refuse her.

Still, was it wise to trust someone that would treat her own family this way? They DID deserve it, though. It was all their fault. You reap what you sow.

"What shall we discuss first? I've got an idea. Let's talk about the Heroes from legend, shall we?"

The queen began speaking.

"I'm actually quite fond of the legend of the four Holy Heroes. It's a little different than my own country's legends, though…"

"How so?"

"Mr. Iwatani, I believe you've discussed these things with Melty. May I assume you have a basic understanding?"

I nodded.

"Well then, as you already know, the Shield Hero does not appear in this country's legends. He was permanently deleted from the stories, and people speak of him as though he were a demon."

"…Uh huh."

The book I'd been reading before I was summoned to this world, *The Records of the Four Holy Weapons*, had no information in it about the Shield Hero. It had been completely blank.

I'd figured that the pages were blank because I had been summoned to fill them in… but could it be that the book had simply been a recording of Melromarc's version of the legend?

Something didn't seem right. I didn't think that my guess was accurate, but I guess I'd have to just go with it for the time being.

"The Shield Hero worked with both the humans and the demi-humans. Because of that, there were many times when the other Heroes considered him an enemy. In the end, however, they were able to reconcile."

Now things were making sense. If that was part of the legend, then it would explain why demi-humans had been so willing to trust me.

"As you know, Melromarc is a human-supremacist nation. We did prepare a special district where the demi-humans could live in peace, but they had very difficult lives."

"Uh huh…"

I'd been in this world for more than three months now. I knew that the demi-humans were basically slaves in Melromarc.

"Because of these things, our relationship with Siltvelt is very bad. Our nations have fought many wars."

The situation was the opposite in Siltvelt, where humans were considered a slave class. Melromarc and Siltvelt were like water and oil.

It only made sense for them to be at each other's throats.

"Now, as you may be aware, Siltvelt's religion also branched off from the Church of the Four Heroes, but instead of worshiping three Heroes, they worship the Shield Hero exclusively."

"I had guessed as much. Seems I was right."

"Yes... Now as for how the Church of the Three Heroes came to be... I imagine that you've already figured that out, haven't you, Mr. Iwatani?"

The original church of the four heroes had branched in two different directions in Melromarc and Siltvelt. In Melromarc it had become the Church of the Three Heroes, while in Siltvelt it became the Church of the Shield.

The queen said that the countries had been at war for a long time, which would mean that...

"I was summoned right into the center of enemy lands?"

I was the saint of their enemy. Who could be expected to treat the saint of their enemy with respect? Humans were not so pure.

The old books of the Church of the Three Heroes were, no doubt, filled with lists of the evil actions performed by the Shield Hero. Similar things happened in my own world. The god of an enemy religion came to be seen as a demon.

It all fit.

Could it be that Trash was prejudiced against me because of the wars he'd fought in Siltvelt?

"The investigations have concluded that all of this trouble was the result of actions taken by the Church, but those actions have also undone much of my hard work."

"You have my sympathy."

"Thank you."

"Yes… Melty, you understand all this, don't you?"

"Y… yes!"

"The major problem remains. When the four Heroes are summoned, there is an important ceremony that is performed that is commensurate to the gravity of the situation."

"But all four heroes were summoned."

"Yes… that is why this problem is so significant."

"If it is such a big problem, why don't the other countries attack Melromarc?"

"Because of my negotiations… though I cannot take all the credit. Much of it is because of your actions, and because of the other Heroes."

"Mother worked so hard. She ran a fever. That's how hard she was working!"

"Melty."

"W… what?"

"Don't be so stiff. Relax a little. You're freaking me out."

"What was that?!"

"Ah… it seems that Melty has finally begun to act appropriately for her age. As her mother, I'm very happy. I certainly won't compare her to her sister, but Melty has cared about the public eye since she was very young. It made it difficult for her to be herself."

"Mother, that's not it!"

"Until you grow up and find yourself, perhaps you should stick with Mr. Iwatani."

"Mother!"

Melty was very angry. She'd really stopped the conversation in its tracks though.

"Why didn't the Church kill me earlier?"

"I believe they wanted the other three Heroes to do it for them."

"So they were waiting for the other three Heroes to be strong enough?"

"I cannot think of a better way to put this, but… the other Heroes sometimes don't seem to think of the future very much. The Church undoubtedly thought they would be easy to control."

"Ah… yeah, I can see that."

The whole lot of them still couldn't get out of the gaming mindset. It was plain as day they'd been deceived, but they didn't adjust to the situation. They never doubted what was right before their eyes.

"Of course, there was a lot for us to do as well, especially regarding you, Mr. Iwatani. Many, many people from the international community begged to meet you."

"That's…"

I remembered that Melty had said something like that.

When I was out on my luck, naked and beaten and alone, people had approached me, and I told them to stay away. The queen realized that I knew what she meant and nodded.

"Because of which, I was able to see through quite a lot of deception."

"What do you mean?"

"I told the council that the Heroes were busy expunging a disease from our country."

To keep the world from war in times like these... she must have worked very hard.

Back in my own world, when I had managed a guild for an online game I played, there had been times when other guild members would throw fits.

It took all I had to put out the fires they'd started. Normally I would have just fired them, but I wasn't able to according to the rules. The queen must have felt the same way.

"When Mr. Iwatani went around the country cleaning up the messes left by other Heroes, that was the final straw."

The other heroes had caused problems, and I had fixed them. That caused the populace to doubt their faith in the Church.

"The other heroes didn't know why only I was being discriminated against?"

"Kitamura was working with Bitch, and Mr. Amaki and Mr. Kawasumi received all of their information from the guild.

People tend to believe in the authority of the people around them. They accept what they are told."

So they would just believe what authority figures told them... I suppose if you didn't have access to any other information, then that was a natural thing to do.

If they'd known that they were being lied to, they would have supported me.

They just didn't know. That's why they looked so thoughtless. Yeah, Ren and Itsuki seemed to have figured it out, eventually.

"When I had finally calmed everyone down and was ready to come back to Melromarc, all of this happened. I never would have imagined that the Church had a replica of the four Holy Weapons."

How could she have known? Who would have expected the Church to have something like that?

"The high priest was a foolish man... When you attacked, he could have turned the weapon into the Shield and survived..."

"So that thing could turn into a shield too?"

"That's correct, though you cannot expect more than one-quarter the power of the real thing."

"So that was only a quarter of its true power?"

If we leveled up, we'd be four times as powerful as the high priest had been? That was hard to believe.

It was just a legend after all. I'm sure that with time a little embellishment had... Wait, thinking back on Fitoria's power made it seem more likely.

Honestly—we were all probably a little too weak to begin with.

If we didn't find some way to level up soon, we'd never survive the coming waves.

"Trash's actions have threatened to end a long period of peace. He was a skilled man, but it seems all he knows how to do is aggravate conflict."

He must have really wanted to keep me out of Siltvelt. That's why he had increased the border security so much.

"Finally... Yes, I wish to do whatever I can to support you going forward. Knowing that, would you still like to go to Siltvelt, tell them the truth, and start a war?"

"Hmm..."

That meant that, if she wanted to avoid war, the queen would have to do whatever she could to protect me.

But to be honest, I really just wanted to say "goodbye" and leave. But I'd promised Fitoria...

And the Curse Series had been so powerful that I couldn't ignore the things Fitoria had said.

"Also, whether it be Siltvelt or Shieldfreeden, shall I tell you what would happen if you were to go pay them a visit?"

"Hm?"

"First the princess and noble daughters would all demand audiences with you. The demi-human women would form a harem around you."

"Ew!"

They'd come after me, wanting to have the Shield Hero's child? After what Bitch had done, the thought of women repulsed me.

The last thing I needed in my life was more unsavory women.

"Certainly, they will give you whatever you wish. If you told them to attack Melromarc, they would rally behind you and march to their deaths."

That didn't sound so bad, but this harem business…

Could I just stick it out? But… if I wanted to survive until the end of this thing, I was going to need the cooperation of the other heroes. Should I ask them to come with me? Would they even agree to?

"All of that would, theoretically, be fine. But remember that no matter what country you go to, those in power and those who manipulate the people's beliefs have black hearts."

"What?"

"'Poor Mr. Iwatani, stricken suddenly by such powerful sicknesses…'"

"I see your point."

"It happened to one of the past Shield Heroes."

I didn't want to know about that.

She was saying that the people might worship the Shield Hero, but those with power—those with something to lose—

wouldn't be happy if I just got whatever I wanted.

I suppose that made sense too. Who would want some random guy from another world to show up in their borders and start changing everything?

I understood where they were coming from, but I also didn't want to die. What options did I have?

"By the way, it seems like you were approached by some adventurers with some false requests…"

"Yeah."

It happened a couple of days after I was summoned. People said they'd join my party, but I'd have to pay them. I had let the balloons settle that matter.

"A couple days after your meeting, their corpses were found—horribly maimed."

"What?!"

More things I'd rather not have heard…

"Furthermore, within a few days a knight's guard was attacked by a number of people and killed. We have not found those responsible. It may be that…"

Siltvelt was an extreme country.

It sounded like both heaven and hell were waiting for me if I were to go there.

Of course, that was only if everything the queen said was true.

"Therefore, I believe that it is safer for you to stay here, as you have finally earned the trust of the people."

"..."

I didn't really want to cooperate.

All the pain and suffering I'd been through wasn't going to somehow disappear just because the queen commanded it.

Even if the queen had been directly involved in Trash and Bitch's punishment, she was only doing what was natural and expected of her as the country's leader.

Now she'd act like she'd done me a favor and ask for my cooperation? Things were too easy for her.

Besides, I respected her abilities—but that didn't mean that I trusted her.

It was easy to say whatever she wanted to.

The truth was that she didn't want me to visit the other countries.

Still, if what she said was true, then I could expect a warm welcome from any foreign country, not just from Siltvelt or Shieldfreeden.

There wasn't anything special about Melromarc.

"..."

I was thinking over all she'd said when the queen kneeled before me.

"Everything that has happened to you up until now has been my fault—my responsibility. I understand that it sounds as if I am asking too much of you."

She lowered her head to me, deeply.

Melty was completely speechless. Raphtalia was watching with wide-eyed amazement. Even Filo seemed to understand that something important was happening.

"But please understand. I don't... No, this country doesn't have any other option left than to rely on you. If taking my head would soothe your anger, then take it. If changing my name would soothe your anger, then you may do so."

"Mother..."

"So please, show forgiveness. From now on I will prevent you from being treated unfairly. I swear it on my name: Mirellia Q. Melromarc. I will sign a magical contract."

This woman...

She'd use her authority to keep Bitch and Trash from being killed then turn around and offer her own life?

Had she offered me Bitch's or Trash's head, I might have thought about for a minute—but I didn't really want to see the queen die.

Melromarc must have really been in a bad situation.

She meant to say that the future of the country depended on... me?

If I wanted to, I could rally the world against them and burn this country to the ground.

But...

"Only once."

"What do you mean?"

"One of your shadows jumped in to save us. And because you helped us put an end to the high priest."

"Which means…"

"I'll trust you—but only once. However, and no matter what happens, I won't trust you after that."

"Thank you."

She bowed to me once more, deeply, and expressed her gratitude.

Was I being weak?

But if I continued to doubt everything, I'd never move forward.

I remembered what Fitoria had said.

There was no time for the heroes to fight with each other. That huge Legendary Filolial would come kill us all if we kept fighting.

The heroes' enemy wasn't a country. It was the waves.

If countries went to war, only to be wiped out by a wave, then none of it meant anything.

And I certainly couldn't forget that, for all intents and purposes, the heroes had lost the concluding battle during the last wave.

There was no reason to make more enemies.

I'd been surrounded by enemies this whole time, but now that was about to change.

I didn't care about what happened to this world, but the only way I could get back to my own world was if I defeated the waves.

I had to focus on the waves… On Glass.

Just realizing that was a big step forward.

The queen rose to her feet and covered her mouth with her folding fan.

"Can you please keep our conversation a secret from the other three Heroes? A Hero, too, is someone's child. If they hear that one of them is receiving preferential treatment…"

She was right. There were plenty of points in the conversation that I'd rather the other heroes didn't know about.

I don't know about Ren or Motoyasu, but it seemed like Itsuki might throw a fit.

Besides, barring any further dramatic developments, it seemed like my lot had greatly improved.

"Fine. I won't tell…"

"Yes. Thank you. I will accept responsibility for future management of this issue."

"Is that so? Then I can finally cross one enemy off of my list…"

"I'm so very sorry. You were summoned here despite having nothing to do with our conflicts… Then you were forced to fight. I wish I could do more for you, but my hands are tied for now. Forgive me."

"That's enough of that. Let's focus on the next step. You said we needed to discuss something with the other three."

"Yes, but I would like you to be part of the conversation.

So let's discuss it at dinner tonight."

"Okay."

Epilogue: Friends Forever

The queen gave orders to her subordinates before walking to the stairs behind the throne.

"Melty… I'm leaving"

"Oh, um… Okay."

Melty looked at me before answering.

"Thank you for protecting me…"

She continued, but was speaking so quietly it was nearly a whisper. Could she have said, "Sorry for not being myself"?

I'm not deaf or anything…. but she could speak up a little. So I made her say it again.

"Huh? What was that?"

"Sigh. If I stick with you, I'll never be safe—so this is a relief."

"What was that?"

Who did she think she was? Oh yeah… a princess.

Melty turned to Raphtalia.

"Hey, don't ignore me!"

"Ms. Raphtalia. Thank you for protecting me. I will work with my mother to do whatever we can to have your village rebuilt. Please look forward to that."

"Yes. Thank you."

"This whole time that I was traveling with you, I've been thinking how much I want this country to be a safe place for both humans and demi-humans to live together. I'll change it. I promise."

"Hey, I'm not done talking! Melty!"

"Naofumi—you're so noisy."

What was that? Before I could yell back she had already turned to Filo. I kept quiet.

...Because that strong-willed Melty was breaking down in tears.

"What's wrong, Mel?! Are you hurt?"

"Not really... No, I'm fine—so don't worry about me, Filo. Hey, Filo. I can't... I can't stay with you anymore."

"Are you going somewhere, Mel?"

Filo could tell that something was wrong. She made a sad face.

"Melty lives in a different world than we do. She can't keep traveling with us the way she has been."

We couldn't just take the future queen around on our adventures.

"Is that true?"

Filo looked like she was ready to start crying too.

"... Yes."

"We can't see each other anymore?"

"No, we'll meet again plenty of times. But I don't think we can travel together anymore."

Melty turned around to look at the queen.

The queen nodded silently.

"So… So we're splitting up?"

"Yes. But, Filo, I can see you any time you come to the castle."

Melty's voice wavered as she spoke.

Melty had really influenced our travels. Everything changed after we met.

"No! I… I want to be with Mel! Master!"

"You got what you originally wanted. Melty is safe. You can't ask for more than that."

"But…!"

"Filo, you can't be selfish."

"U…"

Filo was rubbing her hands, very upset. Melty reached for them.

"I know it hasn't been that long… but I don't know. I feel like I've known you forever."

"Mel…"

"I'm very sad to be leaving you, Filo. But there are so many things waiting for you that only you can do. And there are things for me here, things that only I can do."

"But… but I want to stay with you, Mel! Wah…"

"Filo."

Filo started to cry, and Melty reached out to touch her face.

"It will be okay. If you ever want to see me, I'll be here. I'll be waiting for you, Filo, because you're my friend. My best friend!"

"Even if we can't be together, you'll always be my friend, right?!"

"Of course! No matter where we go, I'll always be your friend."

"Promise?"

"Promise!"

We hadn't been traveling together for all that long, but Filo and Melty had really bonded. At the beginning, Filo had been selfish, a real hungry pig. But Mel had taught her what friendship really was—being there for someone else.

Filo had made a good friend. It was important—these friendships.

I decided that, when the waves were done and gone, I'd give Filo to Melty.

Melty would treat her well, and I knew that Filo would be good to Melty too.

They'd made good friends—both of them.

We were watching the two of them say goodbye when Raphtalia reached for my hand and squeezed it.

I didn't say anything, but I squeezed her hand back. Everything was going well.

I felt like I'd finally made it to the starting line.

Thinking back on it all, after I'd been framed, expelled, and discriminated against… nothing had gone well for me at all.

But things were changing.

I'd be as involved in things as the other heroes… if not more so.

And I had one less enemy to worry about. But the real problem of the waves hadn't changed at all.

Still, I had to believe that everything was better than it had been. I wanted to believe it was better.

"Well…"

—I did believe it.

Looking at my friends, I believed it.

Extra Bonus Chapter: The Fearful Filolial

"Whoa… That monster is STRONG!"

"…"

Fitoria was fighting back the monsters when they came surging from the wave.

"Should we retreat?!"

"Do you think we can?"

Fitoria reared back and kicked a monster as it appeared from the wave.

"Guuuah!"

She kicked it too hard. But the monster was really tough. It didn't actually fall down but disappeared back into the wave.

Had it been a normal person, it would have died on the spot. But it seemed to have survived… I guess.

It seemed like it was formed from pure energy. Fitoria thought about using her weapon, but it wasn't strong enough to handle her attacks.

The wave grew silent, and the rifts began to close.

This was one of the waves from the dragon hourglass that Fitoria was in charge of managing.

That was Fitoria's duty, to face down the waves that happened in areas that humans were not able to enter.

It's what the past heroes asked of her.

"Whew…"

"Fitoria! We've finished pushing back the monsters!"

One of her Filolial subordinates ran forward and saluted

before declaring that all the monsters had been dealt with.

"Good work."

Fitoria looked at the place where the wave had occurred.

Why didn't the four Holy Heroes come to fight the waves?

Fitoria really needed to look into that... If she didn't, how could she protect the world?

She'd heard from her subordinate that the Heroes had been summoned. But it didn't seem like they were doing anything.

For the time being, Fitoria could just focus on keeping the monsters out of her own area, but if the Heroes weren't going to stop the waves that happened in the human-controlled areas then she wouldn't be able to do everything herself.

If they had been summoned, what were they doing?

Who knew?

"This isn't good!"

"Hm?"

When Fitoria had travelled the world in secret, she'd met a strange young girl. The subordinate she'd entrusted the girl too had just come running up.

"Did you see her off safely?"

It had been a young girl that wanted to be friends with Fitoria so badly she'd walked right into a dragon nest. Fitoria had fought to protect her.

It was a very rare thing these days. Normally humans just wanted to control all the other living things around them.

They used Filolials like they were tools, and refused to acknowledge that there were forces out there more powerful than themselves.

Fitoria had gone through times in the past when she'd had to deal with them. It had been a real pain.

The Hero had said, with his dying breath, that they were all supposed to work together to protect the world. But the humans had forgotten, and they tried to do away with Fitoria and the others...

If there weren't any Heroes, there was no point in protecting the humans.

"Ah, I... I forgot!"

Sigh... why didn't any of Fitoria's friends have good memories?

Fitoria put her head in her hands.

"What did you all leave for?"

"We... We..."

"We... what? What? If you can't do your jobs, I'll have to get rid of you."

To be removed from Fitoria's clan was like a death sentence to a Filolial.

Fitoria was in charge of all the wild Filolials.

If you were kicked out of Fitoria's clan, you weren't even a Filolial anymore.

All they could expect was a rough death. That's how strong Fitoria's protection was.

"N... No! Anything but that! Please forgive us!"

"... And? What isn't good?"

"That's right... We saw someone out there that looks like you!"

Fitoria felt the feather on her head move.

If a Filolial grew into a Filolial Queen form, like Fitoria, that meant a Hero had raised her.

It meant that there was proof that Fitoria's successor had been born.

And it meant that the Heroes really had returned.

"What did she look like? What color was she?"

The first thing Fitoria had to figure out was what the Filolial looked like.

"Um... she was white! And there was water running out of her mouth."

"That's not it! She was kind of red! And she had a bunch of hands!"

"She was pink! And she had a bunch of heads all over."

"Are you sure she was a Filolial?"

Fitoria tried to imagine the next Filolial Queen. She was red and white and pink and had a bunch of heads and a bunch of arms.

It would be scary to be attacked by such a thing.

"Uh..."

Fitoria held her head and slowly sat down.

This thing they had described didn't sound like a Filolial at all!

But maybe such things could happen if a Hero had raised her. A Hero had raised Fitoria, and she looked different than the other normal Filolials did.

Did it mean that that was what the Hero wanted? Or maybe she was some kind of mixed breed.

Fitoria didn't want to meet a Filolial Queen with a bunch of heads and a bunch of arms.

She didn't want something like that to become queen either. She didn't want that thing to take over her job.

And besides, Fitoria wasn't scary like that.

If she was supposed to be like Fitoria, she would probably look like Fitoria. It would be weird if she was some other kind of creature.

"What should we do, Queeeeeen?"

A subordinate was asking.

Better not look uncertain.

"Hm..."

Fitoria had just started wondering what the Heroes were up to, so this would be a good time to go see.

"I will go to meet with this Filolial Queen candidate. Let's prepare!"

"Roger!"

And so Fitoria turned into a normal Filolial shape, and set

off for Melromarc, which is where her subordinates said that they had seen the new Filolial Queen.

"What should we do?"

"People will be suspicious if they see us all together like this. Let's all split up and look for the Hero."

"OKAAAAAY!"

After giving orders to the subordinates, Fitoria began to investigate.

The best idea she had was to just ask a domesticated Filolial.

Domesticated Filolials spent most of their time with humans, so they should know what the humans were up to.

They were different from wild Filolials.

So Fitoria went to a Filolial farm, stuck her head over the fence, and asked the closest Filolial.

The Filolial was very black, though, and had an evil look in its eyes.

Was that a name-tag around its neck? In human writing it said: BLACK THUNDER.

"Hey."

"Huh? What the hell? You think you can just talk to Black Thunder?"

The black Filolial was fuming as he looked Fitoria up and down.

"You're kind of cute, though. What do you say? If you

want to stick with me I could have my master make you my concubine."

It didn't seem like the black Filolial really understood Filolial relations.

From the back of the pen another older Filolial came running over in a fluster.

Fitoria would have to show them their place.

She raised one leg and transformed only it, so it grew really big very quickly, slamming it into the other Filolial.

"Fube...."

"You shouldn't speak to a nice lady that way. Keep that up, and it will be the end of you."

Whoops. That hit had made a pretty good sound. She had better use restorative magic.

"Ahhhhhhhhhhh!"

Black Thunder ran off with his tail between his legs.

"You are the Queen! Please, clam your anger..."

The older Filolial bowed his head.

"Very well. I'm not that mad anyway. But I must point out that that Filolial is in dire need of an education."

"I'm sure he is already reflecting on that."

"Good..."

Fitoria received some food from the older Filolial. It wasn't very good.

But it was food she hadn't tasted in a long time, and it made her feel nostalgic.

Over the years she'd forgotten that the humans knew how to make some delicious food.

Fitoria's old Hero master used to make her food all the time. It had been very good.

"I heard that a Hero came through here with a queen candidate. Have you heard about them or seen them?"

"About that…"

The old Filolial explained to Fitoria all that he had heard about the Heroes since they had been summoned.

The Shield Hero had committed crimes and was on the run? He had a blue-haired girl with him?

But all that was some kind of conspiracy?

Hm…

"And what does that have to do with the queen candidate?"

"Right now, the only Hero raising a Filolial is the Shield Hero. I've seen him myself. He seemed like a good person."

"Really?"

"The Filolial was pink?"

"Did she have a lot of heads and arms?"

"No, just the normal amount of both."

Those stupid subordinates had been wrong!

"Do you know where they went?"

"Not really."

"Okay. Well, thank you."

"Come by anytime!"

She left the old Filolial behind and met back up with her subordinates.

They had gathered information too. It sounded like the weirdoes were all on the run towards the southwest.

So Fitoria decided to go to the southwest too.

Where WAS the southwest?

She was thinking it over, when…

"GYAOOOOOOOOOOOOOOO!"

Her feathers stood on end. Her instinct told her that it was the roar of a dragon.

She turned to see a vicious monster with the Dragon King's Fragment crash through the wall of a human town.

Ahead of the monster was… a pink Filolial Queen. And a man with a shield was riding on her back.

She'd found them. Without stopping to think, Fitoria took off running after them.

Squinting to follow them, she was overcome with nostalgia.

Yes, it was the day she'd been born. The hero had looked down on her and smiled.

She almost felt that warm, that all-encompassing warmth, again.

There was no doubting it. That man with the Shield was a Hero.

But Fitoria could feel something else. He had a deep sadness and anger within himself. He must have used the Curse Series.

The curse from a Hero's weapon was very powerful. Fitoria had seen it many times.

But they had to sacrifice much to use it. They ended up really hurting themselves.

There was no doubt in her mind. The deep sadness and pain that he harbored had unlocked the Curse Series.

She wanted to heal his pain. She wanted to help him.

For a moment, she'd gotten sentimental. She quickly blinked and snapped out of it. She was as cold as ice.

This world didn't have time for sentiment.

She watched from a distance as the Shield Hero, his party, and his pink Filolial faced down the dragon monster.

That pink girl must have been the queen candidate.

Of course, she only had one head. They were different sizes and colors, but the candidate really did look like Fitoria.

But, watching her fight, Fitoria didn't think that she looked very strong.

It made Fitoria nervous.

"Sanctuary."

Fitoria cast a spell that would prevent anyone from leaving the battleground.

She had so many questions.

Why hadn't he been helping fight the waves around the world? What were the other Heroes doing?

The world needed the Heroes. There wasn't time for them

to run around a single country.

In the worst case scenario… No, she didn't want to do it—but she could. She could dirty her hands for the sake of the world.

Because Fitoria had promised… a long time ago, Fitoria had promised her Hero…

Character Design:
The High Priest

三勇教シンボル

教皇

Character Design:
The Queen

Character Design:
Fitoria (human form)

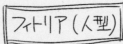

フィドリア（クイーン型）

フィトリア (フィロリアル型)

Character Design:
Myne

マイン

The Rising of the Shield Hero Vol. 4
© Aneko Yusagi 2013
First published by KADOKAWA in 2013 in Japan.
English translation rights arranged by One Peace Books
under the license from KADOKAWA CORPORATION, Japan

ISBN: 978-1-935548-65-2

Written by Aneko Yusagi
Character Design Seira Minami
Cover Design by Yusuke Koyama
English Edition Published by One Peace Books 2016

Printed in Canada

1 2 3 4 5 6 7 8 9 10

One Peace Books
43-32 22nd Street STE 204 Long Island City New York 11101
www.onepeacebooks.com